To June & Bob White
from
Cecily Pile

STADIS PLACE

STADIS PLACE

Cecily Pile

The Book Guild Ltd
Sussex, England

First published in Great Britain in 2004 by
The Book Guild Ltd,
25 High Street,
Lewes, East Sussex
BN7 2LU

Typesetting in Baskerville by
IML Typographers, Birkenhead, Merseyside

Printed in Great Britain by
Antony Rowe Ltd, Chippenham, Wiltshire

A catalogue record for this book is available from
The British Library.

ISBN 1 85776 724 1

For E.M.P.
whose birthday I have borrowed,
and our crowd
wheresoever.

CONTENTS

1	Barbara	1
2	Sir John	16
3	Fabian	51
4	Farmer	68
5	The Experts	91
6	Mares' Nests	103
7	Fisher	123
8	Examination	133
9	Philosophy	148
10	Mr Secretary	162
11	Nearer Home	174
12	'This Thing of Darkness'	201
13	First Player	214
14	The Countess and –	228
15	The Queen	243
16	Goodbye	250

1

Barbara

The village was drowned in cloud. A sheet of rain, not heavy but continuous, hung from the dripping trees and sodden thatch. The tall girl strode through it hardly noticing, in an old grey cloak that had been her mother's, the hood pulled forward; past the motionless white orchards and dusky hawthorn, leaving the last cottage behind. The road began to climb. Here the hedges were wild rose, scarcely in bud yet but rank with new growth; trees were fewer. A belt of limes, planted for shelter, revealed a square little church tower of the yellowish local stone. This was halfway up the hill. When you reached the church the road swung westward, rounded the hillside, and met the rain in full force. There was a wind now, and the girl threw back her head and welcomed it. The heaviness and depression dropped from her, as it always did here, just by the long barn; you quickened your step, and round the next corner saw the chimneys of Aldernaton.

The original stone farmhouse may have been 200 years old. It was now dairy and kitchens and the farm men's living quarters. The 'new' wing, already a lifetime old, was constructed of brick and timber, the brick whitewashed and the timbers pitched against the weather. There was a lime avenue approach, and a windbreak of alder and sycamore; there were gardens down the hill slope, each opening from the other. From the upper windows you could see three counties and the distant, glittering river, and (no matter how gloomy the day) a break somewhere, surely, in the lowering cloud.

So Barbara Dalbie came home and was comforted. For Aldernaton was hers, her very own since her eighteenth birthday; her guardian had written from London, as one grown person to another, what estate she was now mistress of, though in some respects still his ward until her twenty-first year. It was not easy to follow why it should be hers at all. She knew well Sir John was born at Aldernaton. He had often told her of his childhood, and there were old men in the village who remembered him as a boy. His grandfather had built the new wing, in the old King's reign. There had been a Stadis here since the thirteenth century and carvings of some of them were in the church, not very lifelike, but one at least with the long nose and mouth set aslant, the image of Sir John when he smiled. She took his word for the transfer, some arrangement he had made with her father. She could afford now to be gracious, and endure her aunt's plaints and her uncle's exhortations. She had only to be firm, and all would be well.

She came in through the kitchen, shook her dripping cloak and spread it to dry. Aunt Kate left arguing with the cook to stare at her.

'But wet, Babs?'

'But very wet,' she replied cheerfully.

Dear Aunt Kate, with her faded eyes and meaningless little habits – she had been maid-of-honour to the Queen near thirty years back, and still used the phrases of that day, picked up from the court and the foreign embassies. You had to tease her for it, though sometimes you'd be ready to scream. And 'Babs' too. But today, thought Barbara, I will be calm; I have taken the right course.

Aloud she said – 'I went down to the village.'

'If it was old Jarman,' said her aunt indifferently, 'there was a bundle to go.'

'No, aunt, it was not old Jarman, nor yet Granny Hackett. Come into the library and I'll tell you.'

'The library? *Ma petite*, your uncle is in the library. You know well he must spend the mornings on his sermon.'

'The sermon will wait, and you both ought to hear. Indeed, Aunt Kate, indeed there is a good reason.'

Cook and Betty were already open-mouthed. 'Come, aunt,' said Barbara quickly, and drew her along the passage. None of them relished interrupting the reverend Oliver Marbeck; his notions of man's duty temporal and eternal did not include politeness, except to one's superiors.

He said now, 'What is this? What may this mean? I told you, Katherine, I will have no intrusion –'

'I ask your pardon,' Barbara said; 'there is something you should know, and at once. I went to find Gregory, to give him a letter.'

'What folly is this? Gregory was here on Saturday for the farm accounts.'

'A letter for Sir John. I have asked Sir John to come here.'

Her aunt said faintly, 'I am sure he is welcome –'

'Katherine, you are a fool. Barbara, have I yet to warn you this man is vain and worldly, a wine-bibber, a man of loose conversation –'

'I have not found him so.'

'Not found! You were a child, and his visits were not frequent. I tell you, girl, Satan has marked him.'

'You have lived in his house ten years,' said Barbara quietly.

The colour of anger swept over his face; or might it have been fear?

'But Babs,' her aunt was murmuring, 'but Babs, you know there is no vicarage, where else should we live?' They did not heed her.

'And now, girl, he has ended his stewardship. He is your guardian for two years more, that is all.'

She said hotly, 'It is not all. My father died in Holland in his arms; my mother named him on her deathbed. What do I owe him or what does he owe me? Should I not invite him to Aldernaton?'

'But Babs –'

'And I observe you do not ask me why.'

There was an ugly silence.

'Dear Aunt Kate – uncle – I did not mean to be forward. Indeed I did not. May I tell you the reason?'

The vicar spoke heavily. 'You have pained me, Barbara. You have distressed me beyond words. I had hoped to dissuade you from this rash course. I ask it still.'

'It is too late. Gregory set out an hour ago.'

The quill in Sir Oliver's hand snapped sharply. He sat back.

'Then go your ways, but remember what I have said.'

She answered eagerly, 'Indeed I will remember, but please, please hear me. I cannot marry Thomas Wickins.'

'Why then you cannot.'

'But there will be others, others like him. There was even Master Garner, for all his age.'

'Master Garner is a worthy man,' began Sir Oliver.

'Uncle! But you would not have me marry him!'

'Why not?'

Her heart sank. 'You would not, aunt?'

'Indeed, but verily, Babs, you might do worse. With only the purchase of a meadow your estates would join.'

She said with rueful humour, 'I will not be wedded to his meadows. We here, what do we know of the world? You are both so good, but I need a guardian's advice.'

'Well, child, let us leave it so. When should he come?'

'The end of May, I hope. Gregory will bring his answer.'

So Sir Oliver turned to his sermon, and Aunt Kate

returned to the servants – and once more, thought Barbara, they have made me seem in the wrong. But I will never marry Wickins, nor an old man. I will not, though they wish it.

May grew greener and whiter, swallows plastered their cupped nests under the eaves, the plum blossom was over. The rain ceased sullenly, leaving dull grey sky. It was still very cold.

Gregory posted back from London. It was strange to have him ride up to the house and ask for Mistress Dalbie; strange, delightful, and a little frightening. She had used to run to him and to be lifted to his saddle. His rough weathered face smiled down at her impatience.

'Sir John sent you this letter. He bade me say he will be with you the sixth of June. He has writ here to her ladyship, as he unfolds to you in the letter.'

'Oh, thank you, Gregory, thank you. How – was he, when he wrote?' She wanted to ask, was he angry, am I a trouble to him?

'I called on him at Southwark, madam; he was well in health, but distracted with company.'

'What – sort of company? Are they as my uncle says?'

Gregory's teeth parted in quite another smile. He said, 'Look, Barbary, what your uncle says is nothing to the purpose. When did you know him speak a good word of any man?'

'Then you speak, Gregory, for you love him – Sir John, I mean.'

He grinned again. 'Sir John is a proper man and a good master. Never let 'em tell you otherwise. There may be knaves and fools around him. They live on him, not he on them.'

More than that he would not say, and Barbara, eager to be at her letter, dismissed him to rest and eat before his journey into Wiltshire. She walked out down the flagged path and into the rose garden, where at this hour no one would interrupt her. The very feel of the folded paper pleased her. Turning it over she found two inscriptions; on one side 'To Mistress Dalbie of Aldernaton' in a formal hand; on the other, with a more dashing penmanship, the following couplet:

Question the bearer on any score,
He'll tell you he's bound for the Barbary shore.

This made her smile, even as she broke the seal and read on quickly.

Forgive me, Barbara, that I make unhallowed use of your name, when I have but now chidden Gregory for that very fault; tho indeed he takes chiding lightly, and correction drips from him as water from a duck's feathers, when the storm passes up he bobs.

But forgive me, Barbara, for giving so little thought to affairs upon that coast, as to suppose my duties end with your estate. I will come to you, God knows, and play the guardian; a plague upon this Wickins if he plague you further. But indeed what course to follow, to keep promise and serve you best now you are come to womanhood, taxes me much: I am so little fitted to be your adviser in any matter of the tender sort, that I have writ to the Countess, my friend of many years. She is of so good a heart, the kindest lady living, that she will devise some help for you more than a bachelor can well bestow, and one moreover past the hilltop of this life and now going down into the vale; where I thank God he finds himself indifferent well and takes leave to declare himself yours in all affection, JOHN STADIS.

Thursday, 22nd May

She sat for some time with the letter in her lap, in a glow of gratitude and relief. He was coming, all would be well – for she gave no thought to the legendary Countess. Even his written word made her stronger, as it always had; more assured, more real, further than ever from her aunt and uncle. He alone never admonished; he gave good advice with a jest, and treated her as an equal always. He was so wise and kind, so good.

A great white rose, which had balled in the wet weather, dropped suddenly at her feet. The day really was warmer. She would come out after dinner and prune away the poor blotched flowers; thank heaven there was no greenfly yet. She must plan for his coming, invite their neighbours, her own unwelcome suitors included. Backed by a guardian, she could declare herself and be rid of them. There would be new peas, duckling, roast meat, a barrel of Hereford cider and the good wine; she would ask for shortcake and marzipan, and a big dish of cream with the conserve. She would wear her green gown and ribbon knots.

Sir John rode in by a detour, and the village people looked for him in vain. Was that the first omen, Barbara wondered afterwards? There was even, she sensed, a change in his attitude to her; but then they were in public, and she had grown up in the eighteen months since their last meeting. Why, she had once thought him tall; now, as she rose from the courtesy of greeting, their heads were level, chin to chin and eye to eye. The quick smile was ready still in his eyes, for her at least, but his lips smiled less; she thought him overtired. For all that, how well he showed against the other guests, with their loud voices and confident assumption of importance. He sat patiently through course after course of country hospitality, was deferential to the ladies and civil to Sir Oliver; talked foreign affairs with the old wool merchant

Garner, crops with Humphrey Wickins, hunting with young Tom and the Filpot brothers; all with impartial good humour, if somewhat absently. Distracted with company – she remembered Gregory's phrase.

It was later that the trouble began. Her aunt and the old ladies had retired to the parlour, where June or no June there was a comfortable fire. Barbara had escaped to her own room for a few minutes, let her hair loose and sat brushing it by the open window. Downstairs she could hear a chair scraped back and other sounds of adjournment, but the heavier male voices (especially her uncle's) still droned on.

Sir John came out alone. He stood for some moments looking out over the gardens to the distant hills of Wales, and the set of his broad shoulders was somehow desolate. When he turned, Barbara saw on his face a look she was startled to recognise: sorrow, quietened yet deepened by the beauty of the place. He so obviously thought himself unobserved that she withdrew her gaze, ashamed; yet humanly lingered and looked again, to the neglect of her duties.

A clumsy step lurched after him. It was Wickins Senior, already rather drunk. His heavy frame sagged upon unwilling legs, and his coarse face was blotched with purple. Apart from that, he much resembled his son, as Barbara observed with fascinated disgust.

'So you've set her against us, damn you.' She was prepared for the theme, but hardly for the venom of its utterance. Sir John, however, regarded him with weary toleration.

'No, Wickins. The lady made her own choice.'

'Yes – primed by you. You always crossed me, Stadis, but you're master here no longer. Once you pack off, my Tom will win her round.'

Sir John said shortly, 'She refused him. Let him take his answer.'

'Never.' Wickins mouthed the word, showing a set of blackened teeth. 'Never. He'll have her. What is it to you? I've set my heart on it. Let them join the estates, it's no concern of yours now.'

'Is it not? Tom gets the lady and you get the lands: what for? To waste like your own starved acres – twenty of heath and furze to one of pasture? Go and make use of what you have; leave Aldernaton alone.'

'Barren heath, you said it yourself. What use is there in that?'

'What do they in the colonies with worse? Clear, plough and sow, and reap the fruits of their labours. You hanker after the vine that you planted not, but hear me, Humphrey; the grapes are not for you.'

She thought Humphrey would have fallen. His mouth opened once without a sound: he appeared to swell with rage and terror. At last he managed one word – 'Tom!' – and the young men came running. They must have been watching, waiting for the outcome; could even (but she did not think of this until later) have girded him on to this exhibition.

'Better still,' said Sir John, 'since you are too drunk to take it in. Listen to me, all of you, for what I say is final. Mistress Dalbie is still my ward. If she marries without my consent, she will lose Aldernaton: I can yet arrange that. Get this into your addle heads: there shall be no persuasion of her, and if there were, no one here present will profit by it. That is all.'

Three hands had gone to sword-hilts. Sir John's cold gaze travelled from one to the other until they slackened foolishly, like dogs at a scolding. Saying, 'Give your father a hand, Thomas,' he turned away.

Humphrey had begun to curse in a horrible throaty whisper. The elder Filpot said uneasily, 'We had best be jogging.' Between them they urged the old boy in the direction of the stables, and were soon to be heard riding away downhill. To Barbara's shocked senses they left the very smell of their ill-will lying close and sour, like a threat.

She must have leaned from the window, for when Sir John turned back to the house their eyes met.

'I could not help hearing–' she began, but he brushed that aside.

'They will not trouble you again,' he said.

'But you–' Barbara shivered. 'They looked murderous.'

He smiled then. 'Looks cannot kill, you know. Did you think they would attack me here, in my mother's garden – in your garden? I am sorry it was here.' His mouth, so like the crusader carving, twitched a little. 'We must have Ben here with his tobacco, and fumigate it.'

'But will they not lie in wait for you?'

'Not they. All the years I was Humphrey's neighbour we never met without squaring. He'll scowl a bit, and round on the boy when he's sober for mismanaging you. I must talk to your uncle.'

You cannot argue with your guardian out of a narrow casement, with your hair down too. Barbara withdrew, reassured, yet with her chief question unasked. She resolved in her own mind to put it before long.

There was strangely little time for questions. Her aunt or uncle or both were with them mostly, a constraint on speech. Next day was Sunday, and never had Mattins seemed so long nor Sir Oliver's sermon so intractable. His text was Satan walking up and down like a raging lion, seeking whom he might devour, and the development was directed almost entirely at Sir John. The worldly man, the dweller in cities, frequenter of playhouses et cetera ('cetera' were not specified), he depicted in lurid colours as more than halfway on the road to hell. For all that, thought Barbara, how warmly his parishioners greeted the worldly man, and contrast their respectful salutations to the house of Marbeck! There was a difference too in the response. Sir Oliver clapped on his old-fashioned black hat and sailed majestically by, whereas Sir John, cap in hand as he left the porch, was soon the centre of an eager group exchanging question and answer in the liveliest manner. He was stopped again in the road, two or three times, until Barbara, longing to overhear, was compelled to walk on with her aunt. Sir John arrived home one hour later (whereby dinner was kept waiting), having been persuaded into Dame Kersey's cottage. He apologised frankly, but Sir Oliver's humour was not improved.

But dinner was over at last, Sir Oliver removed himself until Evensong, Aunt Kate thought she should lie down for an hour; and Sir John, holding out his hand as he used to the child Barbara, said, 'Come and show me your flowers.'

It was warmer out of doors than in, the sky still heavy and the damp earth smelling pungently sweet. They walked quietly up and down the alleys, content without speech, till imperceptibly the sun came out and was strong through the woollen of her gown. If it could always be like this – she felt with a sudden fierce longing – warm and secure, no sound but the busy murmur of insects; no past to bewail, nor future like a cloud of dread; nothing but the blessed present. She looked at her guardian, and found the lines of his face relaxed and pleasant. He had changed little in all the years she could remember. The well-trimmed beard was perhaps thicker and the hair of his head beginning to recede, that was all: they were both the same shade of light brown, the grey eyes were still clear and the teeth strong and white. He was timeless, a part of her life, as Aldernaton was part of his.

Their thoughts impinged; he smiled at her and hummed little tune.

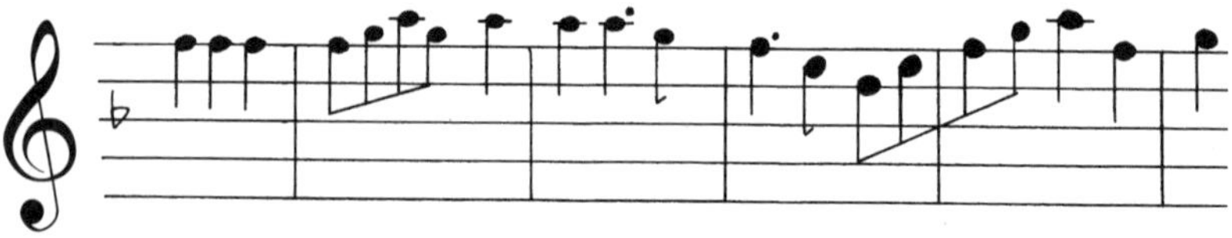

'How does it go? "Then like the humming Bee, then like the humming Bee": that's one of Wilbye's – I'll send it to you. And you hold upper F, like the bee's persistent buzzing.'

For once she could not match his mood. She asked abruptly, 'Must you go?'

He could follow her there too, but would not, answering cheerfully, 'I must indeed, and tomorrow: there are three men awaiting me at Oxford.'

'You do not bring your friends to Aldernaton?'

'My friends I would. These are but hangers-on, some of the bad company Sir Oliver warns me of.'

This was a side-track. 'In what way are they?'

'Well, there is one Nicholas Greenlee, a gentleman of Nottinghamshire, who will have £800 a year if he live to inherit it. I promised some year or so ago to show him London – now he is showing me. He looks like a well-dressed scarecrow, and would be plucked like a crow indeed without advice, so that I dare not leave him in London, or alone anywhere. The others are two in one, or one-and-a-half men: Adey and Crooks, or rather Crooks and Adey, since they were wrongly named; for Adey is crooked and Crooks is addled. They have been useful to me sometimes. Now never trust me but I think I am useful to them.'

'And are they as bad as my uncle pretends?'

He shrugged. 'There are many such in London, who will attach themselves somehow to the court's fringes. They are no good to man or beast, but they know no better. The players, now, there is good in them, for they make us to laugh and cry and recognise our follies. Do not heed Sir Oliver on the players. Some of them are gentlemen, and many are my good friends.'

'And for this – this,' cried Barbara, beginning to stammer in her indignation, 'for s-so little cause – that sermon! I was so ashamed.'

'Your uncle,' said Sir John, 'is some small way to being a puritan: yet he's a good man, and says no more than he believes. He is right enough, there *is* great evil walking with strides across all Europe: but it is other than he thinks. It should not touch you here.' He paused, and said seriously, 'For all that, Barbara, when you are wedded your uncle must find a new home. Promise me that.'

She said, 'It would be pleasanter.'

He added, hesitating a little, 'You can get a good household together – you'll do better in the village than your aunt. I would like to leave Aldernaton the happy place it should be.'

This was her opening. 'But must you – leave it? Can you not return and make it your home again?'

'My dear Barbara.' Sir John spoke almost crossly. 'You have an excellent wit. Use it for one moment, and you will see your suggestion is absurd. If your uncle must go, so must I. Ask your husband else.'

She wanted to answer, 'What makes you certain I will have a husband?' But that is something a girl, however determined, finds more prudent to leave unsaid. Her mouth opened for some retort or other, but what was the use? The still afternoon had grown impossibly cloying; she wanted to run, to burst out of the walled garden and all the stupid irrevocable customs of mankind. She had always thought of her guardian as beyond such boundaries. The disappointment was so intense that she felt a physical pain. He was speaking again – what could it be? Something about the Countess – 'if you go into Wiltshire – she will help you in every way –' but she could not apprehend it. That part of the mind which should attend was dulled with aching fire. Could there not be a world simple and true, where no difficulties arose, where the thought was the deed and the lion and the lamb lay down together – a text Sir Oliver would never preach from? In heaven perhaps, or there was no such place, it was a child's dream and now she must be a woman: but her practical everyday self clung fiercely to the illusion. It would be so easy, it would save so much trouble. All one had to do was to wish it, and act directly – if only the others would wish it too.

They had come in their pacing to the lowest garden. Sir John tried the gate: it opened protestingly, the key shrieking in the lock. She roused herself to say, 'Trueman must oil it, I will speak to him.' She was aware of Sir John's scrutiny, and for the first time in her life was reluctant to meet it. Hurriedly she stepped over the crumbling brick sill, saying, 'Will you walk round the meadows now?' – too hurriedly; he detained her, with a hand on her sleeve.

'Are you well, Barbara? Have I tired you?'

'No, sir. I mean yes, I am very well. I am sorry you are going.'

He said quietly, 'So am I.' But he let go her sleeve and closed the gate. The sun was very hot. They made their usual round through the water meadows, gaining the shadow of the elms. When they spoke again, it was of little things; and for the rest of the day, she noticed, he was perseveringly cheerful. They went to church again – they sat all four after supper in the garden – and Sunday had come to an end. On Monday they breakfasted at five, and by six her guardian was away. Barbara rolled up her sleeves and made busy in the dairy: but all that day, and for long after, she was haunted by the phrases of that bitter-sweet little song,

> All pleasure is of this condition:
> It pricks men forward to fruition,

But if enjoyed, then like the humming Bee,
The honey being shed, away doth flee.

2

Sir John

Horse and man were climbing up out of the Vale of Evesham, close on an hour later, before Sir John looked back. There was nothing to see but a sinuous white mist filling the valley, and the dark line of hills beyond looming curiously near. It was going to be hot. Jewel snuffled, and turned his handsome chestnut head round enquiringly. 'You're right, old lad, why do we wait?' said his owner, fondling the white blaze that named him. 'On, then, Jewel. Keep moving is the motto now.'

They were riding away from Aldernaton, and he could not disguise from himself that it might be for ever. He hoped he had betrayed nothing. It would have been so easy to explain, yesterday in the garden, to break the strict course he had set himself; but it was too dangerous, and too late. He had made his decision long ago: Barbara must never know the truth.

Surely he had done his best for her. Even so, he was uneasy about Aldernaton; the place needed a master. He felt, irrationally, that he was deserting her, leaving a gift to grow into a burden. But the Countess would put that right. (Dear Mary, it was many years since he had seen her, and the world not come to an end yet.) She was a far better helper than himself for a marriageable girl. But reason as he would, his heart was heavy.

The news from Europe, too, he liked not. England was

making peace with Spain, to the Low Countries' disgust. True, the treaty was not yet signed, and by all accounts not like to be; the envoys at Boulogne had been haggling, or keeping each other waiting, or withdrawing impatiently from the meeting; though doubtless the reports had been exaggerated. Meanwhile, the Dutch were still struggling for life. There were officially no English forces with them now, although many gentlemen still joined them from time to time – for the season, as they would go hunting, thought Sir John cynically. It was a subject on which he could be bitter; he had more than once asked the Queen's permission to rejoin Prince Maurice, but had met with a definite refusal. Perhaps she was right; even after the Armada's defeat, it might be prudent to keep one's strength within the country. But that was twelve years ago – good God, could it be so long? – and old King Philip of Spain had been dead two years; and if we withdrew and left them to it, they would leave *us* alone, was that it? But what of the German states, and the long-heralded Protestant League? What of Sweden, once a light on the horizon, embroiled now with Poland? What of France? France would help no one, having made some show of composing their own religious differences, and an honest man might suspect that the true struggle lay elsewhere. What was the cry in Normandy, of Liberty and the Third Estate? That rumour had been ruthlessly suppressed; it *might* be what it seemed, rank mutiny against all lawful government. And in Italy – news was open enough, it was knowledge itself that was suppressed, and the reasonable questing of man's mind. Yet Englishmen still travelled in Italy and saw nothing they would not admire.

Even in England, a too-free speech could be dangerous. Faction and intrigue, rumour and counter-blast were breeding without let; the powerful London merchants became increasingly puritan; and the Queen was growing old. There was no one like her – to her exasperated court maybe it was just as well – but she was the last strong-minded sovereign in Europe. Her power had always been used, brilliantly if maddeningly. When once that imperious grip slackened, who could hold the reins? There would be men in plenty to snatch at them – and plenty to aver they were already snatching. Take Essex, in disgrace just now for his high-handedness in Ireland: the Council had made a mountain out of that. Not that Sir John approved in any way of the Earl of Essex: an impulsive fool, who could not govern himself, much less a colony: but to accuse him, as rumour whispered, of aspiring to the throne was ridiculous. What had he done? As the Queen's Lieutenant-General, he had bestowed a few knighthoods, doubtless believing he had authority to do so. After all, Leicester had done as much in the Low Countries, witness Sir John Stadis. But Leicester had been an older man, and long established in the Queen's confidence. It was stupidly presumptuous of young Essex to expect the same privilege. These brilliant headstrong men were often stupid. One thing was certain, he would never take the Queen's place – the city would not accept him. Where else could the Queen look for an heir, but to the Scottish King, her martyred cousin Mary's son? And he, thought Sir John, is a dull sort of body if we hear aright; the Kirk have had him well in hand, he'll suit the puritanical, but God help England, he is fifty years behind the times. For other possibilities, it was better not to think or speak. Meanwhile, in all but the highest matters, the Council governed rather than the Queen. Since what power they had was kept jealously to themselves and their creatures, men of ability could either sail to the Indies, or hang about Blackfriars Stairs: at their choice. Small choice if the Queen got to hear of one's intentions. Even Drake, after sailing round the globe, must dance attendance to obtain a fresh permit for each voyage.

With such gloomy thoughts Sir John held off his personal misgiving. The sun grew high. He was teased across

Warwickshire by newly mended roads, ten miles of them, fresh-strewn with little sharp flints, and had to search for byways to spare the horse somewhat. It was a relief to reach Banbury and a well-trodden surface again, dust and all.

When at last he rejoined his companions at the little Sack of Malt outside Oxford, he had never disliked them more. Dick Crooks lounged untidily in the doorway, his doublet undone and his red hair ruffled, drinking steadily. There was something pudgy and unformed about his features, justifying Adey's taunt that he must be a seven-months child. This may well have been true, but since he knew not when and where he was born (nor whether, Sir John would add) they were never like to know. He was slovenly and a boaster, and obstinate to the point of stupidity. Why he should stick to Adey was incomprehensible, since the latter lost no opportunity of deriding him; yet they were already a pair when Sir John encountered them in the less reputable taverns round Whitefriars, two years ago. The oddness of the couple had attracted him, and he had shown them off to his friends; Adey and Crooks, or Crooks and Adey – the cause of much mirth if little wit.

Nicholas Greenlee came pushing past him before Sir John had well alighted, a thin and shapeless youth with lank hair and a face which now looked both weak and vicious. He was full of petulant complaint, how he had been taken to this mouldy hedge-inn and left with only old Soakbones here for company – 'on a Sunday too, Sunday in the country – and forced into church for the good name of the house!'

Adey, it seemed, had been off since Saturday on some ploy of his own which he refused to share. Sir John had no wish to enquire into that, but mentally added the Sack of Malt to the list of houses they must not revisit. He put an end to the whining by asking, 'Who breathed the horses, then?'

Nick, brought up short, said sulkily, 'They were in the paddock.'

'Better fetch them in now. We'll make a start when Jewel is rested.'

'Send Crooks, he does nothing but drink. I'm not your horseboy.'

'No, Nick,' (Sir John controlled a desire to slap him) 'but since you are wearying for action, be grateful for the chance of it. I am sorry you were dull.'

'Dull! I saw how it would be, when we first came to this hole. Indeed, Sir John, I take it most unkindly that you did not invite me to Aldernaton.'

'I have told you, the place is not mine now. But unless you wish to spend another night here –'

'Heaven defend!'

'– be a good fellow and see to the horses. Where's Adey?'

'Here on his cue,' said a pert voice behind him. 'The horses are ready but for saddling.'

'Oh, are they so?' It was annoying to be angered at what should please him. Adey was getting too familiar. Standing there now as smug as a cat that has stolen the cream, he roused all Sir John's repressed ill-humour.

'Are you too itching to be gone?' he said irritably, throwing his cap on to the bench.

'I made sure you would be.'

'Since you're so clever, perhaps you have bespoke us a meal? You have dined already, I suppose, with your friends of yesterday.'

It was a deliberate low-line thrust, and Sir John was gratified to perceive that it got home. A red spot burned in Adey's cheek, receding to dirty white; he was silent.

'No? Then will you order? I'm sure you know your way to the kitchen. And remove your friend's tankard; he has drunk enough.'

Temper is catching. Obeying the last command literally,

with a twist of the hand that slopped ale impartially over Crooks' shirt and Sir John's breeches, Adey disappeared within. Crooks growled, 'Send he leave *his* itch behind!' Sir John shrugged and mopped and called house till an attendant came running.

It was a sullen enough party that sat down to meat, Nick sulking, Crooks stuffing away phlegmatically, and Adey silent with fury as Sir John, in his most savage mood, repeatedly got under his guard with another stinging quip. Sir John derived much pleasure from the operation, not the least in seeing with how trivial a remark he could accomplish it, so it be barbed with malice and pointed with icy wit. The people of the inn, sensing this humour, served them with so much dispatch that they were soon saddled and ready. Sir John sent the others ahead along the Aylesbury road and lingered to pay the reckoning; also, pricked by some remnant of remorse, to charm away the effect of his ill-temper. This was easy enough when he exerted himself to the purpose, and he rode off at last in a glow of self-approbation, leaving all smiles behind him. It did not last. Before he had well come up with the dust of his retinue the brief satisfaction had subsided.

> But if enjoyed,
> Then like the humming Bee,
> (Then like the humming Bee,
> Then like the humming Bee),
> The honey being shed, away doth flee,
> But leaves a sting that wounds the
> inward heart.

And he could not be rid of it; neither the tune nor the sting.

Their lodging at Aylesbury was bespoken. He let the trio precede him and made his way in while they were having supper, refused all but a drink, and gave them a brief goodnight. Before the staircase door was shut behind him he could hear the grumbling begin: the old bear was surly tonight. He was, of course. He tore down the fusty hangings from the bed and cast them into a far corner, wrenched the unwilling casements as wide as they would go, and lay tossing and dreaming confusedly.

He was crossing the Channel in rough weather. The ship was small, and shuddered with every wave. The crew were all drunk and the passengers had to batten them below; one man forced his head up through the thin boards and showed the purple furious face of Humphrey Wickins. He was shouting something, but the wind drowned his words. One felt absurdly sorry for him, but could do nothing, for it was a Turkish ship and they were all chained to the oars, three to a bench, Roger on one side and Adey on the other. Roger was dead, of course, a skeleton with long black hair. Adey was white as a corpse except for a red spot on each cheek; he swayed and fell, a sickening weight, across Sir John – who woke to find a high wind indeed, windows banging and doors rattling, and his left arm doubled awkwardly under him, cramped and numb. He scrambled out sheepishly to secure the casement, stubbed his toe getting back, turned resolutely on his right side in the creaking old bed and fell into a deep sleep at once.

At breakfast they met unconcernedly, storms and moods blown over. It was a fair fresh morning and they got away by eight, riding briskly to kill the miles before noon, when they could make an easy day of it. Adey in particular had recovered his poise, cracked innumerable bad jests, and took the others' clumsy baiting about milkmaids, hayfields and the long grass well enough. In return, he entertained them through the tedious part of the journey with discreditable stories of their soberer acquaintances. They made good time, and when any difference arose Sir John had only to say,

'Cheerly boys, you'll lie in Aldgate tonight.' But he had to force himself into his usual tolerance. More than once his attention wandered, and he came back to earth with a jerk to find the others regarding him curiously. Adey, showing more consideration than usual, would laugh and divert the talk skilfully enough.

It was odd how like life a dream could be. A fool might take it as an omen; only a fool, surely, would dismiss it. The restless brain still conning its affairs under cover of sleep would weave such fancies, using chance impressions, truth and nonsense mixed. So the wind and an old house became a ship in storm, and Barbara's smooth dark hair grew on her father's skull, an image of friendship transferred. The rest was nonsense; the other persons in the dream were not worth a mention in the same breath as Roger Dalbie. Yet the dream meant something, or why should it strike so into his very being? The Romish persuasion would see in it a command to pray for Roger's soul; the ancient Greeks, how the fates had interwoven their lives. What should the new man think, that was one half a protestant, one half a sailor into strange seas? No more, perhaps, than that he was growing old, and could no longer ride all day and talk all night like a boy of twenty: that he was somehow disquieted, and searching even in sleep for the cause? Yet he knew the cause well enough. So his thoughts jogged up and down with the rhythm of their travel, and he spoke little and answered neglectingly.

From four o'clock he kept them moving in spite of protests, declaring he had no mind to camp outside Moorgate for the night. Even so, the shadows were lengthening as they rode down Highgate Hill and saw the city spread below them in its veil of smoky blue: a lovely sight at all times, magical in the golden evening, no matter how often you made the journey nor how well you knew the truth beneath the veil – the foul alleys, crowded tenements and stinking wharves; the stews, the bear-pits, taverns and markets, the heaving, rowdy, callous, warmhearted tumult that was London. The present company knew it rather better than most.

'And why,' Sir John demanded, 'do we return?'

'To London, sir? Why do we ever leave it?' said Nick the provincial.

Crooks grunted, 'Home, for me.'

'You ask?' said Adey. 'Because we cannot resist it, you old sinner.'

'And there spoke experience,' Sir John retorted. 'He would barter all the milkmaids in Oxfordshire for a squeeze from Alice Thorn.'

'A prickly embrace! One we'll not share till tomorrow unless we move faster; it's half an hour to sunset.'

They swept through Islington in a scatter of yapping dogs and admiration. It was downhill all the way. The horses caught their excitement and began to race in earnest: past the gipsy encampment, over the little bridge – Jewel ahead; skirting booths and dodging among pedestrians, till they were forced to rein in on the heels of the crowd, all laughing and breathless. Sir John felt ten years younger. A dozen voices greeted him and he answered cheerily. To himself he added, come up, John! It is easy enough to dissemble. They began to file through the Gate.

Alice Thorn kept the Quartern, back of St Mary Axe. She was an enormous woman with a voice and heart to match, who believed in young men enjoying themselves – to wit, plenty to eat and drink and wenches enough within reason. Her welcome lasted half an hour; for by the time she had finished exclaiming at their arrival she had persuaded herself it was expected. 'If I said it once I said it a dozen times – did I not, Winkle?' And the shrivelled little potman would answer, 'Yes, mistress, indeed you did,' and off she would go again,

'Indeed I did, I was *sure* S'John would be back, somethink seemed to *tell* me.'

'Will *somethink* tell her we're *here*?' mimicked Greenlee.

Sir John laughed. 'Well, come now, Alice, have you anything for supper?'

'Ow, yes, S'John, as good a supper as ever you've tasted, have we not, Winkle? And near enough ready if y'r honour'll set down a matter of ten minutes, in the back room, sir, we keep no custom there –'

'Do we not, Winkle?' chanted her guests in unison.

She was not in the least put out, but laughed her jolly laugh, said they were good lads and we would see about it presently, Winkle should serve the front and she'd wait on them herself. 'You shall have a snug night, I warrant, shall they not, Winkle?' And screwing up her huge face in a knowing way, she led them into the back room and prepared at last to leave them.

'A snug night, Alice,' called Adey after her, 'then tomorrow you can hang out your new sign.'

'Why, what sign indeed?' she demanded, ready to box his ears.

'Not what you think I mean. Your sign of Stadis Place. Did he not tell you we shall stay a month?'

Sir John said sharply, 'Adey!'

'Well, do you not mean it?'

'We may stay for some weeks, but I will not have it rumoured. Not for a few days yet. And Alice, a quiet night if you please, never mind your snug one. They that want more can seek it for themselves.'

He meant to shock them, and certainly succeeded. There was a little chill of silence, which they were to remember later. He sat on the edge of the table, watching all four of them as they took in the intelligence. First the hostess, her little dark eyes narrowed, removed herself with a barely civil 'Whatever you wish, sir.' Adey muttered, 'Here we go again.'

Crooks, with unusual penetration, said decidedly, 'He means it,' while Nick, looking from one to another, burst out at length, 'But if *you* turn puritan, the devil himself will follow!'

'He may do so yet, without waiting for me. Go out if you choose, Nick, do but remember I'll not see twenty again.' He added, for the others' benefit, 'I wish now I had kept Orchard House open. We could have rested there a few days.'

'At Southwark?' said Crooks with grand contempt. 'Give me the city.'

'Well, here you have it.' Sir John yawned widely. 'I'll send you out in the morning, Adey, to bring over some of my shirts – and any news you can rake up.'

'The clean and dirty linen together, eh?' But Adey was not smiling. 'Best give me the keys now; you look as you'll be lying abed.'

'And have you off to Mother Bunn's to get your pocket picked? No thank you. I shall be up by seven; can any of you say the same? Ah, here is supper, and Winkle with it: I'm out of favour, it seems.'

'Can you wonder?' Crooks grumbled; but he too had begun to gape, as the closeness of the little room made itself felt. The others were soon yawning too, and had decided before the meal was over that perhaps an early night would suit everybody best. Sir John had been too long at the game to show any sign of victory, beyond handing over the keys and full instructions for the morning.

'And find out chiefly when the Queen is moving to Greenwich, for I will not go to Nonsuch and that's flat. And if any question you, I am in the country, or fallen sick, or what you will to satisfy them.'

The truth would get about, for all that; but he could reckon on three or four days' privacy, perhaps even a week. By then London would be emptying, if today's heat were any sign; there would be fewer of his friends or enemies to face.

The players were gone already, packed up in the last week of May, to tour until the autumn. Why the devil had he come back himself? Well, none but himself would guess the reason.

Alice Thorn had relented. She brought in the drinks with some dignity, and a request that if his people were going over the water tomorrow they might take a dish to her sister in Southwark Street, that she'd had as long ago as Lent if Sir John would believe her, for Lent it must've bin because of the jellied eels which he would understand were the then contents of the dish, indeed the prime cause of its having been borrowed: 'or lent?' he was constrained to murmur. The jest should have been Adey's part, but he had unaccountably missed his cue. Yes, Lent it was, she was explaining, when the point went home and the whole of her great bulk began to shake with laughter. Lent it was and borrowed it was, she'd remember that, would she not, Winkle? But Winkle was serving the front parlour.

'For God's sake,' Adey exploded none too quietly, 'let's to bed at once or she'll have him in here to repeat it.'

'That's enough, Adey.' But Sir John rose, with a frown for his subordinate and a smile for Mistress Thorn. 'Our old rooms, Alice? Then goodnight again, for we are very weary. They shall take your dish in the morning, with or without eels.' He turned in the doorway. 'And Alice – tell no one I am here until I give you leave.'

They were to remember that too.

In all, he had ten days. There was a week of misery when he kept close, or went out very early in the morning on such business as he had. The trio would sally forth each day, to bring back little of interest. The Earl of Essex was still confined to his house by the Queen's order: there were fantastic tales of his questioning by the Council. Penelope

Gaier had been received at court again – too soon, some thought, after what had happened last time. No plague had yet been reported in the city. The first few evenings they spent variously in and around the Quartern; but after three of Alice's 'snug nights' Sir John rebelled, and let Crooks and Adey take him further afield. On Sunday they attended St Bartholomew's in Smithfield – a church large enough, Sir John thought, for him to escape notice, and one moreover so constructed that in the vast side-aisles an unwilling worshipper could contrive to see and hear very little of the service. By Tuesday (a week from his arrival) the first enquiries were being made at the Quartern; on Wednesday he admitted visitors and walked abroad openly. On Friday morning a very young gentleman, dressed from head to foot in orange satin, waited upon him to present a note with the Lord Chamberlain's seal; Sir John Stadis was commanded to Greenwich.

Now that the summons was come at last, he was not sorry. He rode over with Nick only, leaving Adey and Crooks some odd ends to clear up and appointing a rendez-vous in Deptford. At the Palace he found the usual crowd in the anterooms, the usual high buzz of talk, quickly hushed whenever a door opened and as quickly resumed; and so nearly the same faces grown resigned to their interminable wait that he might never have been away. At two minutes to five he heard without surprise that her Grace would receive no one else today. Another exquisite young man, in blue silk slashed with lavender, approached him with a bland apology to the effect that we were busy, very busy indeed for the time of year, or should he say season, and Sir John might perhaps experience a few days' delay in obtaining audience. For this Sir John was entirely prepared. Since the word delay had no meaning for him now, since in fact time stood still and he saw nothing but eternity ahead, he accepted it calmly. The blue silk took its soothing murmur elsewhere, and was replaced by a page, a boy who could scarce be sixteen, intimating in respectful words but with a languor approaching insolence that a place would be laid for Sir John this night at supper. Sir John thanked him gravely, but good God, he thought, were we like that in our day? He liked to fancy they were tougher, his generation; a core of steel behind the colourful clothes, that were cheerful then surely and not merely sickly. But it was all long gone. The valiant youth of Gloriana's golden time had weathered into cautious middle-age. He pitied her now, her spirit rusting in the sheath, surrounded by faction and a talk of trade.

It was perhaps unfortunate that at supper he sat next to Penelope Gaier. She knew him, and knew his reputation, and knew he had always disliked her. In the flush of her recent triumph, he was lawful prey; in his new deliberate mood it amused him to encourage her. He considered her afresh, the thick smooth creamy skin and honey-heavy hair, the full mouth, the too-bright eye: insupportable in a permanent, tedious even in a temporary relationship, but for a fortnight's amble along the Marches, well, sufficient. Besides, the moment when she realised he had fooled her (if the skill had not deserted him) would pay for all. The Marches could be dangerous, of course. For the first time in many months he felt a little spurt of excitement.

To the court in a dull summer they were manna from heaven. The audible whispers, the almost tangible glances were an added spur, enabling him to go through the motions most convincingly. Before nightfall even Nick Greenlee, languishing in the outer halls, had heard the news; by Saturday morning it had reached the Deptford taverns. Crooks hoped it meant the old devil would stay put for a month; and Adey, instead of snapping at him, said thoughtfully it might be longer.

That was before the husband appeared.

Sir John and the aggrieved Nicholas had joined them at

Deptford on Friday night – Sir John in an excellent humour but one plainly labelled 'no questions'. He approved their choice of lodging, altered only two of the lesser arrangements, and laid down a regimen for the ensuing weeks. He would have the barber at eight and breakfast at a quarter past; fence with Nick for an hour, and expect the horses at the door by ten o'clock. Either Crooks or Adey would attend him to Greenwich and fetch Jewel back to stable, bringing him again to the Palace gate by five. They would then all four ride together until supper, during which the evening could be planned. This simple and healthful course left everyone ample leisure, except in theory Sir John. In practice, the Queen was receiving very little at present and he need not expect to be called for. The public rooms were commodious, and there were in addition some acres of not too secluded garden wherein to enact his little comedy: the more public the better, now he came to think of it, since it would afford good cover for his other, true intent. He would dress the part, too. Madam Gaier was affecting white this summer, or a very pale dull pink like a cloudy pearl: his plum-coloured suit for that, and black for her white – all black, not a ruff nor a cuff showing. Faustus or Mephistopheles? She would have to guess.

At church that Sunday, in the preliminary decorous hush that is not yet silence, a whisper sprang to life and heads turned; Penelope Gaier, with rather more colour than usual, entered slowly on the arm of a tall dark-haired man. Few present could identify him, and the immediate gleeful comment was that someone had cut Stadis out; a younger man, too, twenty-seven or -eight perhaps, with a pale, proud face and unseeing stare. Sir John, making his entrance some minutes afterwards, missed the interesting sight, and being placed in a back pew was perforce among the earliest out. The sermon was not so absorbing as to prevent speculation in its hearers, and before he left the building there were several to inform him, gratis, that James Gaier had arrived. He had but one answer, 'Indeed?' and could not perceive how it should concern him.

Black Jamie, as the knowledgeable quickly named him, was not seen that day in the anterooms. His wife made her usual appearance, and the performance proceeded as billed. The talk went either of two ways: that the husband cared not at all, or that he was giving her so much rope she must infallibly hang herself. That he was unaware of her propensity no one for an instant assumed. Sir John, to whom Gaier was unknown, had formed an opinion of him at the time of Penelope's previous exploit: it was a poor husband, in fact, that saw so little of his wife. The gentleman she favoured had been happily dispatched to Ireland. It seemed to Sir John that in engaging the lady's attentions to an end so comparatively blameless, he was doing the husband a service he had ill deserved.

Monday was Midsummer Eve, and a day of great heat. It was pleasant enough on the Palace lawns under the cedars, but to walk, even in a shaded alley, for more than five minutes was exhausting. Sir John, upland bred, stood in a porch and cursed mankind, although the scene in front of him was admirable. Beneath the largest tree Penelope had spread herself and was holding court of her own, with almost every man available drawn to that magnetic pole. He was just out of earshot, but the smile, the glance, the conscious grace spoke clearly; they were directed at him. He groaned. For no reward under heaven, not even the satisfaction of his vanity, would he spend the intolerable day lolling at this woman's feet. Yet something he must do, and quickly; if the Queen should happen to look out of a southwest window some of them would rue it.

He stepped out of cover, and heat smote him like the hand

of God, throughout and over all. The earth retorted it again, a secondary fire; even the cooler grass breathed warmly, and the air ten paces distant was quivering in waves. On such a day there could be but one element unaffected. Walking quickly across the lawn he said, 'Who's for the river?'

The charm worked. At once they must make up a party, send for watermen, acquaint the steward. The young men were soon speeding in all directions, some older people were drawn in, and before long the entire court not actually on duty. A fleet of canopied barges carried them gently into the wind.

There is something unreal about a wide waterway, which the stretch from Greenwich to Gravesend exemplifies. Gliding dreamlike between two widening shores, the poorest part of Kent, with only a tumbledown farm for miles, and the featureless uninhabited Essex coast, one might be removed almost from this terrestrial globe. Sir John felt even more distant. He stood beside and rather behind Penelope, one hand on the back of her chair, and let the laughter and talk lap round him like the rippling water, no more noticed – it did not touch his feet. Alone at last, in some strange region of ebb and flow, his thoughts turned inward: and liked not what they found.

Looking back later, when it became vital to remember the exact sequence of events, he was to find the days before and the hours afterward dimmed and coloured by this improbable cruise. At the time, it was a welcome respite from the life that he despised. Better even the Quartern and her sister houses, a hundred times, he thought; as for hillside grasses or rolling cloud over the Malverns, he kept them resolutely from his mind. He must stay the Queen's pleasure, for the interview was essential to his plan: upon her attitude would depend his next action. He felt he would carry it, either way. There must be no hesitation, and above all, no regrets; only

. . . a sting that wounds the inward heart
With gnawing grief, and never-ending smart.

He could have joined now in a song like that, or one of Dowland's melting melodies concealing tongue-in-cheek, and mocked at his own folly; but Penelope's train were rendering a lively ballad about a money-lender's daughter, with several new verses not displayed in the printed sheet. Among his own friends he would have laughed and contributed a stanza; in this company he felt his lip curl – with scorn of them or contempt for himself?

Penelope, between giggling and saying fie, had almost forgotten him. Now she turned, the titter suddenly shrill, catching him off guard. Their eyes met, and his little game was over. She caught her breath, and flushed. Oddly, he had no wish to press his triumph. He took her hand and bowed over it elaborately, but not in mockery; and when plain Lady Weedon remarked, 'Have you not taken the sun, madam?' it was he who stepped into the breach. True enough, Penelope had gone silent, and the singing presently faltered, and it was a relief to put about. They were two hours out. The tide being still at ebb, they would take three to return – long enough for the incident to be forgotten. The other barges came alongside, flagging spirits were refreshed with food and wine, and the parties re-grouped. Once more their laughter startled the waterfowl; a solitary fisher in a small boat hauled in his line disgustedly and began to row ashore.

The lazy hours slipped by; he stood watching the water till thought itself was expunged. The breeze began to freshen. There was the farmhouse again, and a group of trees he recognised; soon Greenwich was in sight. They were back at the landing-stage, with everyone exclaiming, So soon, and what a long day it had seemed. It was four of the afternoon.

After the river air, an hour's wait in the Palace was

unthinkable. Excusing himself with a brief message, Sir John left the party. There were wherries plying for hire. 'Deptford, y'r honour? Tide's turned – git yer there in no time.' It was quicker than walking, quicker certainly than waiting for the horses. He nodded to the cockney who had hailed him, and was walking in at the tavern door twenty minutes later.

'Good God,' said Adey, 'look who's here.' He seemed amused rather than alarmed; his eyes flickered from Sir John to a corner seat where Crooks and a dark young man sat huddled, their backs to the door.

Greenlee was saying fussily, 'I kept telling you it was time to saddle.'

'Must you be such a fool?' returned Adey with lazy contempt. '*Imprimis*, it is Dick's turn today *secondo*, here's Sir John in person without the aid of a horse –'

'*Tertio*, let's have a drink without waiting for a horse,' interposed Sir John –

'And fourthly – what the devil is fourthly?' said Adey, making no move but to knock on the table. '*Quattuor* – *quarto*, that sounds like the printers' –'

'*Folio*,' Sir John suggested, 'if your list be much longer. Who's the new crony?'

If Adey was not ready for the subject, Nick seized on it; the previous interchange had been above his head. 'Why, sir,' he exclaimed, 'never tell me you have not met?'

'I cannot, till you tell me who it is. Should I be acquainted with him?'

'I know not if you *should*,' Nick began to snigger. 'It is Madam's goodman.' He jumped up and into an exaggerated position of defence.

'On guard in quarte? There's fourthly for you.'

'*Septième*,' said Adey wickedly, 'He'll have at you low-line.' Even Nick saw that one, and began to laugh until he choked.

'You fence in the French style,' observed Sir John with distaste. 'Who waits in this house?' He rapped the table loudly. 'Translated into English, you are telling me, I suppose, that the gentleman's name is Gaier.'

'His name, but not his nature – I never saw a duller. If you ask *me,*' said Adey knowingly, 'the lady's not to blame.'

'You will note I do not ask you. Drawer, a cup all round, including our friends in the corner. What I ask *of* you, Adey, is to govern your tongue a little.'

He would have been more scathing, but with that afternoon behind him, in conscience he could not. The situation had its funny side. Having on purpose led everyone to suspect his intentions, was he now to resent their suspicion? Like the old man in the play, his cake was dough on both sides; but he himself was the baker. It came to him then that for his father's son there might have been fitter occupations.

The drawer planked three tankards accurately in front of them and was across the room with two more while the contents were still swinging. Gabbling, 'You, sirs – gentleman's order,' he was gone and the door shut again, leaving a strong smell of cooking on the hot air.

'For God's sake,' Sir John said irritably, 'have you been basting yourselves in here all day?' Adey laughed lazily, too pleased with himself to answer; then Dick stood up pointing, and the stranger turned heavily to meet his benefactor.

He looks ill, Sir John thought: a chalk-white face and dull sunken eyes under thick brows, a black thatch of hair, and one hand up to his head as if the light hurt it. Poor devil, if he knows his wife at all he got no sleep last night. Aloud he said, 'John Stadis and your servant, sir. Will you drink with us?'

The young man got laboriously to his feet. He was tall, six foot or more, and powerfully built, which made his present condition the more painful to see. For a moment his lips moved experimentally, without sound, then he muttered, 'I thank you, sir.' His manner was civil but troubled; he fumbled for his drink and spilt some, causing Nick to titter uneasily, 'Has he not drunk too much?' Adey offered a chair. He seemed too preoccupied to notice it, until Dick Crooks took him by the arm; he sat down then, and made an obvious effort to gather his wits.

This was neither the neglectful husband nor the cold, calculating one of popular belief. Sir John both liked and pitied him, and set himself to converse pleasantly upon unexceptionable topics. He succeeded so well that in a matter of minutes James Gaier began to look less harassed, and even made one or two remarks not entirely wide of the subject. Seeing him at ease, Sir John withdrew for a few moments. The landlord held him in talk somewhat longer than was necessary but it could have been scarce a quarter of an hour. In that time the climate had changed; Adey was sneering, Nick sly and excited, and Gaier in a state of agitation.

'I thought at first' (went Sir John's account of it later) 'that Nick had been right, and the last cup was one too many. But I soon saw it was not so.'

Adey and Nick were to swear it was so – two oaths against one word. Even the word of a knight would need strong confirmation. Asked how he formed his opinion, Sir John's answer was perhaps not very convincing. He said, 'I thought he was not drunk. Moreover, Crooks looked worried, and it takes more than drunkenness to upset *him*.'

If Crooks were upset by the sight of a man not holding his liquor or from some other cause was never ascertained. There was Gaier nearly beside himself with rage or whatever else, stammering threats and curses. The versions did not quite tally, Nick alleging that he was cursing all women and Adey that it had to do with the Whore of Babylon. The conversation, both were positive, had been harmless till that moment; suddenly, Gaier was on his feet and possessed of a devil. Maybe one of them had happened to mention women – they would not swear to that. They only knew it was lucky he had no weapon, or someone would have bled for it on the spot. Sir John's intervention seemed to inflame him still further, and mouthing something incoherent he rushed stumbling out into the street.

They tried to joke about it, Nick saying, 'Sir John, he has smoked you,' and Adey, 'Look for a challenge now, if he can find one friend to deliver it.' Crooks went to the door to see which way he had gone, but he was already out of sight. No one seemed to know where he lodged. Sir John relieved his feelings with a few caustic remarks upon the character and habits of his followers, adding that they'd plainly provoked the poor wretch, he would tolerate neither that nor their vile guesses, and someone might saddle the horses in half an hour.

Nearer an hour passed before they got started. The whisper of a breeze had come in with the tide; one began to breathe freer and think clearer. In peace and amity they rode up on to the Heath.

It was Sir John who said 'I feel like a ten-mile trot; where shall we go?' Who answered 'I know a road' was never quite established, and it means nothing to say that after a mile or two Adey was leading. Sir John refused to assert even that. He held throughout to his original statement that he had no recollection of the precise course of events; he was mellowing in the quiet of evening, and only became aware of his surroundings, to find they were unfamiliar, when the shouting began.

They reined in. Back along the road (straight and downhill for perhaps two furlongs) was a great grey horse travelling at speed, the rider hunched awkwardly in the saddle in his effort to overtake them. For one horrid instant it looked as if he were headless: but the cries plainly issued from human lips. It was a moment of nightmare, or (more exactly) like a recurring dream, wherein the incidents may differ but the spirit is the same. Sir John was caught back vividly to his dream at Aylesbury, the night of the storm; what that had meant, this too portended. Both were still shrouded from his reason, but a deeper sense acknowledged something, a thing inevitable, turning him in his tracks: a feel of destiny.

While this impression came and went one might have counted thirty, certainly no longer. The four had halted, looking back. It was Adey who gave tongue – 'Ride on, for God's sake, it is Jamie Gaier.' The others added their exclamations. Sir John, awake now, silenced them with two words. He turned his horse and sat with a loose rein, waiting; the others fanned out round him in uneasy expectation, noticing as Gaier drew near that he not only wore a sword but carried a heavy whip. He still came on without slackening, and for a moment they thought he would ride someone down. Then the grey pulled up suddenly, both horse and man panting and sweaty, their eyes bloodshot from the dust and sun. Gaier's shout had become a croak, and his head moved on his shoulders without volition. The appearance wrought in Sir John so great a pity and concern that he must put it into action.

He said at once, 'Can we help you? Are you seeking someone?'

The answer came white-hot: 'Sir – John – Stadis!'

Sir John said, 'You have found him, sir,' and put out a hand to the grey's bridle.

'You are – Sir John – Stadis?' the parched voice continued.

'I am.' (He has been to Greenwich, for certain.)

'Then I demand – satisfaction.'

'You shall have it.' On a quick decision he unbuckled his sword and thrust it belt and all across Greenlee's crupper. 'Take this, Nick, and go home. All of you.'

'But Sir John –'

'Home, or to the devil,' he said equably.

Crooks muttered. 'He's armed.'

'I know, Dick. Thank you.' Even for them he felt a surge of incidental kindness, but he must not take his eyes from Gaier's face. 'Off now, quickly,' he repeated, and louder to Gaier, 'Shall we ride on a little?' Without waiting for an answer he managed the two horses gently ahead.

It worked. The trio let them pass. He pressed Jewel's flank for a quick trot, the grey fell in with his pace, and they rode for some minutes towards the sunset.

'Where are you going?' Gaier demanded suddenly.

'I am looking for a gate.' (Over his shoulder, too, but they were not followed.)

'You shall not escape me.' The black head had begun to roll again.

'No, no,' Sir John said patiently. 'This field will serve us, if as I think there is an entry by the barn.' It was hay time; the field was partly cut and the wagon left ready for next day. Sure enough, there was a gate. He dismounted, Jamie tumbling off beside him clumsily. There was no one in sight.

'We must tether the horses.' Yes, but behind the barn, hidden from immediate view. 'You'd best give yours a rub down,' Sir John continued. As there came no response, he took a cloth from his saddlebag and did the job himself, as thoroughly as he dared; for the sun was very low, and his companion twitching with impatience.

'Now, sir, I am at your disposal.'

Gaier's lips drew back in almost animal fashion; he exhaled slowly and audibly, controlled now, in an icy hatred.

'Take your coat off.'

Sir John did so.

'Look to your guard.'

Sir John remained quite still.

His own sword half out, Gaier paused. 'Your weapon, if you please.'

'I have no weapon, Mr Gaier.' That puzzled him. 'I have no weapon, and I do not mean to fight you. If you are aggrieved by any act of mine, you must take what satisfaction you will.'

'A coward,' he breathed. 'Sir John Stadis! Then by God –' He rammed back his sword-hilt and reached for the whip.

At that exact moment, like the cue of a comedy, they heard voices.

Gaier swore, still in the same cold whisper.

'They are coming this way. Into the barn,' Sir John said quickly. He grabbed their scattered garments and took his enemy by the arm. Gaier threw the touch off wildly, but followed; he too would wish to have the final reckoning undisturbed.

It was dark inside; they collided even in the doorway. When Sir John could make out anything, he saw the place was almost empty, no sacks of grain, no implements, nothing to conceal them; only a litter of dusty straw and old harness, very much pre-harvest. Footsteps were now quite near.

From outside he had seen a high window, a loft surely. Yes, thank God, over here was a ladder and trap. With his free hand he found Gaier's, placed it firmly on a rung, and urged him up. They were both light-footed, and the loudest sound was the rustle of straw; they sank into a heap of it in total darkness.

Four or five men came into the barn. There was a scratching of flint, and the dull glow of a shaded lantern; the thud of something like a box on the earth floor; the clink of metal. Sir John could see nothing, and hear little but the occasional murmur of voices. His impression was that they sat consulting on some plan, and were in no hurry over it. One of them laughed once and was hushed, more as a matter of course than as if they really feared discovery. They were certainly taking their time.

Apart from a slight cramp, Sir John could have enjoyed the escapade. The dry smell of the straw took him back to boyhood; he had hidden more than once like this, playing aboard-ship with a capful of scrumped apples for victual, bound for Africa or the Indies. But this time his shipmate was not playing. Alas, poor Jamie! How in the world had such an innocent achieved him such a wife? I'll tell him all, Sir John thought, and give guidance if I may. After I've calmed him: let him have his revenge first, my back is broad enough – and pleasure will be paid, as they say, one time or another.

'But if enjoyed –' not that: not any tune of Wilbye, it came too near by a fraction. Besides, the rhythm flowing through him even in thought had stirred his yoke-fellow: the straw began to heave. Sir John pressed down a warning hand. The muscle beneath it tensed and went rigid – no giving there; no warmth from the quite considerable store beside him had penetrated Gaier's heart.

'It was a rat.' The voice from below jerked him into alertness. '... understood, then? Wednesday.' They were moving at last, after one hour or two, he had no means of telling. The footsteps made off, some brisk and some deliberate; he fancied they went different ways. Give them a little longer yet; long enough to *s'éloigner*, long enough to remember something and come back. (Expressive tongue the French: take *ramasser* for pick up – compounded somehow of both movements, the stooping and the gathering.) Long enough? Now count a hundred for good measure –

'We may get up now,' he observed aloud. 'Our friends are gone, I think.'

There was no answer. Sir John felt his way down the ladder, still grasping the crumpled wreckage of his plum-coloured coat and Jamie's black doublet. The floor of the barn was now in bright moonlight through the open door.

'They've gone.' He spoke more loudly. 'Come down and stretch your legs.'

In a rush and a slither, Gaier loomed beside him, eyes glinting in the moonlight. He was breathing heavily. He must have lain in the straw there brooding on his wrongs, keeping himself screwed up to the point of action, and the wait had strained his control too far. With no word spoken and as if there had been no interval, he attacked savagely with the whip.

It was thirty years since a hand had been raised in anger against John Stadis. Although a blow was to be expected, this was very much in the plural, with six foot of fury behind it, some fourteen stone in weight and several hours of misery. But remembering the last, Sir John protected his face and let the storm exhaust itself; luckily several blows fell wide. When it began to slacken he turned and gripped Gaier's wrist, quite gently, and let the whip fall. They stood for a moment in silence.

'I must tell you now,' Sir John said as lightly as he could manage, 'that if I have at all wronged you, it is not in the sense you may imagine. I exchanged looks and words with your wife – the extravagance of compliment – no more.'

He paused. There was no response. The little speech, over which he had taken some care, had simply not been heard. When he looked up into Gaier's face he saw why.

The pupils of his eyes were rolled back, invisible, only the whites showing and those dulled to yellow. The lips were held open and the teeth locked. A tremor began to shake him from the head downwards, he swayed, and Sir John was just able to lower him gradually to the ground.

This, in a way, was harder to handle. Sir John bent over his fallen foe and loosened the collar; he struggled feebly, uttering somewhat between a grunt and a snore. What now? Best let him lie, perhaps, although his condition seemed alarming. He was safe enough on the floor, at least while one got into one's coat – an operation of some discomfort. The night air had grown chilly. Cover him up, there was the doublet; easier said than done, he threw it off again and began to thresh about wildly. Already overheated with exercise, if he took cold it might be fatal. Luckily there was a flask in the saddlebag. Sir John fetched it, and without spilling much he was able to transfer most of the contents to Jamie Gaier. The fit, it seemed, was past. For all that, he was relieved when Jamie's eyes opened naturally, blinked, and shut firmly as he slumped back into the straw again. Sick or well, he'd had quite enough of the young gentleman.

He had no idea what hour it was. Everything lay quiet; the moon was high over dusky trees. There might have been a house behind the coppice; he had no intention of finding out. The barn of course could shelter them, but dawn would bring the haymakers. No, they had best get back along the London road, if Jamie's horse could carry him.

He whistled softly to Jewel, and examined hooves and harness. He managed somehow to heave the inert body out of the straw and on to the grey's long back, fastening the arms round the crupper and buckling belt to saddlegirths; a clumsy contrivance, but at a moderate pace it would hold. The small procession moved obediently through the gate.

Sir John's thoughts were curiously sober. He blamed himself entirely for the episode; whether or not Penelope Gaier attracted him, a man of his age and reputation should have had more sense. As for baiting the unfortunate husband, good God, it was no excuse that his irresponsible crew had set that exploit afoot. What was John Stadis, knighted in Flanders, friend of Sidney and Dalbie, doing with such companions? He mused how Sidney's death had left them all the poorer: there was Greville grown sullen and secret, young Essex pert and arrogant, himself cynically haunting the beargarden and playhouse with a congregation of shabby tricksters, sunk lower than the rest. Only Ned Dyer had retired to his beloved Somerset, reading and keeping bees. Happy Edward, whose mind to him a kingdom is! How did the verse go?

> I see how plenty suffers oft
> And hasty climbers soon do fall;
> I see that those which are aloft
> Mishap doth threaten most of all . . .

True enough, Edward, as you knew too well –

> . . . But all the pleasure that I find
> Is to maintain a quiet mind.

There, undoubtedly, was a way out; but for himself, somehow, the time was not yet.

A bramble caught his sleeve, and he found the road had narrowed. Had he wandered into a byway, immersed in these moonshine thoughts? This would never do. Jamie's heavy breathing was unaltered, but he must not be carted round the countryside all night. Sir John turned painfully in the saddle for a wider view. The moon chose this moment to be dimmed with a little veil of cloud, but the Stadis luck brought for compensation a church clock chiming three quarters somewhere away to the left. He knew where he was now, and remembered outside the village a comfortable little inn, tucked away down just such a lane from the dust of the drovers' road: an inn moreover with a new landlord, an old soldier who had known him in Holland. They must be half a mile from the place. Get the poor fool to bed there in snugness and privacy, good Corporal Trott and his wife would keep counsel.

Sir John himself would go back to his home in Southwark: so much only could he yet decide. The strange mood of all-embracing charity still held him, but he knew he had crossed a border, and nothing would ever be the same hereafter. Was it as simple as this, a chance meeting, the whim of a moment: was man indeed pre-destined to heaven or hell? (Not, he thought wryly, that he could be considered one of the elect.) No, there was always a time to choose. He could have behaved differently to James Gaier; fought and disarmed him, run away, or covered him with such ridicule he would have essayed no further. Certainly, choice was free: but having chosen, neither heaven nor earth could undo it; one must take what followed, inescapable, as night follows day. What would follow he could not foresee. He would await the event.

And here, at least, was the inn. He dismounted, grimacing at the unexpected stiffness, espied a light in the back premises, and was soon tapping on the kitchen door.

'God ha' mercy *me*!' said plump little Mistress Trott. 'At this time of the night! Why, Sir John, you give me a nasty turn for a minnit. But come in, do, I was just doin' a bit of smoothing, being as how the kitchen fire was that beautiful it was a shame to waste it, and it wouldn't take long to bring up agin if there's anything your honour wanted?'

'I'm sorry to disturb you, Mrs Trott, but thank God someone was up. I've got a gentleman out here somewhat under the weather. D'you think your husband could help me with him?'

'Well, for certain sure, Sir John, he's only gone up a half hour, we've had the house full of them droviers and it puts us all about – I'll just call him, Sir John, but come in to the fire, do.'

He bent under the low doorway and found himself in a comfortable room, with a wide old-fashioned hearth in which the embers still glowed. The table was piled with new-folded clean linen, whose pleasant fresh smell mingled with the wholesome odours of cooked food. A big clock ticking cheerfully between the candles on the chimney-piece proclaimed the hour of twelve, and almost immediately the spry little middle-aged landlord came in, still tucking himself hurriedly into his breeches.

'Wotcher, corporal!' Sir John greeted him, and he sketched a salute in answer.

'Well, sir, this is a pleasure. I'll see to your friend, sir, but with only the one room empty, and he's drunk I take it, it wouldn't be fitting to bed you together – the wife'll make him up a nice bed in the public room if that'll suit?'

To be in contact with a mature and understanding mind was immense relief. 'Step outside with me,' he requested, and made the landlord briefly acquainted with the events of the night. 'That he's drunk is my fault, he'll sleep that off, but he's a sick man, Trott. Put him in your best bed and look after him, will you?'

They carried James Gaier upstairs and laid him under the worn oak canopy. His face was flushed and sweating. 'If he's fit enough when he wakes, let him go. If not – and I trust you to watch him like a brother – keep him here and send word to his lady – she's at Greenwich – and to his own doctor at home, I think, for she'll not know what to do. I'll write it down for you. It's the other side of Tonbridge, I believe.' He felt in an inner pocket for some coins.

'Surely, sir, you'll be here yourself in the morning?'

'No, Trott, no, he mustn't find me here.'

'But he'll ask –'

'Oh, give him my name if he insists, poor devil; he'll not know where he is or what's happened. You can tell him, anyhow, the reckoning is paid.'

They had descended to the kitchen again, and here Mistress Trott could contain herself no longer.

'Sir John, you're never going out of this house in the middle of the night!'

'I am, though,' he said, smiling. 'I must be at Bankside before daylight, if you will tell me the readiest way.'

She stamped her foot. 'Jacob, say something, it's not right he should go.'

'Better stay, sir,' Trott nodded. 'We can fix it so's you don't meet in the morning, if that's your pleasure.'

It was tempting, and he hesitated. Warmth and friendliness streamed from them, to lull for the moment that sense of lonely destiny. But there were more questions afoot than the affairs of Black Jamie. His followers, where had they gone? How would he meet them, how deal with them hereafter; what change must he make in his settled plan? Such matters were better faced alone in the quiet of an empty house. But food now – 'A meal and a wash,' he said firmly, and had his way as ever.

The rest refreshed him; the five miles' journey through the sleeping fields to Orchard House was almost pleasant, though he had stiffened and felt very sore when he dismounted at his own back gate. Two struck from St Saviour's as he turned the key. Ten minutes spent on Jewel, a rub down and some oats, he'd be in bed by quarter past; the moon was still bright, he'd need no candle.

He felt his way through the kitchen quarters, dark and silent as they ought to be, and emerged into the hall.

There was a line of light. It came from beneath the library door. Thieves? Would thieves pass by the pantry and the silver? He was still no more than annoyed as he strode across and flung open the door, without knowing what he would find. But directly he saw it, in the instant of printing upon his unprepared eyeballs, he knew he had known it all the time.

The curtains were pulled close, and some dozen candles grouped in the centre of the room. Every book in the place was stacked on the floor, with the contents of his cabinet. Two nondescript men in rusty black were searching methodically through the books and papers, turning every leaf, lifting every article, replacing as they went. They worked in silence and precision, and scarcely heeded the open door.

One heard of such things, even now in 1600. Young men home from Jesuit colleges, doubtful travellers in curious merchandise, persons too friendly with the staff of foreign embassies; any of these, it was common knowledge, would have their rooms searched in the small hours, and most likely never know it; they were always away. He would have been away.

But why tonight?

He turned and left them, and took the shallow stairs two at a time. His bedroom door stood open, and the closet beyond; no attempt at concealment here. By the shuttered window was a thin black figure leaning on an ivory-handled stick, immutable, immovable. The Secretary of State had come in person.

The fingers tightened on the carved knob, but the voice was quiet, weary.

'I am grieved for this, Sir John. You were thought to be at Greenwich.'

'As I perceive.'

They faced each other through the veiled hostility of twenty years' acquaintance. The Secretary's pale eyes flickered over Sir John's dishevelled appearance, and away again with faint distaste; from bear-pit to brothel? he managed to convey. Sir John held back his leaping anger. There was a puzzle here to solve. But the room was close, his head reeling, and he ached in every limb. He said harshly, 'What brings you here: some tomfool jest? You are wasting your time.'

The same tired voice said, 'Are we, Fabian?'

'I'm afraid not, sir.' A sandy-haired man came from the inner room. He answered his chief, but kept his gaze fixed on Sir John. He held a paper out to the lamplight, a yellow scroll with a red seal. The Secretary read, his pale cheeks growing paler, and emitted a long exhausted breath.

He said, 'I tried not to credit it. You will not understand that. The world believes us enemies, but Sir John, Sir John, I had sooner have lost my right hand than meet the dawning of this day.' He moved to the blind windows, clutching heavily at the sill.

Sir John took one step towards him, then hesitated. The man called Fabian spoke.

'Sir John Stadis may have something to say.' It was a pleasant voice, honest but impersonal, matching the blue intelligent eyes. The hands were strong, square and uncompromising. There was a long moment of mutual scrutiny.

'Yes,' said Sir John at last. 'I ask to see that paper.'

Without shifting his gaze, Fabian tendered it. It seemed to be the close of a letter in formal Latin, conveying good wishes and enjoining secrecy. The signature was illegible, indeed the wax of the seal half covered it.

'Well,' he said, 'am I supposed to have sent or received this missive?' But even as he spoke, and idly turned the sheet, he frowned in recognition. The reverse bore his own writing, in Spanish: *DAROS EL REINO* – 'give you the realm.'

'Well, sir?' said Fabian. 'You know this paper?'

'I know one side of it. Except for these three words, when last I saw it the sheet was blank.'

The Secretary stirred sharply.

'But the Spanish is in your own hand?' continued Fabian without pause.

'Even so.'

'Leave this, Fabian,' cried the Secretary with sudden violence. 'We are not his judges.'

'Pardon me.' Fabian was firm though respectful. 'If he admits it, we are so much the clearer. The writing, sir, is yours: to whom did you make the offer of a realm?'

The crooked Stadis smile slipped out. 'You both mistake me, gentlemen. The offer was not mine, but God the

Father's, if I read the evangelist aright. St Luke, is it? Fear not, little flock, for it is your Father's good pleasure –'

'To give you the kingdom,' Fabian concluded for him. 'You affirm this –' he took it back, handing it to the Secretary 'to be a piece of scripture, written by you in the Spanish tongue, upon a blank sheet of paper.'

'I do,' said Sir John, and for all his efforts he was gaping sleepily. 'It was many years ago, and I know well no one will believe me. And now, gentlemen, I am nearing forty and have been up since daybreak. May I sleep in my own bed, and we will discuss this matter in the morning?'

Fabian met his chief's eye, and nodded slightly. The Secretary, without another word, limped slowly from the room, and down the stairs. They heard the front door open and his carriage drive rapidly away.

Sir John shrugged, and crossing to the window flung back shutter and casement. His face was dark.

The man Fabian said, still watching him, 'It is out of his hands now. But you have five hours at least – he will hardly see the Queen before seven –' He broke off. 'I am sorry sir, I must leave a man at your door.'

'Anything you like.' Sir John's head was splitting. He tugged his boots off without more ado and rolled on to the bed. The door shut with a click, but he hardly heard it.

3

Fabian

Now in the name of all the gods at once, (thought Fabian), why did I tell him that?

He went downstairs and found the searchers, their task done, tidying up. He locked the library door and paid off the men, who left together, bidding him goodnight: quiet, sober, respectable, like the professionals they were: the undertakers of the State. Many a man's grave had been dug by their labours, and his head left bleaching on the gatehouse. Too many: traitors or heads, whichever way you looked at it. Fabian was not used to feel qualms about his calling, nor did he now; but he wished he were not so disturbed by the case in hand. Sir John Stadis! It was not possible; it ought not to be possible.

He knew, of course, the Stadis reputation. It was not nice, but it had always been open; he spoke his mind and acted as he chose, careless of slander or approval. Did that square only too well with his present attitude? Could such a man, recklessly independent, less protestant than unbeliever, have leaned in the least degree to Spain or Rome?

'You can come in now, Hobson,' he said. 'Our gentleman is upstairs and gone to bed. You'll be relieved at eight. No one is to pass.'

'Begging your pardon, sir, how about the window?'

'He'll not use it. Besides, I shall be out at the back myself.'

By way of making this statement true, he wandered through to the kitchen. It had been searched earlier, before Sir John's arrival. That he had entered by this way was plain; the door was unlocked and there were damp footmarks on the flags. Fabian put down his candle on the dresser and stepped outside.

The short midsummer night was nearly over; a cool air breathed from the shadowy trees. On one hand was a small paved yard, the stables and a remnant of old orchard: on the other, an archway in a clipped hedge led to the garden proper. He took the stables first. Built for a richer man, they would have housed a dozen beasts, but he found only one, a fine chestnut, which roused and nickered gently. He soothed the animal, noting that it had been fed and cared for. Now if the horse could but speak, what a day's work it might save. Part of its tale could yet be told: clods of scarce-dried mud scattered round the threshold matched a streak or two on the foreleg. He picked up a handful and crumbled it thoughtfully; it was brown and sticky, part clay, not the light soil of Surrey. The roads out of London had been dust for a week. Ponds, potholes? Middlesex earth was darker, he fancied. Moreover, the horse had come through the postern or there was no believing old signs: not through the garden, which alone led to the river. They might, in theory, have crossed elsewhere, below the bridge, and worked back, but that seemed too far-fetched in every sense.

Fabian walked across the dewy lawn, unprinted by another tread. It sloped gradually to the river bank and a small brick landing-stage, clean and new-looking; a boat was tied up there, the ropes unfrayed, the bollard unworn. There was practically no foreshore. Some hundred yards of Thames mud gleamed greyly between him and the waterline; the tide was coming in, but only just. Neither man nor beast had landed here tonight.

Very well then, go to: Sir John had come from Kent. He

had indeed been reported at Greenwich in the morning. But Greenwich was only ten miles by the road. Where had he been till two o'clock, that horse and man were so exhausted? Why, if it came to that, had he returned?

For it was not to remove the paper they had found. There had been not even an anxious glance toward the inner room, where matter more compromising might have been expected. He must see that room again (the key was in his pocket), but he was sure, now, he would uncover nothing else. The clothes press had been his first point of search, not a pocket, wallet, bulky seam or double lining had escaped him; he had felt in every cap and examined each boot and shoe. The shelf above had held nothing but some little phials, dusty and neglected. The paper itself he had found, strangely, at the bottom of a chest, under a heap of discarded gloves, frayed ruffs, buckram and broken points: an unlikely, womanish hiding-place. If Sir John had put it there, where was the rest of the letter? If burnt, why not this? Or stay, if this sheet were part of a letter to Sir John, and his reply had been written on the back of the preceding sheet, as thus: 'If all fall out as we have planned, it will be easy enough (to give you the Kingdom).' He had reached those words, say, and the messenger was waiting: no time for flowery phrases or a rounded period. What would he do? Turn the first sheet, squeeze in his ending there, and thrust the superfluous page down in the chest; yes, it was possible. There was an empty inkhorn on the window-sill. He would have meant to return later and retrieve the second sheet.

Or Stadis was speaking the truth: then someone else had found the paper, kept because it had but three words on it for use again. Someone had used it, knowing the handwriting, to bolster up with his name a Jesuit plot, likely enough without his knowledge? The reverse, the Latin, was then the reply, and the paper had been planted to incriminate him: for there were no names named, and the real conspirators would have destroyed the rest of the letter. Strange how all Fabian's inclination cried out to accept this version: but his trained mind told him it was unlikely. Why produce it at all? The success of the whole conspiracy would be jeopardised were anyone to guess that a conspiracy existed. Unless the plant had been intended for a later stage, to divert suspicion when suspicion was aroused, and had accidentally been discovered first? This was going too far too soon, with insufficient data. Well, examination and observation, the two inviolable rules, must find the truth.

The other papers, he had better take them now while he had an hour or two to spare. By six, when the gates opened, he must be at the bridge. He would go straight to Seething Lane and look through the transcripts himself; tavern gossip or straight fact, whatever was known about Sir John Stadis would be there. Then set the search afoot for servants and associates – Farmer must do that, there was no one else to spare – then back here and interview the suspect: a fair morning's work, and one he had little stomach for.

Shivering a little, Fabian made his way back to the library. It faced east, and he was glad to pull curtains and let the morning enter. Spread out upon a table were the results of the search: a locked box, books annotated in the margins, a pile of letters and loose papers with a note of where each had been found. He tackled the box first, and it yielded gently to a fine wire; the lock had been oiled and in frequent use. Estate papers and documents (he began to list the contents) tenancies, accounts, crop records, cottage repairs, fences –

> last will and testament of Henry Stadis, January 1578 ('everything to my son John') –
> last will and testament of Roger Dalbie, August 1586 ('and I appoint John Stadis, gentleman of Sir John Norris's company, to be my executor and sole guardian of my daughter') –

a paper affixed, names, sums of money and dates of payment, May and June 1587–

memorandum of agreement between John Stadis, knight, the vendor, and Geo. Thompson the purchaser (sale of land near Tewkesbury) –

a packet of letters, which he put aside for the moment–

Deed of Gift (copy): Aldernaton: dwellinghouse and those lands known as (etc.) to my ward Barbara Dalbie and her issue.

This last was rolled at the back of the box. As he picked it up, something fell from the roll and thudded between his feet; it was a massive signet. Fabian looked at it curiously. Instead of the usual lozenge, the face was square. It showed the Stadis device of a single tree, simplified into the letter T with two forking roots. The rest of the inscription formed three pairs of reversed letters, one on either side of the T: A-S, S-D, R-P. These puzzled him until he remembered that not only the shape of the letters but their order would be reversed in impression – S-A, D-S, P-R. He wasted a moment working it out, from habit. It was easy as soon as he saw that the tree figured three times; as a T in the top line, as I in the middle, and at the bottom the forked roots served for an A. Of course, it was the motto; STA DISPAR – Stand Apart; dog-Latin like most of its kind, it sounded wrong even to Fabian's hazy memories of grammar. Or STADIS PAR, he thought: equal to anything on God's earth – until now.

He weighed the signet thoughtfully in his hand. It was a clumsy piece, probably old; seldom used now, too heavy to wear, it would be kept locked away in the most appropriate place. He dropped it back in the box and unrolled the Deed of Gift again right down to the bottom. There at its foot was the seal's impression – he might have saved his labour:

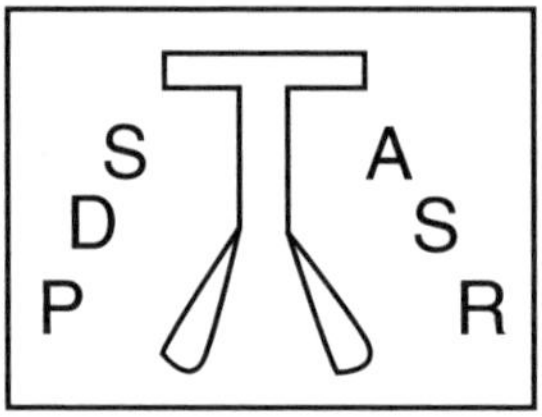

and the date, 15th December, 1598.

Now for the letters. They were tied together neatly and in order, the earliest at the bottom. Fabian turned the packet upside down to read them currently. The first, in a childish hand, began, 'Dear Sir, my mother wishes me write as we are both bounde to your kindnesse . . .' There was no letter from the mother, unless on the back of this a few words scrawled, 'God bless you, your true friend.' The signatory was the child, Barbara Dalbie, and the date '11th April, 1587: at Aldernaton.' Thereafter she had written every month a short note, not always dated but the seasons vividly in the contents: ride on the haycart – quince jelly for supper – ice on the pond – mother fallen sick again – the first lambs doing well. Fabian read on, though this could hardly be his stuff, and the long country days unfolded before him. Mother was 'fallen sick' more often than not: soon it was the accepted fact, and she was either 'a little stronger' or 'hoping with better weather to amend.' In February 1589 she died. After that it was Aunt Kate who figured in the letters, and sometimes a forbidding uncle: 'My uncle says I will never make a scholar, I do but reade to enjoye' – 'Uncle preached today on the sin of idleness' – 'My uncle will not have me to studie Vergil, rather Cicero and Livy who (he says) teach more': and a good deal later, 'I have read your friend's poems with pleasure: my aunt is won over, for she knew his sister and they are of a good family, but says we need not tell my uncle.'

Sir John seemed to have paid regular visits at first, but by

1595 they had dwindled to once a year. 'You coming is so talked of in the village,' wrote Barbara, 'as if the golden age were near. I am sorry we have not now about the house so many who remember you.' The following spring she was enquiring 'if, as we hope, you will visit us this summer.' In 1597 he stayed a month: in 1598 he did not go at all, and since then the letters mentioned only a short visit. They were long frank letters now, full of allusions to his replies. The last was in April of this year. No, wait, here was another, apart from the collection: slipped into a volume of Horace, the *Odes*, Book III –

Faune, Nympharum fugientem amator
per meos fines et aprica rura
lenis incedas abeasque parvis
aequus alumnis –

was it a coincidence that Sir John had placed it there? Had he, when the letter arrived, been reading wistfully of sunny meadows, flocks, and village occupations? For here, as in the poem, was certainly a nymph fleeing from her wooers. 'If it please you to come, sir, you may give me much assistance, and yet if you cannot come but will advise me I will thank you too.' This was written on 19th May, and there was no sign of a June letter. He had gone, of course, who could resist such an appeal? Gone and come south again; reported back at court three days, and now lay here in danger of the Tower. Was there some significance in the sequel? Could the letter be a secret message, the *Odes* of Horace its key? Fabian swore, quietly but aloud. Fantastic as it seemed, the possibility could not be overlooked. He put aside letters and Horace for the attention of a cipher expert, and replaced the other documents tidily in the box.

So far, Sir John was revealed both as a faithful landlord and good friend. As well as providing for the widow and daughter, he had obviously paid Roger Dalbie's debts, selling some land to do so. He had watched Barbara grow up; had withdrawn, though still corresponding freely, to the point where his visits almost ceased; and in that very year, 1598, not only absented himself but made over to his ward, with some conditions, the title to Aldernaton. A betrothal gift? If so, something had gone wrong; she had not married. Two years later she was asking his help against the local fauna (Fabian grinned at his own poor jest). Well, with the uninterrupted series behind it, the final letter looked innocent enough. The sooner it was proved so the better, and he would return the whole packet under seal.

He turned to the loose papers. Nothing here was methodical; they had been found tossed aside or tucked into books. There were bills (mostly receipted), invitations, a note in a vile hand: 'You came not to the Mermaid so send by bearer', an old wax tablet still scored with the memorandum 'Wednesday at Greville's': all trivial stuff. The marked books were equally innocuous. A few passages in the Greek and Latin authors had been signalled out for remembrance, probably at school, for they were musty with disuse; only the Horace showed signs of constant reading. Of contemporary works, a line or two of Spenser underscored might have been intended as criticism. The rest were flyleaf inscriptions of the conventional sort. Nothing else suspicious had been found, neither mass books nor hidden vestments; indeed he had not supposed there would be. The house had not been built ten years, there were no sliding panels nor secret passages, and every cupboard and closet had been subjected to a thorough scrutiny. The tale of the house was now concluded, and it told precious little. Did it seem significantly bare? The furnishings were not the man, and might indeed have been hired with the house; as for things personal, an hour's work would have removed the lot. A man who had entered on a dangerous course might well begin by clearing away inessentials; there was such a feeling in the house, Fabian was certain, as of a soul made ready for departure. He pulled a face over the metaphor, and rose to follow its example.

Sir John's room remained quiet. With a word to Hobson, he set out briskly for the city.

Coming back through Southwark some two hours later, his programme fulfilled, Fabian smelled breakfast on every side. The tenements were alive and busy, and the smoke of their cooking ascended into cloudless blue. The bustle of the streets increased his sense of urgency; through Bankside and out into the quiet of the country road the uneasiness deepened. A sudden clatter of hooves made him fear he was too late, but it was only a couple of market carts rattling emptily homeward. A little light mist still rose off the vegetable fields, and Orchard House lay silent on his right. It was half past seven.

He dismissed Hobson to the nearest tavern, knocked on the bedroom door and entered. Sir John roused at once. Fabian watched awakening give place to remembrance, and (he thought) acquiescence. He said 'I have sent out for breakfast, will you join me when it comes?'

'Thank you. I am sorry my household is so unprovided. May I dress?'

'As you will, sir, but we must talk, quickly, before the guard arrives. When they get you inside I may not have access.' He paused, and added, 'There are those who want a scapegoat. For God's sake, shield no one, not even by silence. Tell me what you know, and I will help you if I can.'

Sir John said, 'Your usual gambit, Fabian? Is that your name? What is your office?'

'To find the truth,' said Fabian. 'If you are clear of this matter, nothing else you tell me will be divulged: if not – nothing on earth can save you.'

'And yet last night – what would you have done in my place?'

'Put thirty miles between me and London,' said Fabian promptly.

'And supposing you were innocent?'

'Even more so.'

'I see.' He smiled a little. 'Well, ask your questions.'

'First, when did you turn St Luke into Spanish?'

'When we garrisoned Flushing – in 1586 it would be.' The answer came readily enough. 'There was little to do that first winter and spring. Someone would make a raid and bring back prisoners; I knew a little Spanish and I used to question them. To fill in leisure, I sat down with a borrowed Bible and tried my hand at translation.' He looked up with the rueful Stadis smile. 'With my reputation, you may find it hard to believe.'

'Worse,' said Fabian, 'it will be hard to prove. Who knew of it? What became of the work?'

'The chaplain had it – what was his name? Walton, Walters, something like that. I was transferred to Norris's company soon after, and never saw him again.'

'And this odd sheet – Chapter twelve, I think – was as far as you got?'

'It must have been. I scarcely remember.'

'Excluding last night, how long since you handled the paper?'

'Some years, I should think. It was in an old wallet.'

'Where was the wallet kept?'

'Nowhere especially – up here, or in the cabinet downstairs –'

He was making a rapid toilet as he spoke, Fabian automatically handing him towel and brush as in some preposterous levee. Catching Fabian's eye, he remarked, 'They say the King of France has forty-seven.' They both smiled. Was it a clever change of subject? Two could play that game.

'Have you an enemy?'

'A dozen. None, I would have said yesterday, capable of this.'

'Do you know this writing?' It was two scraps of cheap paper, the latest of the anonymous letters, announcing in clumsy characters 'SIR J. STIDDIS GOES TOO GRENICH' and 'TRY ORCHD HOWSE TONIGHT'. The subject of the message looked at it with distaste. 'A bad pen, and a writer of small experience. No, I do not know it.'

'Who knew you would go to Greenwich?'

'Half London, I expect. I made no secret of it.'

'Why did you come back last night, or rather this morning?'

Here for the first time Sir John hesitated.

'I will put it another way,' said Fabian crisply. 'Who was with you and when did you part company?' We are getting somewhere, he thought.

Sir John shook his head. 'It can have no possible connection with this business.'

'Then there is no reason why you should not tell me.'

'My companion's affairs are not mine to discuss.'

Fabian said, 'The talk last night in Eastcheap was that you quarrelled with Black Jamie Gaier and were horsewhipped. Is that true?'

Sir John stared. 'Not altogether.'

'How then?'

'It was a bull-whip, I believe.'

Their eyes met, charged with precisely the same degree of mockery. They laughed loud and long, laughed till they cried; they clung shaking and helpless to the bedposts. Hobson, that worthy officer, arriving to herald a laden potboy, looked first alarmed and then scandalised.

'Shall I send the food up, sir?'

'Do, do.' Fabian recovered himself with an effort. 'And now,' he said, 'you had better tell me all about it.'

'Faith, I were best testify with my shirt off, and let the bruises speak for me.'

'In your own interest, you will be asked to do so yet.'

That sobered them both. They fell to breakfast, while Sir John told the story. He spoke simply, with a detachment unusual in a witness. The barn and the whispered colloquy he made no more of than any other incident. Is it possible, thought Fabian, that he cannot see the significance of that?

'So I left him with the innkeeper, and came – home.' He weighed a little on the last word. 'For it is all the home I have, and I was tired. I could have gone no further last night to save my life. To save my life,' he repeated. 'May it even come to that?' He pushed away his plate and wandered over to the window.

Fabian watched him keenly. He was behaving very well in a difficult situation, an impression that no new fact so far could counterweigh. He did not look nor sound like a conspirator. The extraordinary story he had just told rang true enough if for this only, that no one surely would invent it; a story that could be checked, and one moreover exposing him to the scorn of the world he lived in. No one would even contrive it – for assume it would be confirmed, in all substantials – unless for some overmastering reason. For what after all did it provide? An explanation for his sudden return, nothing more. There could be only one cause for manufacturing so damaging an excuse; if the real reason were even more damning. It did not at all exonerate him from a charge of treason; in fact, the weak spot of the narrative might lead directly back to that point. If the rest of the story were invented, would that part have been included? If true and the narrator guilty, would it not be concealed? Or must it be included but minimised, because Gaier's evidence would reveal it?

'Whereabouts did you say this was?' Fabian tried to sound casual, but the intimacy of a moment ago had been destroyed. When Sir John swung round he was on guard again, a faint smile lightening the shadowed eyes. He said quietly, 'I did not know the road.'

'Could you find it again, do you think?'

'Not from Blackheath.'

'From the inn, perhaps?'

'I might. Things look different in moonlight.'

The point of evasion? Fabian was sorry for him, but disappointed. Very well, then, he should have it straight.

'The inn itself – you know that. I must ask you for the name of the inn.'

'And I must leave you to discover it.'

That was straight enough, too, and so was the look that accompanied it. 'In God's name,' said Fabian, exasperated, 'will you begin to see your danger?'

'I see it, though not yet how I came in it. It can hardly be such that an extra day's delay will alter. You perceive,' his smile deepened, 'that I do not belittle your people. You will find it soon enough; the respite may mean the difference between health and sickness to that poor wretch.'

Or life and death, if Gaier should be their quarry? But let it pass; Fabian knew when he was wasting his time.

'And you still think the affairs have no connection?'

'I can see none. None but – it sounds foolish – a feeling I thought I had.'

'A premonition, would you say? You felt it when?'

'Most strongly as we waited for Gaier.'

'"We" being –'

'Greenlee, myself and my odd couple. Adey and Crooks, or Crooks and Adey –' He broke off. 'But this is moonshine and not evidence.'

'And the other occasions?' Time wasted perhaps, but confidence regained.

'The other was a dream, mere nonsense. No, there is nothing to it. No Fate pursues me but my own ill-humour – I have been in the sullens since we came back from Worcestershire.'

'Not in our stars, but in ourselves?' said Fabian.

He grinned reluctantly. 'That's *Julius Caesar* – Cassius, was it? You saw the play?'

'I never miss them – the Chamberlain's; Alleyn's lot you can keep; nothing but strut and spout, and that handsome face of his to fetch in the groundlings.'

'And a good leg and a good foot to it,' Sir John said, laughing. 'And his company standing about like so many hobbyhorses – I'm with you there. For acting, every time, give me Burbage and Will.'

They talked playhouse for some minutes – precious minutes ticking relentlessly away and both of them aware of it – till Fabian pulled out his notes.

'When did you come back from Aldernaton?'

'June the – tenth was it? A Tuesday.'

'In the same company?'

'The four of us: we'd not met Gaier then, not till yesterday, ye gods!'

'Will you tell me your movements since?'

He did so briefly, and (prompted by questions) backward as far as he could remember.

'You were nine, ten days at the Quartern.' Fabian kept his face expressionless. 'Doing what?'

'Waiting for a summons.'

'To court? Just so. But while waiting: had you business at all?'

With barely a pause, he said, 'No.'

Fabian pocketed his tablets carefully. He said, 'You know this is only the beginning. You'll be questioned time and again, and not by me. If there is anything – indiscreet, for instance: anything you have not told me – I beg you most earnestly to do so now. An action may be – not treasonous, which if concealed may yet appear so.'

He said again, 'No, but I thank you.'

'No one you met by chance, or invited to this house? No friend or enemy who may have scotched his own difficulty by making it yours?'

He said firmly, 'There is nothing.' They were both silent, listening for the sound that was to come.

'For my private satisfaction, could you tell me one thing?, Fabian was diffident now. 'In the matter of James Gaier. Why would you not fight him?'

'A guilty conscience, shall we say?' But he smiled again. 'No, I will tell you, for your own ear. It is not generally known, and I think he would not wish it. He is going blind.'

'He told you so?'

'I'm the last person he would tell. No, I guessed it; I've seen the signs before.'

'I see.' Yes, that fitted, although a jury might not credit it. He looked at Sir John with a new liking and respect. This was a bigger man, in both senses of the word, than one at first sight supposed. Fabian noted consciously for the first time his easy strength of body, the authority of his bearing; and if he was not over-tall, in conversation one forgot it. The Stadis charm had not been exaggerated, and was none the less potent for being withheld; as now.

Sir John had dropped the matter already, as though unwilling to take advantage from it, and had turned to the window again. 'A beautiful day,' he said, and it was more somehow than a comment on the weather.

Fabian could only say, 'The house and garden match it.'

Answering the unspoken thought, 'I could not have settled here. I miss the hills,' he said. Then, dismissing that subject also, 'We're on the wrong side of the house, you know. They'll come by the road, I suppose.'

'Shall we go downstairs?'

'If you please. You are in command.' He saluted with a mock ceremony which they both enjoyed. When Fabian motioned him to go first, he was neither deceived by the courtesy nor offended at the precaution. The door duly locked, they descended the broad stairway together like host and guest.

Should I ask more, wondered Fabian, or leave well alone? The minor queries he need not himself pursue. He'd given his man at least three openings, all plainly declined, but the relationship established between them was so uncommon that even now something might come of it – if there were time. They had already had longer than he expected; the tall clock in the entrance hall lacked twenty minutes of ten. And in spite of his outward coolness, Sir John was clearly feeling the strain. He walked up and down the hall, hands in pockets, aimlessly.

What a pity, thought Fabian: with the country crying out for men of this quality, what pitiful waste. He had been kept idle, and others like him, while lawyers and politicians ruled the roost, until this was the outcome. Guilty or not, the possibility should never have arisen.

Abruptly aware of his restlessness, Sir John halted. He glanced up at Fabian with that half-smile, but when he spoke it was directly and seriously.

'It looks bad,' he said. (Fabian nodded.) 'Were I given to protestation, this is not the time and place, and I will not insult you with it. As for the customary trust in one's innocence, believe me, I have no such illusion. Better men have died for less.' He resumed his pacing.

There were horses on the road at last.

'Before they come, may I ask you one favour?'

'Ask,' said Fabian (and prayed, let him not spoil it now).

'My sword is at Deptford, but as you surely know, there is another weapon in the house. It was my father's. If it lies within your duty, will you forget for ten minutes that you saw it?'

'Willingly.' And now, it seemed, they could both smile

again. They shook hands, as outside the troop clattered to a standstill.

Sir John went out bareheaded to meet them in the startling sunlight. There were six horses, one led; four men and a young captain with candid, troubled eyes.

'I am sorry to carry out this command, Sir John.'

'You need not be, Captain Wintring, I am happy to obey it.'

Captain Wintring produced his warrant.

'Sir John Stadis, I arrest you in the Queen's name. You must surrender your arms and go with me presently to the Tower.'

'I am parted from my sword already, sir. Will the surrender of my person content you?'

'If it please you to mount, Sir John,' he replied unhappily.

As he swung into the saddle, 'Jewel!' he exclaimed. 'I had forgot. My horse is in the stable.' He looked across at Fabian.

'The horse will be cared for. I can do that at least.'

'Thanks. Work him if you can. Until I claim him.' The eyes added their own ironic comment. 'I am ready,' he said.

The captain gave a signal; the six horses started forward as one. They broke into a canter, raising a little cloud of dust, and disappeared round the bend. In the silence that followed, a lark was singing.

4

Farmer

When Fabian reached his lodging near Bishopsgate, it was past two o'clock. He went in as usual, into the haberdasher's and through the little door at the back of the shop. This opened directly on to a staircase, at the head of which a narrow passage ran the whole length of the building. The last door on the right gave on to quite a pleasant chamber, light because the neighbouring roofs were lower. There was a small bedroom beyond, and another door by which he could descend to the yard and leave as he chose, either out at the ironmongers or by way of a warehouse to the rear. It was comfortable and convenient, and entirely respectable.

A note had been pushed under the door, double-folded and sealed with plain wax. 'Committed. Come to me on Friday.' Committed! Where was I the while? And if he thought by Friday to have the whole story pat he can think again, was Fabian's comment. He burned the paper, went disgustedly to bed and slept about five hours.

He was wakened by a little bell at the bedhead, caused to ring, with some ingenuity and a quantity of thin cord, from his warehouse entrance. He got up and plunged his face in a basin of water. It was a lovely golden evening.

The visitor was Farmer, of course. He came in showing all his fifty-odd years, and sank heavily into a chair. It had been hot, and his feet ached, and of the dozen or so interviews entrusted to him only two had proved transferable. With his ruddy complexion and plain brown homespun he looked like a prosperous countryman, like enough to account for the name he was known by; he was in fact a Londoner, knew the city like the palm of his hand, and farmed out more enquiries, with more success, than anyone else in the service. Either way, the name had stuck.

Fabian poured him a drink in silence, and he gulped it thirstily.

'I've been to Deptford, and I've been to Greenwich, and then across the water and right down as far as Wapping. I got something, but not much.'

'Will it keep?'

Farmer snorted. 'It's not hot enough to catch cold.'

'Right, then leave it for a bit. Tell me first of all whatever you know about Stadis.'

Farmer's shrewd good-humoured face dropped into cockney-lugubrious.

'Here, what *is* all this? *I* never went to court. You know more than I'm likely to.'

'Not the same things. You know what people say and think, in the gardens, in the eating-houses; what do they think of Sir John? What manner of man is he?'

'I never met him myself. Well, first, he's only a Leicester knight, but he did see real service – not like this lot swaggering about in Ireland impressing the poor savages.' He took a contemptuous swig of liquor. 'He's liked – I'd say well liked, that is, generally. Merry with his friends, pays as he goes, keeps his people well found and never stints the reckoning. Mind you, there are virtuous folk looking down their noses at the pack of them.'

'But the ungodly are not so. Well,' said Fabian, 'warm, eh? What they call a tall fellow?'

Farmer pursed his lips comically. 'Not quite that. He's always Sir John, I gather. He'll go as far as the next man, but in a different way, see? You know what they say about him? He could put up his own sign wherever he goes. Stadis Place. That's what people think of him.'

'STA DISPAR,' murmured Fabian, 'or, "shall I not take mine ease at mine inn?"'

'He's got no place of his own, not in London,' said Farmer. He did not frequent playhouses, being one of those happy souls who find sufficient interest in human nature itself; besides, he was the older London and knew nothing of the new living theatre that was itself a comment upon life, witty, gentle or malicious, and would not have cared for it if he had: so are we wedded to our own generation. Thus thought Fabian, and grinned affectionately at his colleague. In all essentials they understood each other exactly, and worked together very well.

'It fits, so far. Any more?'

'More brings me to today.'

'No, wait then, let's see where we are. I'll give you my side of the picture.' Fabian laid on the table his notes of early morning. His glance rested on the top sheet, but did not see it. He stood in thought for a moment, teasing his square beard with a square forefinger.

'Ever try to clean an old tapestry? I helped my mother do it, years ago. Faded, stiff with dirt, nothing but dim figures and a mass of greenery. No telling whether it was Venus and Adonis, or the nymph being changed into a laurel. You sponge away very gently, a corner at a time, and gradually the picture appears – a bit of blue sky, a cloud, a bird flying: leaves on the trees, a lock of yellow hair. It takes days. If you rub hard, the thread breaks; if you get it too wet, the whole thing may drop to pieces. And all the time you're guessing at the other bits, and altering your guess each day. It got hold of me, even as a boy. I little thought my life's work would be the same.'

'And what did it turn out to be?' demanded Farmer.

'What? – oh, the tapestry. It was Abraham and Isaac. What we'd taken for Cupid with his arrows was the ram caught in the thicket.' He laughed. 'That's the way it goes.'

Farmer nodded. 'You might have known, though. If it was an old piece, much more likely to be out of the Bible than any of these nymphs and things.'

'You're right, Farmer. There's the point. The past, so far as it's known, needs study too. If we try to judge by present appearance, we're apt to see only what we fancy.'

'Like old Jack Gullyman last week,' said Farmer, 'bought a sack of eels off a stranger in Thames Street. They were alive all right, he felt 'em wriggling. When he gets it home and empties it out into the pot, what'd he got but eleven little puppies and a half-brick. Laugh! You should've heard the neighbours.'

'What did he do?' asked Fabian with some interest.

'What could he do? He's a bit deaf, and it might've been his mistake. Said he could hardly drown the lot after carrying 'em all that way, so he drowned ten and kept one for the yard. Got his old woman feeding it with a spoon.'

'Well, there you are,' said Fabian, 'and talking of feeding, I'll see what Mother Margett's got for supper. You might set table for me. There's cheese and a loaf in the cupboard.'

'Bread and cheese for me,' said Farmer, but his face lit up when Fabian came back with a large glazed pie dish and a fresh jug of beer. They dealt with these in a proper manner, while Fabian looked at his notes and made a few more.

'Right,' he said at last, 'let's have at it.' He began to read aloud, but soon forsook his papers and went on talking softly. The sunset flamed in reflection from a nearby window: the chimneys across the way stood up gilded at first, then dark against the darkening blue sky, before his narrative was over.

'Aged thirty-eight or nine. Bachelor. Son of Henry Stedys or Stadis (he spelled it both ways) gentleman, of Worcestershire, and Anne, only daughter of William Warwick Esquire –

whoever he may have been. In spite of the name, he seems to have come from Northumberland.'

'Northumberland, Warwick – now don't tell me –' began Farmer.

'Nothing in it,' said Fabian. 'He was not a Percy or Dudley, a Neville nor a Beauchamp, not even by accident. There'd be stories enough if he were. I find nothing at all. He's been dead fifty years, and there are no known kin. Just plain private gentlemen on either side, no titles, no wealthy alliances. The Stadis line goes further back and we know a little more. One went to the Crusades, another fought at Crécy: after that they lay low, perhaps the estates were encumbered – it cost something to follow all those wars – and cared for neither York nor Lancaster. They kept to themselves, STA DISPAR: the motto dates from then. The next we hear of is Sir John's great-grandfather, in the early years of this century. He had done the King some trifling service, and sent his son to court.'

Fabian drank his beer reflectively.

'They talk of the good old days, but we've come a long way since then. They did seem good for a time: when old Harry was the brave young King astonishing all Europe, when their wars (they thought) were done, trade prospered, even the weather was good and seasonable. And then the years creep by, we grow selfish and cynical, we're round the globe and back and still find nothing good or ill but in the human heart. The nobles' wars for power are finished; no more of up and down, win and lose, the crown on a fresh head after each skirmish: true. But who governs now? A few names, no more – inscribed, they'd go on a thumb-ring. We're free of Rome; are we better for it? On balance, yes; even though we know how few protested truly and how many of the reformers simply wanted money. But there was something to reform, and not all who clustered round the King were seeking favours.

'Richard Stadis, grandfather of Sir John, held some office in the royal household, but resigned it to devote more time to his estates. He was already married. I think one child had died in infancy, but the boy, Henry, was born in the south and made one of the small group of children the little prince was allowed to play with – until, of course, the factions stepped in. It would be that that decided Richard. STA DISPAR – he would not meddle with either party, nor be thought to cadge advantage. He took his family home, and left a reputation so high that when Henry came to London in his turn, years later, it ensured him a warm welcome.

'We had better be clear about this: although Henry Stadis moved freely in Queen Mary's court, he had no leanings towards Rome. There was no suggestion of that at any time. His friends were of either persuasion or of none. Both old and new families accepted the Queen – they did, you know: she was the heir – whatever they thought of her advisers. They even thought her marriage would work out well enough, given time, let the Spaniard learn our ways and not try to interfere. So there's no significance in Henry's Spanish friendships; or his falling in love with a señorita, which came to nothing anyhow, for she had not only two richer men on a string but a sweetheart back at home. The incident is only remembered because it was laughable, and within a twelvemonth he had met and married his proper love. What might be significant (though it's easy to be wise after the event) is that they had no child for five or six years. The times were uncertain, the alliance with Spain was not a success and might become a danger: more and more people were convinced that government was in the wrong hands. And Henry was in London, as far as I can learn, most of that time. He took his bride home, of course, and I suppose spent the summer months at home, but always he came back. That might mean two things – that he and his wife were not agreeing, or that he was needed in London. I think it was the latter. Nothing in his public life could quite account for the high esteem he was held in; unless perhaps (like too few nowadays) the cause was in his personal character, so that he is still spoken of, years after his death, not for what he did but what he was.

'I think, then, that Henry was in the protestant counsels during Queen Mary's reign, although just what part he played we shall never know. Certainly his reputation was already established with all parties as a moderate and honest man who had no axe of his own to grind; and when the present Queen succeeded to the throne and new honours were being distributed, he made himself scarce in the right Stadis tradition. His wife, we may surmise, reaped the reward of her long patience, and a year or two later their only child was born.'

'Wait a minute,' said Farmer. 'There was a whole lot disappeared from the court about that time, Romish sympathisers we thought.'

'Doubtless most of them were. Meanwhile,' he continued, 'I was not yet thought of, and John Stadis was a child in Worcestershire. It's a part I know little of. Aldernaton – heard of it?' Neither of them had. 'Hilly, I believe. Sheep country mostly; the money comes from wool thereabouts, anything else is grown only for their needs. Not that a Stadis would trade. They owned land – Richard had extended the property – they could very well live on their rents. When the boy was old enough they sent him away to school (I think, but I'm not sure, Shrewsbury) and in due course, to the university. In his second year there his mother died.

'That seems to have been the end of a chapter. He left Oxford without graduating, and was at home with his father for several months. Henry still had friends, who would make plans for the boy. He sent him to London at the end of '76, in the nominal care of Viscount Solva; but the Viscount was considering marriage, and John soon had to stand on his own feet. He'd be about sixteen. Anyhow, he succeeded very well: if the entry was for his father's sake, the welcome was soon for his own. In '77 he went with Sidney's mission to the Emperor, the youngest in all that glittering young embassy. With that, of course, he was established. For a year or so after their return he was a page at court.

'In '79 his father died. He'd have to see to things at home. For anyone else that would be the cue to marry childhood sweetheart and settle down, but no: by '83 he was back in London, finding it somewhat changed. His friends were getting married, the Queen was refusing to do so; we were cooling towards France and maddeningly careful of Spain. Stadis was appointed a gentleman-in-waiting, at a time when everyone about the court required not only patience and discretion, but the outward appearance of not needing it. And the storm was beginning to break. There was the Throckmorton plot, the expulsion of the Spanish Ambassador, a growing feeling that war was on the way. There'd be increasing irritation on the part of an able man who lacked advancement. He wanted to sail with Raleigh's expedition to the New World, but was forbidden it by the Queen. Then Holland was further overrun and it was war with Spain at last. He was given permission to join Leicester's army and embarked with the first company to leave – that was Sidney's. Later he was transferred to Norris's, which was seeing more active service; he took part in the siege of Doesburg, received his knighthood, and lost his best friend in a trivial skirmish.

'Dalbie had named him executor, so he got leave to settle his affairs. When he returned, in a month or so, he was used to carry official letters to the General. Leicester sent him back with dispatches, and this time he was ordered to remain in England. There was talk of an appointment, but it went to someone else.

'That is the end, so far, of his career. He was not employed again, for no reason that I can discover, although had England been invaded he was planned to have a command. But times were changing rapidly, there were everywhere new Jacks in office and the old Johns were out. You've seen it happen – I have – in other walks of life.

'I may tell you he behaved handsomely to Dalbie's widow and child, which is no more than one would expect and has no bearing on the present matter, except as the past reflects the future in some measure. We should, I think, consider all we know. He has changed in the interim from a young man of promise, with the world it seemed at his feet, to the figure about town you have described.

'You know how this case was brought to our notice. There were three notes, unsigned, delivered at intervals to the Secretary of State's apartments in such a way as to be untraceable: the first on 13th June thrown in at a window; the second on 21st June, brought to the gate by a nondescript small boy who ran away at once; the third, strangest of all, delivered by an accredited courier who disclaimed all knowledge of it. He'd watered his horse at Holborn and someone must have tucked it in the saddlebag. That was 23rd June – Monday – yesterday, good Lord! We went at night to the house outside Southwark, and found one paper which might be called incriminating; and at that moment, at two in the morning mark you, Sir John walks in. I'll tell you about that shortly, and of this morning's conversation, and the explanation he gave.

'There are a few stray facts worth mentioning. He has been fined twice for non-attendance at church; no hint of dissension, or anything but levity – excuse recorded on the second occasion, "he did not like the preacher". He paid up on the spot, and later retailed the magistrate's exhortation to an admiring audience at the Mitre. He is admittedly free of tongue, and has been heard to speak against more than one notable; but as this country is not Spain, so far that's no treason. Item, he keeps various hangers-on, which you knew: item, he has deeded most of the Worcestershire property to his ward, which you did not.'

It was nearly dark. The last of the sunset lay dull green and purple, faintly ominous.

'Well, that's the background: as much of it as I can see.' Fabian stretched and got up. 'I'll light the lamp, but it's too hot for shutters. There'll be a storm, I think.'

'We're due for it,' agreed Farmer. 'Two warm days and what do we always get?' But this was only perfunctory backchat; his mind was busy with the stuff it had been given, sorting it, matching strand for strand. The two men pursued their linked and separate thoughts.

At last Farmer drained his mug with decision.

'You've got a lot there,' he said unexpectedly. 'You've been delving for that.'

'Not deep. An hour's work if you know where to look.'

'And you do. True. Think you'll need it?'

'Who knows? I needed it this morning. Now –' He paused. 'Having talked with him –'

It was no use trying to explain. He would trust the man with his life, having talked with him, yet could not tell if he were guilty of the worst kind of betrayal. Put like that, it sounded mad. And the one man to whom he could infallibly have told it was at Hetton-le-Hole or Whatton-under-Whichit, not to return till autumn. Fabian had never yet discussed a case with anyone outside the ranks of his own calling, but he felt the need to now.

He said aloud, 'That's another thing: every blessed soul we want is going to be out of town. I've got two good men in Oxford, keeping their ears open.'

'Are you telling me?' said Farmer feelingly. 'I've had some already.'

Fabian grinned. 'Sorry. I'd not forgotten. Give me your end now, will you?'

He did not at once comply, but sat thoughtfully rubbing the bridge of his nose in a characteristic gesture.

'You know, that's curious, what you've just told me. I knew most of it but it seems quite different the way you say it. I suppose it's all according to how you look at things. Put it like this. Here's a man of good family, with a nice bit of land his father and grandfather were content to end their days in, and for some reason or other he's not toeing the line. Drink, women, money troubles you can understand, but not treason. Now where I am we trust nobody, let alone at court, least of all in politics. See what I mean? It gives you a different outlook.'

Fabian began to speak but changed his mind. The different outlook was what he relied on.

'Not that you'll miss a point on that account,' went on Farmer, 'for you never have before, and you're making very sure I should not. So what's worrying you? If you're afraid to prejudice me, no need: you can take it I'm prejudiced already.'

He was right, of course, and because of it they were a formidable combination; the differing viewpoint and the converging aim, straight to the centre: and the heart of the target was truth. Take it as an ordinary case. He was quite right.

They exchanged the rest of their information, and Farmer's as he had hinted seemed of little value. Greenwich was quiet. It had heard of Black Jamie's quarrel, and any who missed Sir John concluded he was lying low. Of Jamie himself there was no news, and Farmer had not enquired, not then knowing the rest of the story. He was able to confirm that Sir John had made one of the river-party, that it had got back rather sooner than expected and that after they landed no one remembered to have seen him; those in the garden assuming him to be in the Palace, and *vice versa.* At Deptford rumour had been busier: it was currently supposed that there was a fight and one had slain the other – either, according to the speaker's fancy – and ridden straightway to Dover. This was the common talk of the waterside. At the house where Stadis had lodged, Farmer had been taken for a man of the Lord Chamberlain's enquiring into the matter, and had encouraged this belief, the better to keep it secret.

'Only to the innkeeper, of course – and it's lucky old Trimblewick gave up last year, he'd have known me at once. Used to take the missis there when we were courting. It's a well-known place – whitebait suppers, and that sort of thing.'

There was not much to be got from Trimblewick's successor. Yes, Sir John had been there four days himself, and paid a fortnight in advance; he had not mentioned when he desired to leave. He was a gentleman one would not question – an absolute gentleman, yet with a pleasant manner, easy of converse, if Farmer could follow him? 'Oh, *absolutely*.' His people were here still and might be spoken with – later, yes of course, and unobtrusively – the business should not be breathed to anyone, in this trade one must always be discreet.

He tried the drawer and the horseboy a different way. Much custom? Always when the court was at Greenwich, and the light evenings too. Strangers? he could not say, he (the drawer) took no note of faces, they were shorthanded this summer and he had to help in the kitchen. But coming and going, ah, plenty of that, especially lately with this new party that were staying; it was riding here, riding there, bring 'em to the door on the stroke, the grey's gone off his feed, rub down the chestnut; all of them giving orders till a fellow hardly knew where to turn. It was not so much the gentlemen he minded, the knight was what he called civil, and as for the poor silly young gentleman, no one in his five wits would heed him more than a fly. But the others, they were out of a different stable, he'd seen their sort before, Master know-all especially that was so fussy about the grooming and cared so little for the horse: off his feed indeed, when even a child could tell you all the animal wanted was exercise. And so on, until Farmer had managed to divert the flood. All this company, he supposed, was good for the house; they'd bring more custom? Not as much as you'd think, though mind you they'd only been here five days and things were warming up now, there'd been three or four callers today already and it just went to show how some people would believe anything, but for our part we never repeated rumours. They'd heard what was said, then? Oh yes, everyone had *heard*, and if Gaier was the blackhaired man who'd been in yesterday morning no one could wonder, a face like that (from the man who never noticed faces) was not to be trusted.

From much more of this stuff, and by dint of describing an imaginary friend he'd missed at the week-end, Farmer extracted the fact that no one had sought out Sir John there, nor had he been seen to converse with any but his own people. They, of course, had talked with all comers, but strangers had been few and could be linked with reasonable certainty to the known frequenters of the tavern. As for the parties of an evening, they were served separately; Sir John was usually out when they came and avoided them when he returned. He had kept reasonably early hours.

The place itself, Farmer concluded, was harmless. He'd gone for a stroll, and looked in again about noon on the chance of seeing something of the Stadis party. Luck was with him; he arrived as they were dismounting from their ride – a fruitless one, for Greenlee, it could be no other, was grumbling that they might have saved their labour, and Adey shut him up pretty sharply, saying what was the point of lying in bed all morning, and at least they need not go that way again. Farmer guessed they had ridden out to look for Sir John in the direction they had last seen him take. They were evidently not swallowing the rumour entire, but were considerably puzzled by his disappearance, and Adey at least (as the only brain of the party) was more worried than he would admit.

'Though what worries *him*'ll be where the money's coming from. No more sack and spices, but small beer for him when this lot's gone; as go it will, and shortly – they were sitting down to a dish of buttered crabs when I came away.'

'What did you think of them?'

Farmer shrugged. 'Much what the stableman said. Young Greenlee's the silly gentleman all right – more money than sense and more sense than wit: dresses in all the newest fashions at once, apes every man's vices, and has no virtue of his own to be ashamed of.'

'Could that be a pretence?'

'I doubt it. I saw them half an hour together, and again after dinner when I'd put Jackson on to them. I'd arranged to meet him down by the river at one, to describe them, see. Then he was to follow me back without being seen, and not lose them till relieved. There's another man joining him this evening. They'll report to me in turns at the Turk's Head.'

'Good. Sorry to halt you – you were saying –'

'Well, I got into talk with them afterwards – at least Crooks, the redhaired one, was drinking mostly, but the other two did his share. Know-all was Adey, of course, although that's hardly a fair way of putting it: he's older than the others and he's got a head on his shoulders. I could see what the man meant, though; I know the sort all right. Quick-moving and quick-witted; dark hair sleeked back and mustachios oiled forward, more hair to his top lip than ever he'll have on his chin; talks rather too much on purpose to see how the other fellow'll take it; bit of a military air, but that's misleading. He'll tell you himself he's been a soldier – "for pay, but not for long". As a matter of fact he has – I made enquiries when I got back. He was taken as a lad in mistake for some other boy, and got no nearer the wars than Gravesend. I fancied I'd seen them before, Adey and Crooks, or Crooks and Adey as Sir John puts it. He's got a proverb about them, "Crooks is addled and Adey is crooked". Though mind you that's only his humour, when he entertains his friends. How the pair of them got a living before he turned up I'll not bother to repeat to you; it was usually questionable, but never criminal.'

'That's what he meant, then,' interrupted Fabian. 'He had mentioned Adey and Crooks and stopped abruptly, as though if he continued I might get a wrong impression.

'Or to draw attention and lead you to suspect them?'

'No,' said Fabian. 'It could be that; I can only tell you it was not. Well, what about this couple?'

Farmer looked at him, but made no other comment.

'I'd seen them before right enough. They've hung together for seven or eight years with half London to vouch for it. Adey's what? Twenty-five, twenty-six near enough, and Dick Crooks some three years younger: useful to show off to, I suppose. They've never been mixed up in anything dangerous. Crooks was a foundling, and if Adey had any family he soon made sure of losing them. I'd not be surprised if he was somebody's bastard, only the sort he is'd be sure to boast about it. He's had schooling, too – the grammar school at Enfield it was. That shows you.'

'No harm in going to a grammar school,' said Fabian, mildly amused. 'I went to one myself if it comes to that.'

'Yeah but *you* got some good out of it. Not, as I say, that he's likely to be in anything really dangerous. If Jackson's the man I take him for we'll soon know. Well, that's the inner ring; unless you want more on Greenlee?'

'Greenlee's genuine. Nineteen years old, son of a Nottingham mercer who's made his pile and bought his crest and wants dear Nicholas to see the world. But for last year's invasion scare, he'd be in France or Italy. Pity.' A thought struck him. 'Why's Adey worried about money? Nick has plenty.'

'Ah, but Nick likes him not. They're cat and dog together. They were talking against each other the whole time, Adey just sneering generally, the other one digging away at one point – how impatient Adey was, how slow he thought the rest of the world; how they had to give him the oldest nag to ride, he'd founder a horse of any spirit; that sort of thing. Spiteful as a monkey. It's true Adey was on a steady old grey – I had a good look at the horses for future use. Greenlee's is a roan, not too well broken – he thinks it looks big to go prancing about – and Crooks has a great piebald carthorse, sixteen hands at least, one white ear and one black.'

'If the three keep together we'll not mistake them. You've drawn a lively picture. Well?'

'Myself, I think they're not in it. He'd hardly trust them with anything serious.' He looked at Fabian across the lamplight curiously. '*Can* you tell a man by the company he keeps? This lot was a surprise to me. Not the sort of company, I was prepared for that, but somehow –' he shrugged. 'I dislike it when a man surrounds himself with people so much younger.'

Fabian nodded. 'It argues a lack in him somewhere, a chink in the armour? Perhaps. Though Greenlee at least was thrust on him, and he has friends enough of his own age. I've got a list as long as your arm to work through, and there are still the servants –'

'I've started on them. Orchard House was closed up on 4th June, that's three weeks ago tomorrow, and the household dispersed. There were three of them lived in, and a woman from Blackman Street used to come in in the daytime. The cook is now at Wapping, and I've seen him. He says they were all paid up to Michaelmas, and parted on good terms. They understood they would not be wanted again as Sir John was giving up the house. The indoor man, Tom Wilson, actually left on the first, because he'd had word his mother was ill, but he got his money like the rest. The mother lives at Ivinghoe in Bedfordshire. The gardener was a Surrey man and that's all they knew of him, except that he was courting a farmer's daughter up Clopham way and he'd most likely go there. I've put someone on to that, and I found a man who can bring me news of the Wilsons. But they'll know very little, you'll see. He sent them away for that purpose.'

'It almost looks like it.' Fabian stood up restlessly. 'Is that thunder, or a cart in the next street?' It ceased while he spoke, as unidentified sounds always do. 'I wish it would storm and have done. I could believe anything tonight.'

'I've never seen a storm upset you before.'

'They used not to. We none of us get any younger.' But it was not the weather troubling him. He must pull himself together.

'No,' he said resolutely, 'to begin with there's no use making too wide a cast: we must narrow the time a little. Keep clear in our minds what we're fishing for. Any contacts which could lead to Spain. Any unusual incident that stands out against the background. The usual too, within limits, but only as a background. Take May and June: this month when things began to move, last month as leading up to it. Instance, he was called away to Worcestershire; I rather think that was unexpected. If so, it meant a change of plan. Find the changes, and you come near to discovering the plan.'

'How long was he away?'

'Six days including travelling. He stayed only Friday to Monday, and was back in London on the Tuesday night. That was 10th June. Quick going.'

'Long enough to meet someone on the way.' Farmer was thumbing a calendar. 'But he went to Deptford on the 20th. What did he do for ten days, with the house at Southwark shut up?'

'What indeed?' said Fabian. 'There are two separate questions there. The what he would not tell me, beyond that he was waiting to be called to Greenwich. The where, which he was quite open about, was not far from here – they were lying at the Quartern.'

'The *Quartern*?' Farmer was genuinely shocked. 'A place like that, for a gentleman – can you understand it? That woman, Alice What's her name, 'll find herself up before the magistrates one of these fine mornings, or I'm a Dutchman.'

'It belongs to his younger days, I take it. That's no concern of ours, unless you can see him meeting a foreign agent in Mistress Thorn's back parlour? No, what puzzles me is how else he spent his time.'

'If we knew that we knew all.'

'I wonder.' Fabian began to pace up and down the room. 'He lied to me, twice. Once when he said he had no business there: a direct lie, and he must have known I would know it. Once indirectly, when I asked where the paper was kept – he broke off, and I think he remembered where he had seen it last. Did he change the subject rather than tell me, or because someone else had seen it too?'

'Does it make any difference?'

'Only that the rest of his story may be true. But look, it's late and you've had a hard day. We'd better wind up for the night.'

Farmer nodded. 'I must show up at the Turk, if it's only for half a pint.'

'I'll walk along with you,' said Fabian. 'There are two things I want of you tomorrow – and use someone younger, no need to kill yourself. One, find James Gaier. Two, which may amount to the same thing, who met in the barn? Find the barn first, in fact. A barn with an upper storey, in a new-cut field, visible from a road, anything up to ten miles from Blackheath. Not the main Kent road or he'd have known it. And two or three miles from that, I should guess, the inn where he left Gaier.'

'Assuming the story he told you was true.'

'Yes. Test it anyhow, but I think yes. What's on your mind?'

'The times.' Farmer frowned in concentration. 'How do they tally? Not too well. The court party gets back from the river, four-ish. Stadis returns to Deptford, half-hour or three quarters; say an hour indoors, that brings it to six at the outside when they set out riding –'

'Later: they had Gaier there in talk half an hour at least.'

'Say half after six, then; and suppose they rode for an hour before Gaier caught up, which I doubt: then what? The two of them go on – it'd not be far – come to this barn, start a quarrel, hear a noise and hide: I still make that only about eight o'clock. Then when these other men have gone they come down and have it out properly, Gaier has this fit, Stadis humps him on to the saddle and takes him to the nearest inn, and when they get there it's midnight? There's an hour or two astray somewhere.'

'He was deep in thought and missed the way: says he'd no notion how far it was. He'd be at walking pace because of Gaier.'

'All the same –'

'Yes, it's thin right enough. That's what makes me think it's the truth. He's not fool enough to invent a palpable absurdity.'

'Unless he thought you'd think that. No, how's this? They reach the barn at eight if you like: they've come to meet the other men, who arrive after dark, perhaps singly. They're proposing their next step. During the talk Gaier's taken ill and they concoct this story to account for it. Stadis gets left with the body, and has to stay in hiding till the conspirators are safely away.'

'And what about the quarrel? It started before they left Adey and company.'

'Faked, to give them an excuse to leave.'

'Sir John's part was no fake; I helped him dress this morning.'

'They came to blows later, maybe. Or Gaier's out of it; Sir John was meeting the conspirators when Gaier fastened on to him and refused to be put off. That's it. There'd be a quarrel all right. He was playing about with the wife, everyone said so.'

'Or else that was a fake? He said he was not serious. But if so, why tell me, and destroy its usefulness? It would be a good cover – ostentatious pursuit of the wife, staged quarrel with the husband, an evening's absence well accounted for. Difficult otherwise, with so many hangers-on, to ride off to a secret meeting.'

Farmer's brow wrinkled again. 'But that brings Gaier back into it.'

'Find him and we'll see.' Fabian handed him his hat. 'Till then, we're making bricks without straw – or rubbing a hole in the tapestry.' He reached for his own hat, but checked himself. 'On second thoughts, you'd best not be seen with me for a week or two. I'll walk up to Seething Lane after you've gone.'

'More paper-work?'

'Much more.' He showed his list. 'More family histories. And someone must be sent up to Worcestershire. I'd like to go myself, but the Chief wants me on Friday. If Fisher's finished in Norfolk I'll make *him* work for his living.'

'Well, try not to sit up all night,' said Farmer as farewell. His ponderous, reliable footsteps receded downstairs and clapped across the yard. There was a flicker of summer lightning away in the west, but it seemed a long way off.

That night's work was not as informative as the morning's, or perhaps day-sleep is less refreshing than the night's. Fabian went doggedly down the list of names, copying all available data in his own private shorthand. He filled several sheets. Most of the entries were concerned with family relationships, monetary status or particular services rendered; very few were discreditable. More than one name he passed over with a glance; their lives were open and above suspicion, as he thought even Farmer would admit. By midnight he was not thinking at all, but wrote mechanically, the words and symbols present to the eye but not the mind; relying on an inner sense, which seldom failed him, to bring sharply to his attention any matter deserving it. This useful faculty had made him much envied, yet it was less a gift than his own extension of the art of scrutiny, developed out of hard work and long practice. The man in charge of the enquiry, he always said, should carry out such preliminary tasks himself: they gave him a grasp of his subject from the beginning, and enabled him later, when dealing with the many reports he could not personally investigate, to discard irrelevancies with a surer touch.

His mind now, as he worked upon the borders of sleep, was occupied with Farmer's observations. Good old Farmer, still the same, a mixture of shrewdness and simplicity, he could always be relied on to spring a surprise. Fancy old Farmer being scandalised at the mere mention of the Quartern. You'd have thought him hardened by now to the worst revelations of human frailty. And so no doubt he was, in theory, but the descent from general to particular may be sudden and shocking. Yet on Farmer's own showing he'd believe anything of the court circle. Well, well. There was a solid core of respectability in many a loud-mouthed Londoner (hence the puritans' success), and Farmer was not that but discretion itself, a married man and a grandfather. One ought perhaps to discount in some measure the popular estimate of Stadis as seen through Farmer's eyes. A reputation for wildness is easily got and very hard to lose, increasing from mouth to mouth; people will always say something of a well-known figure, especially an aloof one – the fewer facts to bite on, the readier they digest the pap of fiction. But was he indeed aloof? Had the motto and the family record combined to make Fabian think so? Sir John's habits were unknown to him: all he knew was what he had seen for himself, a disarming sense of the comic and a calm refusal to be hurried in the face of danger. It was too soon to impute motives to his actions, too soon to say positively what those actions were. He could be all he seemed and yet a conspirator, the more dangerous for that reason.

Meanwhile, this looked the last for tonight; poor Ben Jonson a little dashed, one fancied, by the soberness of his company – and but one line of quarto to his name! But that one in virtue of the scholar, you could almost hear him saying. True, Ben, for this record stoops no lower, and where else thou consorts let the officers of the ward make answer. Fabian grinned to himself as he refolded the sheet: a good jest gone to waste, since he could never use it. The lower degrees in these lists were well known to him, though few of them knew him by name. The square-built man, hair sand-coloured – talks but little: that's how it would go. And that was where he must go, for a great part of his information: the several comfortable houses he usually frequented, inconspicuous for all his size, sitting back in the darkest corner where he could watch the light on others' faces, hear their talk unheeded. Not the alehouses of Farmer's orbit, but a better sort of place where thronged the wit and the sophisticate; law students, young nobility, gamblers, gossips, writers, players and all. There would be something to glean, though not yet, not too soon; give the news of the arrest time to leak out, as it would. Tempting to think of precipitating it, but such a trick seldom worked. A watch must first be kept on the associates. Adey was taken care of; there were three more at least might repay attention. Any one of them, for just so long as he thought himself safe, might lead to the conspiracy. If only it were autumn! But those who were still in town, the poor, the unsuccessful or the discontented would be the more likely to talk. And here, and here – his pen-point stabbed the paper – he must put someone on to those two, even if it meant all summer. But for the most part his notes were singularly barren. There was nothing on Gaier; between them they would have to supply it.

He quenched his candle and went into the next room, where a pale-faced clerk handed him the evening's transcript. There was nothing new, and nothing about Stadis – even with several trained ears stretched ready to receive it – but a much-garbled version of the Greenwich rumour. Early yet, of course, but disappointing. He left a message for Fisher and certain other instructions, and walked home through the quiet streets by moonlight, startling the watch as he came suddenly round a corner. Luckily they knew each other by sight, and a suitable explanation was easily found and accepted. And so to bed, to turn this week-long day the right side up again. Midsummer Night, indeed! It was nearly morning: but dawn would bring no hunter's horn, no friendly Duke to smooth out all this tangle; and Puck, if he visited the city, must be cackling with malicious laughter.

5

The Experts

The next few days were blessedly cooler, and Fabian moved about the delicate task of questioning those that he could reach. He hated this stage of an enquiry, with its remorseless multiplication of data and as yet no clue to their usefulness; one could so easily be bogged in the morass of it, and forget all sense of direction. To Farmer he longed aloud for the dry land of evidence – one little piece of it – something to stand firm on, to warrant issuing subpoenas and put a stop to this hole-and-corner business.

There was one strong consolation this time: a good horse at his command. He had no scruple of conscience at using Jewel as it were against his master; the animal must have exercise, as well with Fabian as another. He did wonder idly if the horse would be recognised, but in London at least most people are preoccupied with their own affairs and would take it as a chance likeness. If anyone were sufficiently interested to challenge him, that in itself would be worth knowing.

So he set out on foot each morning for the Borough, where he had left Jewel (under the improvised name of Hewins) in the Tabard stables. He might have found cheaper accommodation, but only at a house of the first repute could he be certain the animal would not be hired out 'by accident' whenever his back was turned. And Jewel was worthy of his setting. It was a pleasure to bestride him. He eased every encounter, anyone so well mounted being at once accepted as a gentleman. There was too an interest as lively as any human conversation in watching him respond to the slightest signal, or look round seriously for further instructions. When they took the road past Orchard House he was patently enquiring, but content to trot on. So indeed was his rider, on whom the scene there played had made such a powerful impression.

This morning's call, thank God, was of a different order. He was bound for Lambeth Palace, to ask the whereabouts of a cleric named Walton: or Walker, Walters, Walmer, he would not stickle for the form of it, whosoever had been with the army in Holland. That at least was a straightforward question, although there might be some difficulty in the answer. The Archbishop's under-secretary looked worried enough, but he was a very young man, to whom fourteen years ago must be ancient history – he was probably in petticoats at the time.

'Certainly if he has a cure we can find him. It would be easier with the Christian name – there are a great many parishes, I fear.' He brightened. 'I could show you the parish lists.'

Fabian explained patiently just why that method of approach would be no use. Just then, an older man promised to make full enquiries within a week, and with this Fabian expressed himself content. Even a waggon-wheel turns slowly when you first begin to push. With enough encouragement, a clear road and the right direction it may eventually roll downhill of itself.

That was Wednesday. The following day, acting upon Farmer's advices, he rode out to the little village of Hatcham and found James Gaier, saddling his horse with a not too steady hand but otherwise safe and sound. He answered a few simple questions civilly but without interest, and as though he had never heard of Stadis. Jacob Trott, hovering in the background, spoke up.

'He's been like that the whole time, sir, ever since the Captain brought him in. As harmless as a baby, but not quite in his proper mind. He's going to Greenwich, that's all he will say. The last few days are a blank to him.'

'Has anyone been here to see him?'

'No one, sir. Only myself and the wife. The Captain, Sir John I mean, told us to look after him. Do you come from Sir John, sir?'

'I saw him on Tuesday,' Fabian answered truthfully.

'Then will you see the gentleman safe to Greenwich, if it's not out of your way? I'd go myself, I was just getting my boots on, but he'd be a bit impatient with me. A friend of Sir John's will be fitter.'

Fabian promised, feeling ridiculously guilty. He had indeed no intention of letting Gaier out of his sight. 'And talking of sight,' he added in a lower tone, 'help me take a look at those saddle-girths, or he'll break his neck in the first mile.'

He nodded competently. 'Leave it to me, sir,' and called to his wife, who drew Gaier inside for a parting word. While they made all secure, Trott told Fabian what he knew: that Gaier had sought a duel and Sir John had refused it, and that the violence of Gaier's rage had induced some kind of fit. Did he foam at the mouth and become rigid? Sir John had not said. Had he fallen since? No, for they had kept him in bed till this morning, when he pleaded so and seemed to be so much better. The violence was all spent, leaving a curious innocence and docility, and but one fixed purpose: he must go to Greenwich. To do what – whom should he meet? Trott did not know. Did Sir John not mention the barn and the meeting there? Did he ask you not to speak of it?

Here Trott looked up from tightening the last strap, and met Fabian's gaze squarely.

'Look, sir, if there's anything behind this, why not ask him youself? I've told you what he told me. There was nothing secret in it, only to spare the poor gentleman's feelings. I've known the Captain a good many years and he's one of the best, believe it. Now if you'll excuse me, I have the house to see to.' He made a dignified little bow, and walked away.

That was the real thing. Indignation can be counterfeit, but not the look in an honest man's eye when he thinks you beneath contempt. That hurts. Fabian turned to follow his quarry, wishing very much that he had left this end of the job to Farmer. But at least one point was settled: Trott had no part in any conspiracy. His statements could therefore be trusted. Sir John's story was so far corroborated, and no one had approached Gaier since then. That did not clear Gaier, needless to say. As they rode, Fabian looked at him afresh. He had been ill, that pallor could not be simulated, but he sat straight in the saddle and held himself easily, and appeared in some way to have matured during the last three days. Fabian here smiled: he was making the comparison as though they were old acquaintances, so clear Sir John's description had been.

The smile seemed to catch Gaier's attention, although he was half ahead and could not have seen it. He slackened pace a little to allow Fabian to come abreast, and thanked him courteously for his company. He had an attractive smile himself and a very pleasant voice, and no one casually watching him would guess he was nearly blind. The previous agitation of mind would have made him clumsier, and might account for an altered appearance. He responded adequately to Fabian's conversation, but was not talkative; his mind was elsewhere.

When they came to the main road he halted. There was a certain amount of traffic, and thinking he might shrink from it Fabian offered to take the lead. Gaier looked at him intently, but assented.

'This is the Greenwich road,' Fabian reassured him, 'by way of Deptford. Last time I expect you came across Blackheath.'

He shook his head. 'I am making my first visit now.'

'Indeed?' said Fabian.

As he intended, the single word pricked home. Gaier brought the grey alongside.

'I trust, sir, you do not mean to be offensive, that you seem to doubt my statement.'

'Can truth offend?'

'I hope not.'

'Then you were at Greenwich on Sunday.'

'You are mistaken, sir.'

'You came, I think, on Saturday,' pursued Fabian. 'On Sunday you joined your wife. On Monday you quarrelled with Sir John Stadis and rode after him across the heath. There were at first three men with him and the tallest had red hair.'

Gaier stared. 'You are under some strange error. I will not be offended, for I have that to do that calls for all my calmness. No, sir, I see where you mistake: this Stadis you have now twice mentioned must be my good Samaritan. When I was taken ill on my journey a gentleman befriended me and brought me to this place: so the innkeeper says, for to speak truth I was in no state to remember.'

'And when was this?'

'Why, on my way to Greenwich.'

'On Saturday?'

He began to tremble.

'It is now Thursday. I ask you to believe you had already been to Greenwich, and all fell out as I have told you.'

He put a hand to his head. 'This is like witchcraft. I have travelled there so often in my dreams, rehearsed so many times what I must say – or do –' He broke off. 'You seem as well-disposed as you are well-informed. Tell me in charity what else is supposed to have happened.'

Fabian told him.

He let out a long breath of relief.

'Then – my wife –'

'Is well, I trust,' said Fabian cheerfully. 'In any of your dreams was there a meeting of five or six men, by moonlight?'

He shook his head. 'Your story is all new to me. It may be true, I cannot gainsay it, but I know nothing, on my honour, since I started out from home. I am – you may have noticed my sight is not altogether perfect, and I have been much preoccupied. Too much, perhaps.' He gave another shake, like a rough-haired dog scrambling out of water deeper than he thought.

When they passed through Deptford High Street, a man carrying a little sack detached himself from a group across the way. Fabian moved his hat as if he found it uncomfortable, settling it further back on his head. The man untethered a waiting pony, threw himself on to its back and trotted off ahead of them. The signal had been given and received, and Farmer's people knew their job. Fabian could now part from his suspect when occasion offered, knowing that his movements would be duly followed. There ought to be no need, but he could not afford to take chances. And just in case he was mistaken as to the nature of Gaier's dreams, he invented for himself some business within the Palace grounds. He helped Gaier alight, and they parted with a friendly handshake. Fabian sought out an official of his acquaintance and gained admittance to the Palace, where shortly he witnessed a curious little scene. In a sudden hush Gaier entered, took his wife by the hand from the midst of a party, led her in silence to the gate where her horse had also been brought, in silence caused her to mount, and they rode away together. His wits were gone, some said: others that he had at last recovered them.

'So they lived happy ever after?' said Farmer later that evening.

'I hope so. Time will tell, but I'd lay on it.'

'Not if he has the falling-sickness.'

'It may not recur. He had been working himself into a state for weeks past. He is greatly in love with his wife. Somehow out of this confusion he has now plucked the right answer. I thought so as we rode, without knowing exactly what he would do.'

'You took a big risk, though,' Farmer reproved him.

'He might have waited till the Queen appeared, then out with a pistol and shot at her.'

Fabian smiled. 'Or his wife. But he was carrying nothing. I made sure of that first; of the saddlebags, outside the inn while he was saying goodbye; of his person when we dismounted and I tenderly held him from stumbling against a wall. One way and another a good day's work – and for our purpose absolutely useless.' He flung his weight on a chair, and such was the solidity of the Margett furniture that it did not even creak. 'I've not given up Gaier; he'll be watched from now on for possible approaches – both he and his wife could still be part of the campaign: but if so, he's the best actor I've ever met, on or off the boards.'

'All right then; you've cleared away some dead wood. Let's take another look at what's left.'

'Where is this barn, by the way?'

'Choice of two,' said Farmer, pulling a face. 'You and your hayfield – they've been making hay all over Kent for the past week. We can rule out the first, I should think, it's halfway to Chislehurst. The other one's a goodish step along the Bromley road. Even worse, they must have done some travelling.'

'And come round in a circle, to end up where they did. Possible. I suppose you found the inn by accident?'

'Good luck and a regular old search. I had three of the boys on it separate, like, looking for any house with a mysterious visitor. Once we got it I checked back to the barn myself. There's a maze of little lanes. A horse or horses had stood for some time in a corner, out of sight of the road and right away from any cart-track. It could easily be the place.'

'Who's the owner?'

'Summers, Esquire. Bedridden two years, man and his wife take care of him, saw nothing, heard nothing, bolt all the doors at sunset and never receive callers. It's a tumbledown sort of place, grass a foot high in the orchard and a few scraggy hens picking about. The field's let to the nearest neighbour a mile off. He was there himself with the men till seven and they knocked off then, reckoning the weather'd hold overnight, and seeing what day it was – he was taking his wife and children to Bromley to the fair. They all went home together for a spruce-up, and they passed nobody going the other way – everyone was off to the fair too. He's a good honest country sort, yeoman-farmer, name of Ralph Baker, well-known and well thought of. It was him told me first about the old man never leaving his bed – he's almost the only visitor.'

'Summers. Summers. Never heard of him. Any kin?'

'There's a nephew.' Farmer looked pleased with himself. 'They directed me to his house and I called there, and he's away from home and not expected back for some weeks.'

'Are we getting warmer.'

'May be. And that's not all. Where do you think he lives? Lewisham.'

'Well?'

'Throckmorton lived at Lewisham.'

'So he did. But that was years ago,' Fabian objected. 'What do you suppose – the place to breed conspiracy; or treason a condition of the lease?'

'Laugh if you like. These things are not mere chance,' said Farmer solemnly. 'Am I to look for young Summers?'

'Yes, look by all means; and you might find out whose tenant he is; you never know what may help. Anyone, in fact, who could have been at the barn or connived at a meeting there, and who also – this is the point, I think – had entry to

Orchard House, or contact with any who did. It's a tall order, Farmer. Sir John entertained there quite often until recently, generally a large party. Unfortunately no one I've spoken to was lucky enough to have been invited.'

'I'd better smooth up to the cook again. He might not know who was invited, but he'd remember times when there were only a few. This sort of business would be kept to a few.'

'Yes, but what better than to invite a whole horde in which your few are included, and take them aside while the rest of the party makes merry? Less noticeable that way. We could do with the names of all his visitors, and see who coincide most often.'

'Chances are he'd keep suspicious company away from the house. Meet them along the Strand, or walking in St Paul's Churchyard. You've only got to brush a man by the sleeve, like.'

'One suspicious person came to the house,' said Fabian. 'Must have – to have seen the paper.'

'I forgot about the paper.'

'I know. We forget it because at present nothing else fits in with it. But that's our best way in. Someone knew where that paper was and what it was: someone who knew or guessed enough of the business to take fright and inform us. That's the man we want. The principals will be cool and wary; they're in it up to the neck, and short of definite proof we'll get no change out of them. But the one who's got his feet wet and is afeared to catch cold – he'll talk.'

'Then I wish he'd begin,' said Farmer gloomily, 'he – or she?'

'Not she, I think, considering who's in question. No woman would betray Sir John Stadis.'

'Not one he'd thrown over?'

'I doubt it. Anyhow, he, or she if you will have it, *did* begin. It's our move now. I've started a few hares, but they're running in all directions and I'm blest if I know which one to follow. You know what we want next?'

'A statement from Adey,' said Farmer promptly.

'Right. And the others, of course. The time for secrecy's gone by; we'll have it out in the open.

'Come to think of it, that's our work,' said Farmer with one of his unexpected flashes of insight, 'bringing things into the open. Like it says in the Bible, what's whispered in a dark corner will be shouted from the house-tops. I used to wonder about that as a boy, whether it was thatch or what, and how they managed not to put a foot through the rafters. But I suppose they had flat roofs like you see sometimes in Italy.'

'I suppose so,' agreed Fabian abstractedly. 'There's been plenty of whispering, but after today the story's split wide open; it was Gaier they'd cast for the corpse, and nobody will think the other way round for a moment. At a guess, the truth's out already as if the town crier'd had it. Tomorrow –' He paused in annoyance. 'Tomorrow I go to the Chief, I'd forgot that too. You can handle Adey: better you should, for he's seen you once and he might loosen up. Your man has picked up nothing, I take it?'

'Not a crumb. They've behaved completely as usual, only young Nick's asserting himself and chucking his money about with no Stadis to restrain him. The other two look as though they'll make hay while the sun's still shining. Adey rode into Greenwich today to ask after Sir John – that's fuel to the fire. He'll have heard the fresh crop of rumours, and be the less surprised when I turn up.'

'Try not to scare him,' suggested Fabian. 'If he knows about the Tower, well and good – if not, lead up to it in your own time.'

'What I most want to know,' said Farmer, 'is which way they were left in the dark. Were they surprised he went off, or only that he stayed away? There's a difference.'

'What time did they have supper? Find that out. If he went

out without a meal it looks as though he expected to be back.'

'Or hoped they'd think so? He sent *them* back, remember. Did he just ride off and leave them without a word? Why has no one been to Orchard House to see if he's there?'

'The house was shut up. The lease was running out. They expected not to go back there.'

'Then why did he?'

'You know,' said Fabian, 'I've been over all this till my head ached. If Gaier is innocent, why lead him straight to the conspirators? If not, why mention them at all? If either, the business being concluded, why should Sir John not ride back peaceably to Deptford? Even suppose the meeting gave him instructions, there was little he could do till morning.'

'Say he'd learned that he was betrayed. They told him at the meeting.'

'If anyone told me that, I should fly; not walk straight back into the net. And once again, the house was closed – or supposed to be; unless that was a blind, prepared in advance to cover his retreat. He might hide there a day or two and get away one night, by the river.'

'Why not that same night?'

'He was dog-tired,' said Fabian shortly.

'Or he'd had orders to stay there, to expect a message; someone would visit him by night?'

'I thought of that too, but he was ill-prepared for a wait: there was no food in the house and he brought none with him.'

'Not prepared for hiding either,' said Farmer.

'But if for none of these reasons, why oh why did he come back at all?'

'To get the paper.'

'That's what puzzles me. I've seen a good many men confronted with their own hand, and they act either of two ways: break down, or brazen it out with denial. This was nothing of the sort. The paper surprised him, I'll lay all I've got. He'd forgotten its existence. As far as that goes, his story could be true. But that's not all. The bed was made up ready to sleep in, and aired too – I put my hand inside. There was clean water in the ewer, not a layer of dust such as you'd expect after a fortnight. Not knowing at the time how long they'd been gone, I guessed no more than three days.'

'It looks suspicious all right.' Farmer got ponderously to his feet. 'Well, leave me alone with Master Adey. I know how to tackle *him.* And I'll make sure of seeing the other two separately, or get Jackson to do it – he's a nice smooth-mannered sort. He's friendly with them already, but I told him to lay off questioning until you gave the word. Then we can put all their stories together.'

'Tomorrow, then,' said Fabian. 'I wish I could change places with you.'

Farmer grinned. 'So do not I. Good luck with his mightiness.'

'Good news, I hope: he should have heard from the cipher people by now if nothing else, and perhaps identified the seal. Then we'll begin to know where we are.'

But that would have been too easy.

6

Mares' Nests

Fabian presented himself at Mr Secretary's town house at the accustomed time, to find that gentleman not yet arrived. After an hour in a stuffy little back room he heard a hopeful bustle, but was still kept waiting half an hour more before being ushered into the presence; and the presence was moody and irritable and inclined to discuss every question under the sun before the Stadis case. Fabian always came prepared, as he thought, with everything, only to have his chief's needle-brain prick unerringly into the one subject he had not. This time it was the man referred to as Melton, cause of Fisher's recent journey, the report on whom he was expecting that very night. That Fisher was only just back in London weighed nothing, nor that the business was comparatively trivial; which (as soon as he could get a word in) Fabian pointed out.

'And he stays a month in London before accompanying his cousin to Plymouth. Till then he is well watched and can come to no harm, and I have use for Fisher in Worcestershire.'

'Worcester? What have we there?'

'The Stadis ward, with an aunt and uncle. His childhood home and his old neighbours.'

'Oh. Yes, of course.' But it seemed to Fabian that he spoke grudgingly. 'That is necessary, you think?'

'Yes, sir. We know he made over the place to his ward more than eighteen months ago. There may be a link there.'

'Very well, if you say so.' He withdrew into thought, and Fabian once more had to summon up his patience.

'The ward. The girl Dalbie. How old is she?'

'Nineteen or twenty, sir.'

'Old enough,' he muttered.

'To be confederate? I venture to think not.'

'Well? What have you to tell me?'

'Not much at present. We are stopping what gaps we find.' He gave a formal summary of the investigation.

'Is that all?'

'So far. I have been hoping for a lead from the papers we found. Have you had a report yet, sir?'

'Papers?' He had grown distant again. 'Let me see.' There was a deskful of them, tied neatly in packets, and for a man so methodical he took curiously long to find the right one. Used as Fabian was to his chief's odd humours, he could not help feeling there was something extraordinary happening.

'The document.' He flipped it contemptuously with a fingernail. 'The Latin, I may say, is faulty: a boy at school could do better. They are using indifferent agents.'

'They?' murmured Fabian, he hoped encouragingly.

'The Spanish, one presumes.'

'You have not yet discovered the sender?'

He shook his head. 'The signature is disguised; even the wax has been deliberately blurred. De Vasquez? Sandoval? I wonder.' He produced a newer paper, laying them side by side. 'Here. This is a copy. See for yourself, they are identical. The seal, I think, is fairly drawn.'

It was in fact a remarkably good copy of a blur. The only salient feature was some sort of animal, at least there were four legs discernible, in an attitude Fabian supposed to be rampant although it was not very upright, with a diagonal line that might be a bend, a staff, or just a smudge. He ran his eye over the wording too; there *were* one or two mistakes – a mis-spelling, a wrong case - the kind Fabian could remember making himself, but the meaning was quite clear. He looked up with a smile.

'Copy found correct, sir. Even to errors.'

'Take it to the College of Heralds yourself and enlist their aid.' (Fabian's smile vanished abruptly.) 'I have reason not to let the original go.'

'And the letters?' asked Fabian. (Lord help us if he's been sitting on those too.)

'You will not need the letters. I agree they are harmless, except possibly the last. It is in no known cipher, but contains a close allusion to the book in which it was found. You remember the Ode, perhaps.' He began to declaim it in the sing-song voice of a pedant, accentuating the rhythm grotesquely. 'The likeness ends with the first verse, but the allusion would be to the later part - "*Cum tibi Nonae redeunt Decembres*"; when to thine honour December's Nones come round – where it speaks of the wolf mingling harmlessly with the lambs, a feast in the meadows and the population dancing. Which is as much as to say, by the fifth day of December our hopes will be joyfully fulfilled. Coupled with a reference to the old altar smoking again, it is not hard to believe an invasion intended, its purpose to restore the Roman faith. In conjunction with the sealed paper, I think it would convince a jury.'

A medley of retorts chased through Fabian's mind, of which the mildest was 'preposterous!' That fustian stuff? A meaning picked perforce out of a printed page, the author 1500 years dead, even the type set and the book bound a generation ago? An allusion so open, that anyone who knew the verse could at once complete the message? And such a message: invasion in December, as if anyone would be fool enough to try it. 'And Christmas in London, I suppose,' he heard his own voice say cuttingly, 'like William the

Conqueror.' At the same time, he saw only too clearly that a London jury would indeed believe it; and in spite of that, it might even be true.

He added 'We have first to prove the main point: if Sir John had dealings with the Spanish. Your odes and letters are no more than corroborative evidence.'

'Do I not know it?' The words came fiercely thrusting out. 'Go on and prove it. That is your work. Prove it, without recourse to the girl's letter. We can say the leaf was turned down in the book, or – prove it, anyhow, and he will confess the whole.'

'But sir, the letters should clear her. It will be easy to confirm their story. If they are harmless, so is –'

He interrupted without heeding. 'Her name must clear her. Whatever you find. That is an order.'

'Sir?'

'The blame is to be his, not hers. As of course it would be: a girl who never left the village. Remove that look of surprise,' he added coldly. 'She is her father's daughter. The people would not relish it. There are few names they still venerate, dead or alive, and Dalbie is one.'

So that was the dilemma. 'You give me little help,' said Fabian slowly. 'Is the girl not even to be investigated?'

'That is for you. I do not wish to know of it. Only, I say again, there must be not one breath against her. If you doubt anyone's discretion, leave her alone and find some other way.' Then, as Fabian's face showed his distaste, 'It should be easy. He has Catholic friends.'

'So have I – so, I dare say, have you. They are as open as daylight and as loyal as we are ourselves. I have told you once, I'll be no heretic-hunter. They are watched already in precaution; if their actions prove innocent, *finita*. That's all, where I'm concerned.'

And if it was over-blunt, the Secretary made no sign. In his precise, colourless voice he put a question on some other point of detail, which nevertheless changed the subject so effectively that Fabian could not afterwards be sure it was deliberate. He had quite hard work to bring it round again, and ask outright for at least a copy of the examination, if he were to make any progress in the Stadis affair. And when it appeared the examination had not yet been taken, he was past showing surprise or irritation: it was all of a piece with the case so far, a series of delays for which no one could be blamed and checks in the most expected or unexpected direction. He did advise, with all the earnestness he could muster, that this essential preliminary should take place at once; although the damage was done, the prisoner had had time already to work out any story he intended to tell. (It was a great deal later when Fabian wondered if that too had been deliberate.)

So he got away at last, his shirt and thinnest suit sticking to him, from the little white-faced man still muffled in his dusty velvet, and the close room to which no servant was ever admitted.

Here was a setback if you like, and the statements from Adey and company did little to restore his spirits. They confirmed the circumstance in which Sir John had left them; they could not understand why: they had tried to tell him Gaier might be dangerous, but when Sir John looked like that, and spoke so, it was better to obey than argue. They had stood irresolutely for some minutes watching the pair of them out of sight, and then there seemed nothing else to do but trot back to Deptford. It was about sunset when they got on to Blackheath. There was a fair there just getting into its stride, and they were tempted to spend some time on it, but it would not be safe to leave the horses; moreover Nick was encumbered with two swords, his own and Sir John's, and thirdly and chiefly they wanted a meal first. So they spurred on home, and came out again on foot after dark to the fair. There Nick became separated from his companions, who thereupon enjoyed themselves very much, meeting several old friends (together), lending a hand at one of the sideshows while the owner went to have a drink (Adey), and bowling the black-man's hat off six times in succession to win a genuine imitation amber necklace (Crooks, but having no use for such trinkets he had let Adey have it for sixpence). When they decided to go home it was a simple matter to pick up Nicholas, lying as several people had described to them, dead drunk behind one of the booths, all his ready money gone and even the empty purse stolen. They had sobered him up enough to get back to Deptford, and all crawled into bed as quietly as possible, wishing to defer Sir John's comments till the morning. Morning in their case had not been much before ten, and they were astounded to find Sir John had not been in. It was Adey who insisted on the search party, including the groaning Nicholas, but it had been a waste of time; up on the Heath they could not agree which road to take; Adey still thought they'd picked the right one, but they rode for the best part of an hour without finding any corpse or sign of combat, and gave it up and came back to dinner. When evening came and no Sir John, and as Nick kept saying they should have turned to the left, Adey ruthlessly had them out again to take that turning, and after a couple of miles they found themselves at the foot of Eltham Hill and knew they were on the wrong road. After that they stopped searching. By that time they'd heard all the rumours and half believed them: that is, Adey pooh-poohed every story on principle, Crooks thought Sir John might really have come to some harm, and Nick pointed out that the chief rumour was so near to what they knew themselves that it must surely be true. How else should anyone know of the quarrel at all?

It was at this point that Farmer, in conversation with Adey, had begun to show his hand. Were they still worried about Sir John? Had they cause to be – a different cause, perhaps? Did Sir John often leave them at short notice? He had done so, but usually left a note or message for them. In the absence of instructions, Adey felt it would be better not to interfere. He'd made out to the others he was as fogged as they were, but for himself he had an idea there was perhaps – well, private business – he could understand there might be things Sir John would hardly wish to tell them. 'You might think I'd want to make out he told me everything, but I'm not conceited enough for that,' was how he put it. Farmer thought he was sincere, because beneath the remark was the faintest undercurrent of hurt pride. What's more, he said frankly that the rumours were absurd: Sir John knew how to take care of himself, and would never have harmed the fool, only disarmed him somehow: he did things that seemed crazy until you found out the reason, but there was always a method in it. So then Farmer had asked outright, where he really thought Sir John was, and he answered candidly he had not tried to guess; there might have been something afoot – he'd been secretive lately – and full of humours, but they were used to *that.*

'Then I put it to him, what about Orchard House? And he gave me a funny look; his tongue said "the house is closed", but his eyes were asking what the dickens I knew about it, and something else too, grappling with a new thought – "What d'you mean, Orchard House?" and I said, "He went there, Monday night." I was watching him all the time,' said Farmer, 'and at first he looked relieved. He burst out laughing, and said "What, has he been there ever since? The old –" and then he must have seen from my manner there was more to come. He said, "Look, who are you, what *is* all this?" or something like that, and then I told him straight, he's in the Tower. My word, I never saw such a change. Talk about wiping the grin off anyone's face! He turned the colour of that paper. He opened his mouth and no voice came out. At last he forced out an uneasy sort of laugh and says, "It's not true. You're trying to frighten me." Then he takes another look at me and sees it's true all right, and sits down suddenly holding on to the table. So I called for some more drinks. He soon pulled himself together when we were alone again, and then the questions poured out – when, why, what happened, what's he accused of? All I told him was, the charge will be treason. He sat there and stared as though he could hardly believe me. "He's done nothing, they'll have to let him go." That's what he kept saying over and over. I hinted there was pretty strong evidence, and he all but called me a liar. I tell you, I was surprised. I never thought Adey would stand up for anyone but himself.'

'The Stadis touch,' said Fabian. 'Yes, he commands loyalty. There can be danger even in that.'

'How do you mean?'

'Danger to himself if he is innocent – the very protestations of others on his behalf are suspect; if guilty, danger to the state – there'd be too many people thinking whatever he did was right. Danger either way; that would be why they chose him.'

'They?' Farmer queried in his turn.

'The enemy. The Spaniard, if you like, though that remains to be proved. We have all presumed the Spaniard, from the three words written in Spanish.'

'Yes, well, it stands to reason. There's one thing, though: why reply in Spanish to a letter written in Latin? Or is it all the same to you learned clerks?'

'No, that is curious, agreed Fabian. 'Perhaps the Spanish came easier to him: he'd practised that in the wars, whereas schoolday Latin's a long time ago. It soon rusts unless used often. Mine has, I know.' He stopped, suddenly remembering the thumbed Horace: but Farmer took the pause as signal to continue his report.

He had questioned Adey as to Sir John's movements, pointing out that if he had done nothing harmful there could be no harm in replying. This well-worn piece of counsel actually seemed to hearten Adey. He gave a clear account of their activities since the spring, and the names of most of Sir John's visitors, promising to write down any more he remembered. He declared there had been no strangers at the house and that he would have known if there were. Messengers? There were few – little boys usually. Of course there was the agent from Worcestershire, he came three or four times a year, but this year only once so far, in May. He never stayed at Orchard House, but lodged in the city somewhere. He brought the rent from the farms, letters and suchlike. It was four, no five weeks ago. He came on a Thursday, spent an hour with Sir John in private, went off presumably on business and came back on the Saturday for final instructions. Apart from that, Adey knew nothing of Sir John's correspondence and had seen no letters delivered. His account of their recent journeying agreed with Sir John's. When he got to their sojourn in the city he became noticeably less talkative, but admitted after some hedging that Sir John had more than once refused to go out with them or had sent them on trivial errands. He asserted firmly that there was nothing unusual in this, and then he had suddenly refused to say any more.

'I think he saw where it was leading and shut up,' said Farmer. 'Especially when you hear what we got from the others.'

The invaluable Jackson had gone roundabout with Crooks and Greenlee. Crooks had taken a liking to him and was less taciturn than usual, and Nick was too glad of an audience to care who it was. He was soon telling all he knew and a good deal he did not. Jackson heard every detail of the journey to Oxford, of Sir John's meanness in not letting them lodge in the town, the horrors of country inns, Adey's amorous adventures, Crooks' liquid capacity and all. It was not easy to sort the grain from the chaff, but now and then Crooks put in a word of confirmation or correction. In this way he learned it was Sir John who had insisted on getting back to London, and who tried to keep their presence at the Quartern a secret. Of course he had to hear all over again the events of Midsummer Eve, but embedded in that narrative, like the jewel in the toad's head, was some useful information about their daily life and habits. It supplied, for instance, an answer to one of Fabian's questions concerning Orchard House: Crooks and Adey had orders, whenever they went there, to make a fire, put warming-pans in the beds and re-fill water-jugs from the butt – an hour's work at least; Crooks grumbled about it. They saw nothing suspicious in this (though Adey had not mentioned it), being too used to Sir John's whims. Another point which stood out clearly was that in spite of Nick's boasting, Sir John had taken none of them into his confidence, even in matters like his visit to Aldernaton; he had simply announced it the day before and expected them to make ready. And although Nick was quick to seize on questionable incidents, and they all had some complaint or other, very little discreditable to Sir John had in fact emerged.

'What we *have* got,' said Farmer in conclusion, 'is the good beginnings of a daily history – Jackson has written it down according to the calendar – and a line or two more to follow up. The Quartern, for one: I can go there now, armed with this information, with some hope of success.'

'Something else we have, if I'm not mistaken,' Fabian added. 'Most of the time they hunted in couples: Crooks and Adey, Nick and Sir John, or Sir John and Adey, Crooks and Nick. I'll mark out on the journal – like this – the statements that are already confirmed by others. Unless they're all in it, and I feel more and more they are not, we need not question the times they were together. Apart from Sir John, do you see who's left alone on one significant occasion?'

Farmer followed his finger down the page.

'Nick – at the fair. When he was dead to the world.'

'Was he? Can we prove it? Even if he was, who spoke with him beforehand? Could it, in fact, be scatterbrain after all?'

'You mean Nick Greenlee's only acting silly, and that he really is in the conspiracy?'

'I mean it's still possible, but Lord help us, a fair! A hundred people might have seen him receive or pass on a message, and thought nothing of it. A drunken ass, throwing his money around and as good as asking to have his pocket picked. What would you think? "A fool and his money are soon parted," and take no further notice.'

'I might get proof,' said Farmer doubtfully. 'I know a man who knows the fairground people. They rest up for a bit and then go on to Mitcham or somewhere. And I'll put the boys on to anyone who saw him. If we get reliable eye-witnesses, will that content you?'

'Content!' Fabian grimaced. 'Four days, and we're nowhere. No fault of yours, Farmer, you've done wonders. Keep on is all I ask.' He pulled the seal-copy, carefully folded, out of an inner pocket. 'Look at that. I was all afternoon at the College of Heralds. They'd not been shown it before. Four days! And of course, they are puzzled. It could be a Boar of De So-and-so, but for the staff: or someone-else's Centaur, but the legs are not long enough – bah! The fact is, they've seen nothing like it. It's deliberately blurred, of course. The only thing certain is that it's no English seal. And they've taken a quick copy and will I call again next week. And the old man's bleating about the Nones of December – that's in the book I told you about. It's all wrong, Farmer. There's such a smell of fish about the whole business that if they tell me this object is a mermaid with a golden comb I'll not be surprised.'

'Well, it's Friday: what else do you expect? And talking of Mermaids, that crowd that meets there on a Friday – Stadis was one of them: what about it?'

'Dispersed for the summer. I know them all. Yes, they know Sir John and he has joined them sometimes, and I'd stake my last penny on the lot of them. Not everyone can get into that circle; not the sort we're looking for; they're different worlds and hard to mix. And the only thing that justifies us spying on them and all the good plain simple men as well is to keep the dirt from spreading. It's a canker, Farmer, a disease, that fouls friendship and stifles honest laughter. All faction stinks, all, whatever side it takes. Yes, we're infected too – the difference is we know it.' He subsided angrily, alarmed at his own outburst.

Farmer was looking at him in astonishment. 'What the constable's the matter with you?' he demanded. 'Just because you get a difficult case–' He paused, and his face softened. 'Look,' he said more quietly, 'let me tell you something. I may not know Latin, but I'm old enough to be your father, and if I put it a bit awkward, try and take it as it's meant. You're doing a good job. Keep that in your head first and foremost. It's needed. It's dirty work, of course: so's a collier's. They put up with dirt on their hands, why should we be so particular with our hearts? Someone's got to get dirty, till they clean the world up good and proper – as if you could do that by city ordinance – and it'd better be someone that can see straight, and face what he sees, and never twist it to his own advantage. Like you. A man, not a politician. And if it clogs your stomach sometimes, well, eat plenty of lettuce and forget it.'

'Thanks, Farmer.' He was stirred more deeply than he knew how to admit. 'You're right as usual. We're both right, but yours was the better speech.' He grinned and held out his hand. 'If you do see a bit of dirt–' They shook.

'And now,' said Fabian briskly, 'I tell you what I'll do: leave me Jackson's calendar, I'll fill in the rest that we know. By Tuesday–' he checked himself. '*When* I get the month's general reports, I'll set them alongside in the same way. If any of our old clients was within ten miles of this lot, we'll pull him in at once on suspicion. At any date this year,' he added. 'I'm ranging wider now. This is no four-day matter, I knew that all the time: they say a tree's roots spread as wide as the branches. Very well. Four weeks or four months be it, we'll have it out in daylight at the last. I'll start on the old reports this evening. And Fisher leaves tomorrow for Worcester whatever the weather and whosoever's plan it spoils. Can he do your Bedfordshire errand on the way?'

'No, no, that's taken care of. I put the cart before the horse there,' confessed Farmer, 'and told him to get a signed statement if the man can write. That may save us a day later on. The rest of the bunch I'll see again myself – there's a whole lot more I can ask them now.

'When you want me, send. I'll have news or eat this hat for dinner.' He put it on as he spoke, grabbed his worn leather budget and made for the door. 'Keep your heart up, lad,' he added. 'The picture's not coming yet: maybe that's only because we're not clear what to look for.' And he stumped away downstairs.

You never spoke a truer word, thought Fabian: is that lock of hair the mermaid's after all, or the seaweed I want it to be? But Farmer's trust must be lived up to. He took his own hat, before resolution could waver, and went out to give instructions covering another dozen names on the list. Then he called for new pens and shut himself up with his task.

He rode out of the city with Fisher in the morning, to fill in at first hand the details of his brief report, and to give him the background of the new assignment. Fisher was a quiet young man, with a shy smile that won every motherly heart and obtained for him confidences his elders could not hope for. His one fault was lack of imagination, but this in his present capacity was something of a virtue too; he remembered everything he heard, very nearly verbatim, and passed it on without trying to interpret it. Fabian could not wish for a better substitute, and although instinct cried at him to do this job himself, it might be wiser he should not. Let other hands bring in the evidence and no one could accuse him of partiality. He could promise to sit in the middle of the web and deal justly, whatever his feelings, with all that arrived.

When he got back the day was well worn, and there was nothing more he could usefully do until Monday but escort the Margetts to the home of their married daughter at Brentford, a long-standing engagement. In a way he was glad of the respite. His thoughts had been churning up and down to no purpose long enough: let them stand, as the good wife did her cream, to thicken. So when the Brentford folk pressed him to stay at least the night he accepted with a clear conscience, and ended by travelling back with the old couple on Sunday evening. The quiet, the sweet country air, the unaffected welcome he had enjoyed refreshed him; his brain began to work again of its own accord.

This was the line it took. How would the enemy approach such a one as Sir John Stadis? What argument would they use? Here was no case of fanatical devotion, no personal attachment to their prince or to their cause; on the contrary: he came of one of the first protestant families, with a high tradition of public service and a record the reverse of self-seeking. The customary inducements, the appeal to greed or pride seemed rather out of place. Religion, on whichever hand, was unlikely to be a motive – he had shown himself indifferent to it. What could they offer? Money? He had certainly signed away his heritage, with as yet no abatement of his accustomed spending. Power, place, advancement – what blessing would they bring? In his chosen life here in the city he was the prince of good fellows; to those who surrounded him his word was already law. For what would he exchange his ease? Perhaps for action – any sort of action, the extremer the better – to assuage some inner longing. A decision taken, bridges burnt behind him – was there not some hint of this in his behaviour? Fabian cast back in recollection to the day of their interview. There had been something he could not put a name to, some awareness, inclining him to the belief that Sir John knew just what he was doing: some feeling too open for guilt, too private to define. And the previous night, when he had burst into the bedroom and confronted them, what was that first impression of Fabian's, so difficult to recapture now that he knew more of its subject? Not surprise, that was the wrong word: shock? Surprise came later, with the document. Shock without surprise, the shock of the expected come at last? Not quite that either. It might be only his fancy, Fabian admitted. Nevertheless, if he could read a man's mind once and once only, that was the moment he would have chosen. He felt uneasily that even now he held the key to it, could he but recognise and put it to use.

So what did it add up to, all this reasoning? Religion, no: power, not likely: money perhaps – and stronger than all these, some appeal to his generosity, a threat held over someone dear to him? But could there be such a person? The one close friend of his youth was Roger Dalbie. He had taken Roger's death hard, several people had testified. Since then he had, it appeared, rather an easy intimacy with many than a deeper feeling for any. He had changed too in the last couple of years, people said, losing interest in his old diversions, become moody and unpredictable and distant even from his friends. There could be no one for whom he would risk being an accessory, unless – perhaps – Roger's daughter? If she were indeed involved, would he think it his duty to shield her? He had been trying for some time to sever his connections with Aldernaton; he had paid his debt to Dalbie's memory by doing as much for the girl as her own father would have done – more, Fabian suspected, for the

Roger Dalbie he remembered had been dazzling, delightful, and impecunious. Was the Chief's last order based on something more than misgiving? Had Sir John assumed the part of protector, or was he being cast for it without his knowledge?

At this point speculation reined in with a jerk. Between Sir John and Mr Secretary was an old antagonism which neither had troubled to conceal. If the business was fish-like before, it now began to smell even less pleasant, and Fabian had to remind himself it was still no more than conjecture. He must reserve judgement. There could be a dozen different explanations. Say the Chief knew what he would not tell, it might be better for Fabian to discover it, even as it was better Fisher should go up to Worcestershire. There were degrees, it seemed, of impartiality, and he only hoped it would be unnecessary to invoke them all. He had a moment's absurd fantasy of Fisher falling in love with the girl and refusing to give *his* evidence, and so on through the whole gamut: though the Lord only knew who could replace Fisher. There was that boy with the pointed chin who showed promise, but he was too young yet...

The reports began to come in. Fabian studied especially those from the coastal towns, with London, Bristol, Milford Haven. He had a map prepared, as well as his date-chart, and plotted the movements of all relevant persons thereon. He sat long into the night poring over the conjunctions thus revealed, some of which threw light on an entirely different problem, but on the Stadis case no single beam. Every known foreign agent was satisfactorily accounted for: no stranger in any way suspicious was known to have crossed Sir John's path. Turn the sum this way or that, the net result was NIL.

He thought he had something at Lambeth, for his kind helpers welcomed him smiling. They had identified the man he was seeking as one Hezekiah Walters, who had undoubtedly accompanied the army to Flushing in '85. Unhappily (although we must not question the Divine Providence) he was no longer with us, having died four summers ago at Billericay in Essex. He left a widow, they added hopefully. Would she have his books and papers? There was an anxious pause. They looked at each other, and said several persons could vouch for her. It dawned on Fabian they must have thought there was a legacy. He corrected that impression as kindly as he could, and trusted the lady's hopes had not been raised. No, no, they assured him, only the present incumbent had mentioned she was in straitened circumstances. He would be the man to consult. It happened he was in the building now, in the next room to be exact. They introduced him and tactfully withdrew.

The frail scholarly-looking priest, whose name Fabian did not catch, had obviously travelled all the way to London simply in the hope of assisting his colleague's widow, but his disappointment was solely for her. He put it aside and prepared to give what help he could, but shook his head on hearing what Fabian wanted. There were no papers at all. Walters' death had been suspected as a case of pestilence, and the villagers' fears had outrun discretion: they had burned everything, from roof to ground, and the wife, who had been visiting relatives, came back to find herself husbandless and homeless too.

'I am sorry.' The old man was distressed. 'I suppose I must not ask you more. But surely,' he added earnestly, 'the truth will come to light some other way.'

'I hope you're right, sir.' Fabian rather awkwardly brought out his purse. 'If you could bring the lady to believe that this is from a friend of her husband's – repayment of a loan, perhaps –'

He smiled. 'I will take the lie on my conscience. But pray do not scant yourself, for I see you are not a rich man.'

'Call it a gift by proxy. I have small enough chance to do good deeds of my own.' He was thinking of it as Sir John's gift: the parallel was close enough. 'Tell me,' he said abruptly, 'can a man be both good and evil? Generous, open, universally liked, yet for one fault or for one act condemned?'

'We are all imperfect. The law condemns, but only God can judge.'

'Yes, yes, I know.'

He said, 'Forgive me for troubling you,' then went back to trouble his subordinates and the next person on the list.

And if he would turn cynic, why at least he had been spared a journey into Essex.

He did not see Farmer for a week. In that time he had covered much paper and torn most of it up again, exhausted the College of Heralds, who said at last, in the person of a high official, that they could do no more: and received a curious bit of news.

'Listen to this, Farmer – no comments till the end.' He read from his cramped shorthand: 'Burglary at Catford, night of 23rd June. Burglary at Bromley 25th June. Three men taken in the act of entering, 29th June, at the Grange, Foots Cray, two got away and one picked up later at Deptford; the four now being held at Maidstone awaiting trial. Confessed to many crimes of the same sort. The leader escaped, dresses like a gentleman, brown hair, and brown eyes, wears a ring set with two rubies and a gold locket in the left ear – et cetera.'

'23rd June – that was Midsummer Eve.'

'It was so.'

'Four held and one escaped?'

'Yes.'

'They sound like our conspirators.'

'Do they not,' said Fabian bitterly. 'We must get their movements, of course. I'm going down there tomorrow: no risking some bumblehead put the question to them with the answer inside it. But they're the ones all right; I feel it in my bones.'

'Then we're back where we started.'

'Worse: two milestones at least in the wrong direction.' He told Farmer of his other disappointments. 'So unless you have something for me –'

'I've found young Summers.' Farmer was looking sheepish.

'Summers? Oh yes, the nephew. Where?'

'You'll laugh when I tell you. He's in the Clink. For debt. Been there eight months. Dipped a bit deeply in expectation when his uncle had the stroke, and the old skinflint refused to cough up. I've seen the process, and I know the creditors, *and* the crowd he used to run with. You can rule him right out.'

'We'd have to, anyhow; the barn means nothing now. Let's face it, we've been wasting our time. Any more, while you're about it?'

'News, but nothing to handle. Adey and Crooks are back in London; their fortnight at Deptford was paid for, and it's run out now, and they've gone to ground somewhere – I can put my hand on them any day in the week. Nick's broken with them, I think. He was mucking about with a mixed sort of crowd up by Lamb's Conduit an hour ago. We'll keep an eye on him.'

'They're not at the Quartern this time?'

'Lord, no. Not one of them's gone near the place. If there's any trouble they mean to be out of it. I got a long story from the woman Thorn – a thorn without a rose and no mistake, just as I thought, nothing they can touch her for, of course. Nor him, if it comes to that. Evidence of suspicious behaviour, no more. She knew all along he was up to no good: if she said so once she said it a dozen times, did she not, Winkle? Winkle's the drawer and handy-man. Halfway between his and hers you'll get near to the truth. There was something under cover all right.'

'He went out in the mornings.' They had stopped using Sir John's name long ago, but they knew who was meant.

'I know. Winkle confirms it. He tends to like him, so that'll be true. He went a different way each morning.'

'In case he was watched.'

'Looks like it. I'm working on that still. And we're filling in the picture out at Southwark, who went, who stayed, what they did there – not many names, but pretty good descriptions, right down to the shape of their noses – you'll recognise them sure enough. The man Wilson's a godsend, a natural imitator – he's only got to think of a face and it's somehow there in front of you. I went up to Bedfordshire myself as soon as I got the first report, and persuaded him back with me. The mother's recovered, and he'll never get employment there. He's at the Elephant at present, can be seen there any morning.'

'Good work,' said Fabian heartily.

'Not so good. It still tells us nothing. According to him all they did was talk, talk, talk. He's a trifle simple.'

'Never mind. I can fit all this in. But I want more, though.' Fabian smoothed out the crumpled sheets with a determined hand. 'We go back two years at least – when his friends say he began to change. I want to know every little thing – who was with him and where, how he looked, what he laughed at –'

'Where he itched and when he scratched,' grumbled Farmer good-naturedly.

'That too. Nothing is too trivial. We still know nothing, therefore anything may prove important.'

'May not,' retorted Farmer. But they both began to feel more cheerful; there was still one hope on the horizon.

7

Fisher

When they met again two days later, it was at Seething Lane.

'You've just missed Fisher,' Farmer greeted him. 'Came in this morning, and gone off now to get his dinner. He spoke to me, but maybe you'd rather hear it from him yourself.'

'Anything stand out?'

'Yes and no. You'll send him back, I expect – him or someone else. Shall I send after him? They know his ordinary house.'

'No, let him alone for now,' said Fabian. 'If you've had your own dinner, come in here and talk to me.' He shut the inner door behind them.

'Well, how are your burglars?'

'As we thought. Three of them did the Catford job; it was timed for Midsummer Eve an hour before sunset, when they knew there'd be nobody at home. They met the fourth man about a mile off, by arrangement, and he took them to the leader at a special rendez-vous. It was fairly new country to all of them, they're not able to swear to the exact spot, but it *was* a barn with a clump of trees nearby and a waggon in a field, they did hear horses moving about cropping, but being town rats not country rats thought they belonged to the place. They sat in the barn an hour or so, till the moon was right up, sharing out the plunder and plotting nothing more serious than the next bit of thievery.'

'So that's that.'

'Or is that what we were meant to think?'

'Here, here, here,' said Farmer, 'what's on your mind this time?'

'I wish I knew. Nothing I like the sound of – or can put a name to, yet.' He began undoing his doublet with impatient tugs.

'You've been stewing over this too long,' said Farmer sympathetically

'Stewing's the word. You try wearing a quilted lining in July.' He flung off the garment and jerked a flat package out of its interior. 'I called on the Chief this morning and he gave me this. The first examination – yesterday: sixteen days after the arrest. I suppose he knows what he's doing.'

'Does it tell us anything new?'

'I've not had a chance to look at it yet. We'll go through it together, after you give me Fisher's story.'

'As far as I've got it,' said Farmer. 'I might miss something, and there may be all sorts of things he noticed or thought at the time –'

'Does Fisher think? I've often wondered. He's a good man, though. Never mind the little things, he'll put them in the report. Suppose I know nothing, and begin at the beginning.'

They seated themselves on the hard chairs that the office afforded. There was no need for Farmer's apology; he had mastered the facts, of course, and shut his eyes now the better to recall them.

'Aldernaton's a house on a hill. *The* house on *the* hill. Village two miles away in the dale, church about a mile. Two ways in from the south, the second from some hamlet three or four miles off but in the same parish – they join below the church, so there's just the one road going on up the hill. You have to go up to go down, Fisher said. He went right on past the house first time, so he could turn back and make out he'd missed his way. It goes up best part of another mile, and suddenly drops away and you see the country all laid out below you like a map, little fields and hedges and farmhouses and the brook winding in and out. The farms are part of the property, six or seven of them, he's not certain – all green and rich-looking. Then beyond, where the brown heath begins, that's Wickins' land. Humphrey Wickins of Baindon. When the old man died, Henry Stadis that was, Wickins offered to buy the place, but the son refused him. There's been no love lost between them ever since.

'It belongs to the girl now. They like her in the village. She's good and she's straight and her head's screwed on the right way, not like the aunt that has no more sense than a silly old hen. They'd be glad to see her married to a proper sort of man, but where's she to find one? Tom Wickins, he tried hard to get her, but she sent him off with a flea in his ear, and good luck to her. He's no fit husband for a girl like her. Takes after his dad, a glutton and a waster. They could do better than him for a landlord, they'd rather the girl stayed single only it seems a shame, like; but that's how it is, she's not brought herself to fancy anyone, not any of the neighbours' lads nor those fine folk that came from Glo'ster last year. They'd be after the estate, and she knows it. And her without a penny to her name only a while back. A good name too, they admit, but it's not as if she were a Stadis.'

Fisher had posed in the neighbourhood as a carpenter (to which trade he had actually been apprenticed), going north to an uncle and working for his living on the way. He called at every house of any size, and was usually given an odd job and a meal. At the larger places he threw out hints of dry rot and got permission to go over the upper storeys, prepared if he should find any to make out it was a long job, he'd not be staying and they'd best call in a local man. There were plenty of small repairs at Aldernaton and he managed to spend two days there. It was all in the report, but to sum up, the house had held no secrets. Books in the parson's study were fewer than one might expect, but all properly of divinity. In the young lady's room he found a packet of letters: they were from Sir John to his ward up to last year, nothing more. The ribbon was firm upon them and tied in the original bow, for the colour had faded; if any papers had been removed the loops would not coincide with the previous tying, and it had taken him longer than he'd liked to replace it exactly. He had read them all and reproduced them afterwards to the best of his excellent memory. There was nothing there. He had got very little from the household; most of his information was gleaned elsewhere.

At Shirecote, residence of Simon Garner, wool merchant, he found the outward signs of great wealth and no work for such as he to do. The house was still fairly new and everything handsome about it. Old Garner was suffering from the gout and a married daughter had installed herself recently to nurse him; no young bride for him – so much money would not be allowed to pass out of the family. Fisher's next call, Monk's Croft, in contrast was a bare untidy place, the brick showing through the plaster. There seemed to be no one at home, until he heard barks, cheers and excited voices from the direction of the stable, and discovered the entire Filpot household engaged in a rat-hunt. Contributing a modest two to the total bag of nineteen, he was welcomed generously and his offer of work quite naturally accepted. He did not charge them very much. They were a young, noisy, cheerful family, five brothers, three of them schoolboys; they had lost both parents in a year and Martin, the eldest, could be no more than twenty. He had been hoping to ask Sir John Stadis' advice on the June visit, but old Wickins' behaviour had put paid to that. Now he would have to consult an uncle whom none of them liked, but Tony was leaving school at Christmas and something would have to be done. These confidences were not just blurted out to a total stranger, but emerged while he put in some hours of solid work, with the enthusiastic if unskilled help of the younger boys. Fisher had gone so far as to hint that Martin could do with a rich wife; the suggestion met with much scorn and had plainly never occurred to them, nor did Martin appear the kind of man to plot and scheme for an heiress.

The news of Sir John's arrest had not reached Worcestershire, or so Farmer inferred from Fisher's story. He was told of him on all sides and had plenty of openings to question further.

'Makes out he *did* once hear of a Stadis in London – Sir John was it? Would he be any kin? So he gets the whole tale – mostly from the old dear at the Woolpack, down in the village; she'd been milkmaid or something up at the house in Henry's time – all about what a lovely baby he was and grown into a fine man of course but still young-looking, and walked into her parlour this very last month and kissed her on both cheeks as if he'd not been a week away. Mind you, it's seldom he comes now, and only to be expected, what with his London friends, and serving the Queen like he does – they say she thinks the world of him.

'That's how the women talk. The men spoke up for him too, allowing he's not quite the man his father was, but a man all the same, and never too proud to take you by the hand like some they knew – and been in foreign parts too, and knighted on the battlefield. They can all tell the tale of how it happened, and whose life it was he saved, some German prince that was one of the allies, and how he shoved him in the ditch for safety just like a bundle of straw and went back into the thick of it after plain Ned Phillips of Bermondsey, and brought him out alive too. Only they'd not know Ned's name,' explained Farmer, 'getting the story from others as they did: I put that bit in, knowing myself that it's true.

'The men on the whole disapprove of the property being transferred. No one can understand why he's done that, and gone off and left everything. It's not like him, they say. It's true the agent has run the estate for years now, but he always looked to Sir John for orders. They'll treat the young lady as mistress right and proper, but not stand any nonsense from Sir Oliver. That's the parson. Courtesy-title – they're old-fashioned in those parts. Name of Marbeck, married to the aunt, came from Lincolnshire ten years ago when the girl's mother died. Sir John moved heaven and earth to get him the living, went into Worcester and saw the Bishop himself seven or eight times. Thought it would be best to have her own kin bring her up. Regrets it now, they reckon, though it's not the sort of thing he'd speak of to anyone. Could be Sir Oliver that keeps him away – no comfort with *him* in the house always harping on your sins. Not but what he preaches a powerful good sermon, but why not keep that for Sundays? Sir John used to come home for Christmas always, and in the summer he'd stay two or three months, but all that's changed; he'll come for a couple of days, that's all, and though you'd not call him different from his old self, it's as though he had something on his mind.

'Fisher says they'd talk about this quite openly. They're not simple either, but hard-headed farming folk, and if they thought anything needed covering up for Sir John's sake, covered it would be. The only thing he heard against him was one old crab-face saying perhaps the girl *was* his own daughter, and the others rounded on him at once, told him he had a dirty mind, everyone knew she was born in Northamptonshire and Dalbie never left his wife from the day they were wed until he set out for the wars.'

'And that's true too,' said Fabian, 'though how they knew it across two counties . . . Peddler's talk, perhaps. Always listen to country gossip: it's the best weather vane I know.'

'Well, that's about all but for movements. Fisher has the names of those who visit the house. Sir Oliver has never left the parish since he first set foot in it, and that means his wife too – she waits on him and clucks round after him. The girl used to go visiting as a child, though not often; now she's grown she stays home and lets the world come to her. The people from Gloucester were some kin of the mother's: they'd neglected her all the years she had nothing and came clustering round when they thought there was honey in the pot – and how they heard *that* was the wonder. They came uninvited, and the girl, who's no fool, must have been plain with them: they've not been seen again. Then there was a houseful of company last time Sir John was there, invited to meet him, match-making mothers and every man who thought himself in the running. The girl got up after dinner and said thank you kindly but she was not intending to marry anyone, present company least of all.'

'*Oratio directa.*' Fabian could not help smiling. 'She was plain with them, too. Directed, I wonder, at whom?'

Wickins mostly, Tom Wickins, Farmer supposed. Fisher had been to Baindon, of course; the old man was not at home when he called, or he would not have penetrated as far as he did. There was not, be it noted, a book or paper in the house; it was old but in good enough condition, the timbers all sound and no false panelling. Tongues wagged in the master's absence and shut up the minute he was reported on the skyline, but they had let out quite a lot. It was Humphrey chiefly who wanted the match; he and Tom had argued so long beforehand that they left themselves barely time for the journey, some three quarters of an hour. Still, they'd set off in good spirits and seemingly at accord. They returned not long before dusk, at roughly the time they were expected but in very different fettle, both savage and sullen. Tom slammed straight to bed, his father sat up and drank himself into a stupor, and they hardly spoke to each other for days afterwards.

'There'd been an almighty row over at Aldernaton, old Wickins spitting out threats, Sir John cool as a cucumber shutting everyone up with a couple of words. Wickins and his crowd went off in a huff and *they* have not been seen since, by the girl of course. That's what she got him there for – Sir John, I mean: to clear the decks for her. So everyone reckons.'

'And that,' said Fabian, 'is where our story began.'

It was shaping up very well, the outline firm and unmistakeable. So this corner *was* a pastoral, nymph and satyrs in the traditional manner but against a grey-green English background, the house on a hill dominating the skyline. 'He built a chimney in my father's house, and the bricks are alive this day to testify' – why should that line come suddenly to his mind from a play at least two years old? It came ready grown and authoritative as though pertinent to the occasion, lending its own hint of sadness within comedy to the scene he had been piecing together. Pastoral-historical-comical? It fitted, too: he could almost see the rest of the pattern – only, if he were right, it would not further his investigation one whit. Unless, said reason's chill within him, that dark patch should be the ram in the thicket after all?

And prompted by his words, Farmer was murmuring the old rhyme,

> I'll tell you a story about Jack-a-Dory
> And now my story's begun:
> I'll tell you another about his brother
> And now my story's done.

Had he seen the point too? Better not mention it, it might have no connection. 'Brother' here was comparative, of course, like 'who is my neighbour?' and 'am I my brother's keeper?' Or, to take the metaphor further, do I send anonymous letters accusing my brother of being up to no good? Not unless I was in London at the time, said common sense firmly asserting itself.

'Has any of this lot been in London recently?'

'I was coming to that. Tom Wickins left home the second week in June, exact date unknown but soon after the row at Aldernaton, supposed to have gone to his uncle's near Bristol: certainly back at Baindon by 21st June – he was seen riding a mile or so off on the Saturday by the local blacksmith, who shouted after him, he was digging his spurs in so, but he took no notice.'

21st June – he'd never get back from London the same day. He could have sent the first letter but not the second nor third. He could have sent the first and made arrangements for the second and third: or was he really in Bristol all the time?

'Then there's the agent,' went on Farmer, 'and this is what made me sit up. He was in London the third week of May: that agrees with Adey's story. Fisher says he was late going, he should have come in April but the weather was so bad he kept putting it off. He was back on 29th May, went straight up to see the girl, then home to change his clothes – he has a house in the village – told the housekeeper to expect him when she saw him, saddled a fresh horse and rode away again directly. And *he*–' He paused significantly.

'Has not been seen since?'

'How did you guess?'

'I have the second-sight. You know, you might have told me that in the first place.'

Farmer grinned. 'You said start at the beginning. Well, what do you think? Are we getting warm at last?'

'I'll say that when I get the evidence. Any evidence. But it is a lead: the only one, unless this yields us any.' He tossed over the unopened packet. 'I'm sending Fisher to Bristol: clear as we go. And I want a good older man to ride openly to Aldernaton and ask for the agent, with credentials we can supply. See to that, will you, and bring him here by tomorrow.' He scratched a rapid memorandum. 'Any comment, before we go on?'

'Only – I see you're confident at last.'

Fabian smiled back. 'That's part of the act.' But there was a difference, he felt it, in the whole structure of the case: the first lap was over, he was settling like a runner into his serious long-distance stride. In this rhythm he came into his own, and could give out a certainty he was often far from feeling, till the very clerks in the room outside would nudge each other – 'He's on to something this time.'

'Come on then, let's have the seals off: this is what we've been waiting for.'

8

Examination

The preliminary enquiry. Presiding, old Lord Ambrose – clever, that: a friend of the family; respected, kindly, not a courtier in the accepted sense, shrewd enough but with no great pretension to wit – if he finds against him the whole world will be satisfied. Conducted by – yes, clever again – no brilliant legal luminary but an unknown junior, carefully briefed, of course. Secret as it was, there was to be no possibility of a whisper, no faintest hint yet of the colossal weight of law and influence piling up against the prisoner. For an instant, his hand still on the title-page, Fabian sickened of the whole business; even though he knew, and better than most, how well it could be justified, how often indeed it was, by the fact of a full confession. Then he firmly turned the sheet.

> ... understand this is not a court of law but a court of enquiry ... establish the truth ... not under oath, but I do ask you earnestly to consider...

'You can skip that page,' he told Farmer irreverently. 'Come to where the questions really begin.'

> QUESTION: On the fifteenth day of December in the year of our Lord 1598 you disposed of your property at Aldernaton in the county of Worcester?
> ANSWER: Except for certain outlying farms – yes.

Q: Tell his lordship how you did this.
A: By Deed of Gift.
Q: To whom did you make over this valuable property?
A: To my ward.
Q: Quite so: to Barbara Dalbie. In consequence of what did you do this?
A: I had promised her father as he died to provide for her.
Q: Could you have done so and yet retained this property, your birthplace?
A: I suppose so.
Q: You have, in fact, provided for her liberally for fourteen years, ever since her father's death?
A: Yes.
Q: You could have continued to do so, to the same extent, for the rest of your life?
A: Yes.
Q: I put it that when you decided to make over the property to her, it was because you had embarked on a treasonous enterprise, which if discovered would cost your life.
A: That is not true.
Q: What then was your reason?
A: I wished not to disturb her: she is happy there.
Q: You were lodging meanwhile at Southwark at the messuage known as Orchard House?
A: Yes.
Q: Your own house?
A: No. It belongs to the Archbishop. I took it on a five-year lease.
Q: When does this lease expire?
A: At Michaelmas.
Q: This year? In less than twelve weeks' time?
A: Yes.
Q: Where did you then intend to live?

A: I had not decided.

Q: You expect his lordship to believe that you disposed of your heritage, knowing that in so short a time you would be without a roof over your head?

A: That is hardly the position. There were many choices open to me. I simply had not made up my mind.

Q: You had made no decision on the fourth day of June last?

A: That is so.

Q: Then why did you on that day dismiss the servants and close Orchard House?

A: I was going into Worcestershire. Wilson's mother was ill, so I let him go early, and it was hardly worth while keeping the others.

Q: What did you plan to do until Michaelmas?

A: I should have spent some time at Deptford, the rest in London.

Q: Lodging where?

A: At some inn or other.

Q: Would this restless existence content you?

A: It sorted with my mood.

Q: Why were you restless?

A: I – was dissatisfied with my way of life.

Q: You were perhaps in money difficulties as a result of your Deed of Gift?

A: Hardly that. I should have to be somewhat thriftier. That was why I did not renew the lease.

Q: You were dissatisfied, and not so well off as in the past. I put it to you, that for a promise of money you agreed to help the Queen's enemies.

A: No.

Q: You admit you were disaffected.

A: Nothing of the kind. I said dissatisfied, in myself and with myself.

Q: In what way?

A: As any man might be, in his fortieth year and nothing to show for it.

THE PRESIDENT: Your life had not maintained the promise of your youth?

A: I accept your lordship's emendation.

And suddenly Fabian could see the speaker clearly, hands spread in the slightest gesture of distaste, tired eyes mocking his own detachment and the obscurity he could no longer claim, knowing that before the case was ended (whatever the outcome) there would be no shred of privacy remaining: everything good or bad, large or small, each detail the self keeps hidden must be dragged remorselessly into the common light of day.

The questioner had harked back again:

... You held the Queen's commission in the Netherlands from 1585 to 1587?

A: I did.

Q: While with the army you acted as interpreter?

A: On some occasions, yes.

Q: Your knowledge of the Spanish tongue being extensive?

A: Enough to be useful: not extensive.

Q: How did you come by it?

A: My father had Spanish friends, in the late Queen's reign. He taught me a little, and I improved upon it when we took prisoners.

Q: Did you correspond with your father's friends in Spain?

A: Not often.

Q: How recently have you done so?

A: Not for twenty years. Twenty-one years – I informed them of his death.

Q: Did they reply on that occasion?

A: I think so. Yes.

Q: What was the substance of the reply?

A: The usual expressions of grief, I suppose.

Q: You have said that you did not write again. Did you send messages by word of mouth?

A: No.

Q: Did they not send messages to you?

A: Never.

Q: I have it here recorded that Señor de Mendoza, when he was ambassador to this country, greeted you in your friends' name.

A: Have you the exact words recorded?

Q: I am here to ask questions, sir, not to answer them.

A: Well, I put it to you (in your own phrase) that he said something like, Delighted to meet you, I have heard of you from my dear friend del Fuego – to make conversation.

Q: Then you remember the conversation?

A: I did meet the Ambassador, perhaps twice. It is many years ago.

Q: Did you speak with him in Spanish?

A: Good God, how should I remember? I may have aired my *Buenas noces*, certainly no more. We spoke nothing but trivialities – the weather, I expect.

Q: But he met you and spoke with you, and would remember you on his return to Spain?

A: I cannot answer for his memory.

Q: It would, however, be a reasonable supposition?

A: You can hardly expect me to entertain it.

Q: No, sir, it would be contrary to your interests to have it supposed. To his lordship I am sure the connection will be obvious, particularly when it is recalled in what circumstances Mendoza left these shores.

PRESIDENT: Mendoza, let me see. Was he not involved in the Throckmorton plot?

Q: He was, my lord, up to the hilt, and was requested to leave the country. What more likely than that he contacted many others whom he had reason to believe friendly to Spain: that he kept a note of their names, and made use of them later? Sir John admits that up to the year 1580 he was exchanging letters with Señor del Fuego: that in 1584 he twice met Señor de Mendoza: and that in the Low Countries in 1586 and 1587 he had converse with many Spaniards in the course of his duties as interpreter. When we now find in his possession a treasonous paper, I submit that the connection is proved.

A: My lord, I protest against that statement. There is no such connection, and no letters have reached me –

PRESIDENT: Sir John, you must confine yourself to answering the questions put to you.

A: I beg your lordship's pardon.

First score.

Q: I have here a sheet of paper bearing on one side the conclusion of a letter in Latin, on the other three words in Spanish which are alleged to be in Sir John's handwriting. I ask him to examine this paper and tell us when he saw it last.

A: On Midsummer Eve, or strictly speaking Midsummer Day: it was long past midnight.

Q: Where did you see it?

A: At Orchard House, in the hands of a gentleman who had been searching the place.

Q. An officer of the Crown, my lord. This officer asked you, sir, what you knew of the paper?

A: He did.

Q: You admitted you had seen it before?

A: Yes.

Q: And that the Spanish words on the reverse were in your writing?

A: I admitted, I have never denied, that I wrote the Spanish: I denied then, and do so again for his lordship's information, that it was the 'reverse' of the paper. When I wrote those words the rest of the paper was blank. I know nothing of the alleged letter, the portion bearing a seal, and had never seen it till then.

Q: That is what you told the officer?

A: It is certainly what I told him: it is also the truth.

Q: When, prior to 24th June of this year, had you seen the paper?

A: I had seen it about six months earlier when looking through an old wallet: I remember wondering why I had kept it, but as the paper was good I put it by again.

Q: Was anyone else present on that occasion?

A: A roomful.

Q: Did you mention it to anyone?

A: No, why should I? I was looking for something else at the time.

Q: Which was –

A: My lord, I really think this is irrelevant.

PRESIDENT: It may not be relevant, Sir John, but please answer: the questions are not without method, it may be possible by enquiry among your friends to prove the truth of your statement.

A: Very well. Let me see. We had been talking of love, but idly, and not without a few jests against some bachelors of our acquaintance; I said I had some verses of Dyer's which might astonish the company:

I looked through a box of old papers and finally found what I sought.

Q: Can you remember any of the verses, anything your friends might identify?

A: Only the last, I think. Do you wish me to repeat it?

Q: If you please.

A: I may not have every word correctly:

This was a dream, it was not day,
And heaven was never won that way
Nor shines not for our hardest need:
Loving is not enough: I find
That silence can be –

no, that's wrong -

That silence still is left behind:
Thought must to thought if you would
have thought breed.

I will write it down if you like.

PRESIDENT: I do not altogether follow the argument, but it is probably immaterial. Well, then: you were discussing these verses by a Mr Dyer –

Q: Sir Edward Dyer, my lord.

PRESIDENT: Indeed. Thank you. Yes, Sir John, be so good as to make a copy of the verses you remember, and write also the names of the parties present. One of them may have seen you put the paper aside, even though his attention were not especially drawn to it. The examination will now continue.

It could have been the letter that they saw. Farmer at his side echoed the thought. 'It could be the letter, whether the rest of his story is true or not.'

Planted there so that he would discover it before witnesses? What would he do? Ye gods, what *would* you do, confronted with that knowledge: either if you were guilty, and one of your friends had betrayed you; or innocent, finding your friend to be a traitor?

'Hoy,' said Farmer, 'I've finished this bit. Is there more?'

'Not much. Where are we? "I suggest, Sir John, that if this paper now before us was indeed in your possession earlier than 23rd June (six months before, I think you said) it formed part of a letter you had received...' And so on, making much of the old story about his father and the Spanish girl. That got nowhere, and they adjourned *sine die.* An old trick, of course, to keep the poor wretch in expectation. As a matter of fact, they're continuing today, and putting some questions of mine, I was promised, if the lawyers re-worded them successfully.' Fabian sketched a question-mark in the air. 'They're still in the velvet-glove stage, but what do you think so far?'

'Well, first, he'll not help himself that way, will he?' Farmer picked up the script again. 'Is that how he always talks?'

'To the life, I should think.' Fabian gestured impatiently. 'Does he know what he's up against? Does he care?'

'They showed their hand pretty openly, I'd say: too much so for a start.'

'I think I know why. It's not going to be an easy case. They want to look back and say he had no defence from the beginning: that he knew the accusation and could find only the flimsiest of excuses.'

'Yeah. They would do that. But they'll need more to go on.'

'There'll be more.' He saw the case dragging on, as such things could when a matter of policy intervened; month after month, the questioning more frequent, the answers more irate, till the suspect was tightening the rope round his own neck with every word he uttered. Material was plentiful already, and they would not scruple to use it. 'More of this kind.' He pulled a paper at random from the sheaf in front of him. '"I heard Sir J. Stadis aver, when the court lay last at Windsor, that the Queen's grace had used him ill, and he had as lief offer his sword elsewhere. Mr Greville being present, with five or six other gentlemen, desired him speak no more of it."' This was about ten in the morning walking on the Brocas, having all bought cowslip balls from the woman in Peascod Street – 'and so on. Tcha! And that muck's a signed statement, Windsor!' he said wryly. 'I know someone who lives in the town. You go to the Brocas meadow to *pick* cowslips, but the courtiers wouldn't lower themselves to do that.'

'He'd been overlooked, he was bitter, but he may not have meant Spain,' said Farmer reasonably.

Days passed. Fabian had his answers, all quite plausible and all incapable of proof. He had more of the verses attributed to Dyer, but the names did not materialise: Sir John had professed, on second thoughts, not to remember them – had seen, perhaps, that someone might be incriminated? or at least that no evidence they could give would be likely to assist him.

The news from Bristol served to confirm Tom Wickins' visit; he was now betrothed to a young cousin, a merchant's only daughter, and would console himself with her moderate dowry for the loss of higher hopes. Fabian crossed him off the list, not without misgiving.

The nature of the case had imperceptibly changed. Instead of the former dearth of material he now had reports in abundance, but a growing number of them were closed accounts. The narrowing field should have revealed one clear direction – not so here: rather, each road he took turned into a blind alley, and he had every time to retrace his steps and start again. Or it was like one of those problems in mathematics where you find yourself arguing blindly on and on from one premise to another and getting no nearer a solution; most likely for the same reason – that somewhere in the early stages there had been a false assumption. But which, and where? He could not find it. He read and re-read his notes; he had each piece of information double-checked with a grim thoroughness; he made himself ridiculous the length of Bread Street quoting pseudo-Dyer, but got no one to recognise or acknowledge it. He even went to considerable trouble finding a Nottingham man to verify Nick Greenlee; it was Nick beyond dispute – 'And that,' as Farmer remarked, 'shows nothing but the state you're in.'

It was now the last week in July. They had just finished reading the latest part of the Enquiry: as an example of wearing tactics it was notable, but its contribution to their sum of knowledge was precisely nil.

Fabian slammed the sheets together edgewise; on the bare table-top they rattled like hammers. He shoved them back in their cover, his big fingers surprisingly deft.

'No more reports – you can take that lot away. The answer's here somehow – in what we knew from the beginning. Think for a minute.'

Having said that, thought refused him. His whole consciousness contracted to a miserable awareness of failure: not only failure to unravel the mystery, that might happen to anyone, but in something more important, as if he had let down humanity itself; his own hope, perhaps – the man in the Tower had none. He looked at Farmer, solid and good-humoured, impregnable as the Tower itself, and stifled the feeling.

'Well? What do you make of it?'

Farmer spoke decidedly. 'Someone else drank the beer and he's carrying the can back.'

'I think so too. The point is, does he know it? Has he stepped in voluntarily, knowing we can fasten nothing to him, to protect someone whose guilt would be apparent?'

'If so, why is it *not* apparent?'

'Exactly. Why? We have everyone's movements from the beginning of June: who's crowded out of the picture? Who are we supposed to lose sight of, while Sir John goes capering about in the moonlight?'

Farmer wrinkled his nose. 'You have the list: what is it, six – seven – eight of them?'

'Eight people are being watched continuously: not one has moved a finger out of turn for five whole weeks. Even the underlings we've not had a cheep out of this fortnight.'

'The agent. The man Gregory.'

'Gone to Scotland. Yes, carrying letters, they admit it. And no, we have not traced him. I grant that. But the explanation's plausible, whatever they thought at the Enquiry. There'd been bad news from Italy. Everyone was passing it on to friends.'

'Oh, ah, that Signor What'sit, condemned for some book he'd written? I was wondering what that means,' said Farmer.

'Bruno. Signor Bruno. He observes, that is just permitted; he thinks, therefore he is dangerous; he publishes and will not withdraw so he is "handed over to the secular arm," as they have it. What it means is a very nasty death in return for showing us the universe. Tell me this country was not much better fifty years ago and I say so much the worse for England, and God help us fifty years hence.'

'He knew him, then?' Farmer side-stepped the controversial. 'I thought he'd never been to Italy.'

'Bruno came here. He attended his lectures. Not at Oxford, it was after his time, but here in London, at Greville's Wednesday evenings or what have you. They were breathtaking. Think of it! A living universe, the heavenly bodies moving in natural sequence round the sun and our earth one of them – the old Greeks would have given their ears for it. And to learn this, not in a school from pedants but from the man's own lips who had the wit to piece it out – no wonder he was impressed: no wonder the present news upset him. Reason enough for a dozen letters to Scotland, above the three he has admitted: it was even the reason for his melancholy, or part of it – the only one he gave.

'Would it keep a man two months away?'

Fabian shrugged. 'And so we're back to Gregory. No hint of treason there. His past is open. He has worked all his life for the Stadis family, comes and goes regularly, when in London lodges always with the same family this twenty years, corner of Silver Street: brings presents for the children – that sort of thing.'

'He'd be the very man for it; known and respected everywhere, familiar in most of the great households –

'If he were he would be.'

'You think not, then?'

But Fabian was past thinking. 'The cry is out for Gregory: when we get him we shall know. Till then –' he leaned back with an air of exhaustion – 'what on earth *have* we got?'

'Let me go through the papers again.'

'I wish you would. I almost know them too well. And ask yourself just one question. Why was Sir John pushed on to us at that particular time? For it comes to this, Farmer – either of two things: this whole web of events was woven to conceal one fact: or else –' he paused, flattening both hands on the table – 'or else there is nothing to conceal.'

There were still two other questions: who brought the Latin letter (as a possible lead to who sent it), and what was Sir John's business while staying at the Quartern? These lines of approach had by no means been neglected, but so far without result. The first was now a matter of routine, implicitly something to be looked for in every other investigation however remote from the Stadis case. The second Fabian had charged himself with, for it might touch affairs of delicacy. Following nothing but his nose, he had for some time been making a thankless pilgrimage round the Inns of Court, the task easier if incompleter for the vacation. Though lawyers make holiday their chambers must be kept habitable, and servants have been known to know of their masters' clients if not their business; and lawyers' clerks may well be unable to take advantage of the vacation at all. He already knew who had drawn the Deed of Gift, but expected nothing from that quarter – and got as much, wrapped up in what might be termed the Snub Indirect. He was looking for something secreter, someone, not necessarily shady but perhaps in difficulties, who would take any business with no questions asked. Maybe in his heart he was not expecting to find it, which fact would make the actual discovery more shattering.

He came late to the Turk on the evening of 1st August, and at one glance Farmer knew something had happened. Fabian sat down quietly, and pushed away the tankard before him.

'Have you got it at last?'

'Something,' he replied.

There was a silence whilst others came and went around them. Then still quietly, 'He was planning to leave the country. He found a broken-down lawyer who happened to be from his old school. He put everything in his hands.'

'Everything?'

'Not the estate, of course. His disposition of the remainder. Instructions to pay. A list of letters to be delivered one week after he left. Not the actual letters – he was bringing them later. No one else was to know.'

'When was he going?'

'He was not sure. After going to Greenwich. Some event there was to decide it.'

'Reason given?'

'None. But it's damning enough.'

They had the place to themselves by now, but were still speaking almost in whispers, without inflection, heads a few inches apart. Fabian was staring down at the wet rings on the table.

'There may be an explanation. If only he'd told me! I gave him every chance.' He made a helpless gesture.

Farmer said kindly, 'You want him to be innocent.'

Fabian swore. He got up and crammed his hat on saying, 'Take over, will you? Lest you're right. I'm going down to Plymouth on the Melton business.'

Farmer opened his mouth, and shut it again. Then he too rose, saying only, 'They know you.'

'They know me and I know them, and a damned good thing too. Here I'm blest if I know anything.' He turned in the doorway. 'Find Gregory. Keep your eye on the rest, but find Gregory. If he puts a foot wrong or calls at a suspected house we'll get them yet. And – if you can –' he hesitated – 'send word to me when anything breaks.'

'If *you*'re still whole,' said Farmer, grinning. They shook hands, and went their separate ways.

Two days later at the White Hart in Salisbury Fabian was accosted by a London lad just arrived.

'If you're Mr Hewins, there's a message for you from the Turk's Head. They found that old brown hat of yours you lost in April.'

It was their set phrase. Gloves would have meant Gregory; the hat was what they were really waiting for, a witness who admitted carrying secret letters to the suspect. In every case on record, such a find marked always the beginning of the end.

Against all reason, Fabian rode on his way despondent.

9

Philosophy

Fabian turned back from Plymouth on the morning of 22nd August with every reason to find the journey pleasant. The weather had been cool, with so far only enough rain to lay the dust. In the course of his mission he had learned four things anew – that Tamar water is as wet as Thames, that every man has his price, that two can play at that game and that dead men tell no tales. Apart from an awkward little gash on the forearm the business was happily concluded – a nasty bit of business, now wound up neatly and finally and without public outcry: a good week's work, and well worth the effort expended. But the back of his mind was uneasy. Put it down to shame, pity, disappointment or remorse, he had run away from the Stadis case. He had left the job entrusted to him in sudden fear that he should bungle it, and gone off to play the hero in a smaller, easier matter – that there was danger in it had been a mere sop to his conscience, and he knew it. As far as that went, his quilted lining had come in handy. Had it not, or had his foot slipped before the other man's, his earthly troubles would by now be over. There would be no one to mourn him. He had stayed single as much from choice as from necessity, the nature of his work so far precluding the idea of marriage. His lodging was comfortable, but he was not wedded to that – he might set out any day unwittingly and fail to return. A peaceful old age did not enter into the picture; it was not for him, or he was not for it – certainly he had done nothing special to deserve it. Yet here he was, turned thirty-five and past the halfway mark. He had brought nothing into the world, but had always counted on taking out of it at least a quiet conscience, until now. He had never run away until now.

For such gloomings, now the excitement of his task was over, it was possible to blame the climate. These damp soft mornings did not suit him. Did damp breed melancholy? He inclined to think so.Write upon the subject while it happened to be fashionable, and gain an undeserved reputation as philosopher – many had been made with less. What said the Duke in the play last season? 'I think of as many matters as he, but I give God thanks and say nothing.' A shrewd hit, and the audience had roared.

But these mornings always cleared up – or did they? Eleven came, and this one showed no sign of clearing; by noon he was really wet and looking anxiously for an inn. When he found it the folk there were emphatic; the wind was westerly and freshening, if there was no haste he should not think of riding on. They lit a fire in the travellers' room and removed his outer things to dry in the kitchen, leaving him to the company of a fine pair of branching staghorns and his thoughts.

A whole afternoon with no work to do was something new in Fabian's experience. He lingered pleasurably over his meal and after; he stayed by the fire for some time, encouraging it with the little logs provided, or watched for contrast the pelting rain outside. Then, being long used to method, he sat down deliberately with his back to the window to anatomise conscience.

Start, as ever, with the immediate fact. Well then, *imprimis*, it was no weather to travel. There was nothing to stop him lying up for a few days now his work was completed, but the rain might be as bad last as first; he could not spend the rest of the summer in Devon waiting for a fine day. He wanted to go on – the why, examine later – but first there was the horse to consider. The journey down had made them firm friends. He had travelled carefully at first, trying not to overdo his distances, for he rode much heavier than Sir John, and fixed in his mind for some reason was the thought that Jewel was no stayer. After two days he began to revise this opinion; and when one afternoon they took the wrong road, adding several miles to the tally and leaving Jewel as fresh as ever, he banished the mistaken idea completely. So distance alone need not hinder him. As for the rain, they were now eastward bound; it should be mostly behind them. He thought if he did not force the pace they could travel at least all forenoon, provided they then dried off, ate well and did not have to face the elements again that day. Yes, he would do so would it still the nagging inside him, and – already at the thought he had turned optimist – it could hardly rain for ever.

Now for the why: what reason had he for unrest? There was nothing he could do – he had possessed Farmer of every detail. The case itself might be over, that is, out of their hands and waiting solely on the necessary legal action. Was he longing to convince himself this was so? Was the last revelation too much to believe without documentary proof? He had been stunned enough at his own discovery of the lawyer, but never doubted that was true. Was he so puffed up that he could not take someone else's word for a change? No, the sting lay in this – he feared his own judgement was affected, that instinct for truth that had never failed him before. It was this fear which prompted him to flight; he knew quite well he would never deliberately conceal evidence, only he might misread it. Yet treason (like murder) will out at last, and when that day came could not be misread. Why then, he had no cause to blame himself. No cause where duty was concerned: he could honestly affirm it. This conclusion should have cheered him; perhaps it did. At all events, he kicked the fire into safe shape and went to look for livelier companions.

The rain stopped before sunset, leaving a clear-swept sky, but next morning was wetter than ever. It kept this sequence three days, as the thick Devon accents had prophesied, during which Fabian covered less than twenty miles. Conscience or no, it looked as though nature herself, hitherto abundantly in his favour, would oppose him now his face was set towards London. And then, whether because he was further inland, her force seemed at last to be spent: it still rained, but slackly and without decision; days were warmer; wrapped up against the rain he sweltered. The countryside was changing. He was out of the wet lands and felt suddenly on the high road to home.

Perversely, now he could make better time the sense of urgency had left him. He was not indispensable. He'd had the devil's own luck in the past and an almost infallible sixth sense; if these were now deserting him, other men with more orthodox methods could take over. He had said often enough to Farmer, 'You'd have got there the long way round – I took a short cut and it happened to be right.' Well, the days of short cuts seemed to be over. He must himself learn to use the long way round.

One thing he could do – Sir Edward Dyer lived in Somerset; to call on him would not be far out of the way. In an inner pocket was still a blank sheet of paper cut to the exact size of the latin letter and folded carefully in the same way; wasted labour now, Fabian reflected, but it might serve as a peg to hang questions on. What he would ask he left to the occasion – he could trust his tongue still if not his judgement – but to be so close and make no move at all would be, he persuaded himself, both stupid and inconsiderate. Dyer was not on his list of suspects, but he had no idea how things had gone by now. If all was known, his visit would do no harm; if not, he would be saving someone a journey.

He must enquire first if any stranger were in the neighbourhood: it would not do to bowl on another man's pitch.

So on Tuesday morning, after due assurance, he found himself riding through a peaceful little village. The rain had ceased. Behind still unbroken cloud the sun began to be felt. There was no sign of life from the cottages he passed but a sleek black cat lazily washing itself on a doorstep; everything was clean, trim and prosperous, and more than half asleep. Enchanted country, old Geoffrey of Monmouth's Land of Summer, wherein did its magic lie? A quiet unbroken since before the Conquest, life circumscribed by the changing seasons, a simplicity three parts illusion to one of conscious worth. How much more could be illusion: the village, older perhaps than Lleyr or Arthur yet no different in externals from a dozen you might pass tomorrow; the unseen inhabitants whose chimneys breathed contentment but whose days were an unending round of scrub and bake, plough and hoe; even, maybe, the very man he came to seek?

What, then, was known about Dyer? He was the poet of the 'seventies, before Sidney wrote or Spenser's star had risen, his reputation achieved without publishing a line. It was thought that he refused to publish. He had left the French tradition, toyed with the Latin, condemned popular ballad-verse and produced his own best work in simple colloquial English. The same sort of contradiction showed itself in his life; he had been both courtier and philosopher, in the throng but outside it. Some said he was a Rosicrucian. His career had been not unlike Sir John's; he too had served the Queen when permitted and then faded into the background, only he was older; he'd been one of Gloriana's young men, always at her heels. Rumour had it that at one time he was really smitten; true or not, he had never married. He must be fifty at the least and had given up public life a good many years now. Fifty need not be old, of course; look at Farmer – but then Farmer was the world's eighth wonder anyhow.

And this must be the place, a pleasant manor house of the smaller sort, with windows glinting and the same unhurried curl of smoke from its chimneys as those of the village displayed. The sun was full out now. And suddenly the charm seemed false and alien, the languor overpowering: a magic insidious as that poison that lulls first, then terrifies with one instant's realisation of *too late*. It lasted but the instant, and then Fabian was dismounting in a shady courtyard and wiping the sweat from his face, with a rosy-cheeked maid waiting open-mouthed to know his pleasure.

The master was in the garden and this path would lead to it; 'and will your honour please keep to the path, for 'tis very wet still, and footsteps do injure the turf.' Do they so? Fabian smiled but obeyed, curiosity leaping up in him to meet the renowned philosopher-poet.

Whatever he had expected was not this: a figure squatting by the border, clad in an old rough coat and shapeless felt hat, one hand holding a flower-pot and the other carefully parting the stems of a clump of carnations, so intent on his task that the approach of a stranger could go unnoticed. He was counting aloud – 'thirty-three, thirty-four, thirty-five' – and punctuating the numbers now and then with little wordless sounds of disgust.

The wet earth steamed in the sunshine and fresh aromatic smells arose.

He straightened up as Fabian stood beside him. 'Look at this,' he commanded, with no show of surprise. 'What do *you* do about slugs?' The flower-pot was half full.

'Tread on them?' Fabian offered.

'Hmm!' It was not a laugh nor a grunt but something between the two. A pair of shrewd eyes surveyed him. 'It's this wet summer,' their owner added in explanation. 'Played havoc with the beds. You have no garden, of course.' If the last sentence was not actually spoken, the effect was the same.

'I labour in a different field,' admitted Fabian.

'Hmm. Thought so when I heard you coming. *Auctoritatis Gradus Sonoris* – the firm step of authority, but with a difference. I wonder what?'

The question, Fabian judged, was rhetorical. He said, 'Speaking of authority, may I ask you to settle a point – about gardens?'

'No authority; *amateur*, as the French have it – a terraphile. But I was born here. Ask away.'

'Would you plant herbs where you could tread on them?'

'Herbs? What for? Herbs are for use to cure or comfort –' He broke off, and began to chuckle richly. 'Oh, I see where you are. A nice point. No, I would not, not anything that lives and grows, nor would any but a pompous, pragmatical, selfish – never mind. God made other men of earth but not him.'

'You set my mind at rest,' said Fabian gravely.

'These paper creators!' The stead gaze still searched him.

'Are you an apiarist?'

'Call it beekeeper. Take poor George Peele – as good a fellow as ever stepped, but even he – "His helmet now shall be a hive for bees" – do you mark the absurdity?'

'Metal would be too cold, is that it?'

'Right.' The regard was friendly now. 'Warmth they must have, of substance that has lived. Wicker hive – straw skep – in the desert a dead lion, if you believe old fables –' he coughed his little high-pitched grunting laugh again. 'And now,' he said, 'honours even; shall we leave fencing and come to your business?'

'It may not sound much different.' Fabian looked down at him apologetically, the way in suddenly revealing itself. 'If I have the honour to address Sir Edward Dyer.'

'You are addressing him; the honour I begin to doubt.'

'Then I appeal once more to your authority, this time in the matter of a poem.' He saw interest quicken; that was only natural. Steady now – too soon for conclusions. The brisk little opening skirmish was an affair of humour, not caution;

it must please the poet, now something of a recluse, to test out new acquaintance thus, and Fabian was gratified to feel he had acquitted himself not too badly. But now these trifles fell away like a dropped cloak as one measures one's distance and waits for the signal: the real bout was to begin.

In this game there was no advantage. Fabian had the advantage of surprise – he knew his adversary, who knew not him – but only if Dyer were innocent of the affair. If he were part of the conspiracy the weight of knowledge was on his side. Set against that the ever-present fear of the guilty that even the simplest remark might betray him: advantage neither way. The next move at least was Fabian's; but to move is to show one's opponent how he must defend himself. So fencers may remain a long time immobile, trusting to the menace of stillness, till the weaker is forced into an incautious movement: or the bolder disengage and tempt the other with an open target.

Fabian disengaged. He had by heart the verses quoted in Sir John's examination; both they and it seemed curiously unreal in this peaceful setting. Doubtless his own appearance was equally so. He deliberately played up the incongruity, standing large and unrebuked upon the sacred lawn while he repeated, with a solemnity the words had not deserved:

Sidney, lend me your sonnet-quill
Or come beside me if you will
And let us both our cares rehearse
In some old formula of verse:
Yours to assuage, mine only to make worse.

You that loved verse and music well
And were so richly held in grace,
Yet had no force with love to dwell,
Teach me mine own unhappy case –
– The parts transposed – my tenor for your bass.

And yet not base, though troubled pen
Betray what eyes can see:
I must be sullen when (poor when)
I most would pleasant be,
While all the world looks on, and only she.

This was a dream, it was not day
And heaven –

He stopped there; for the last few lines a kind of intentness had clouded Dyer's face: he might have been going to speak but thought better of it. Fabian gave him time. He remained silent.

'Have I missed out a verse?' said Fabian casually.

Only then did Dyer's expression change, from close attention to surprise.

'No. Odd you should ask. There *was* another verse once but it was expurgated.' He looked ruefully amused. 'Does the gap show so badly? But you did not break off for that, I take it.'

'I thought perhaps – you were reminded of something.'

That thrust was parried. The gaze held firm but the voice was a thought colder as he answered.

'No. You had a word wrong: I will correct it. Not "betray" but "relate". "Relate what eyes can see".'

'Curious. It was told me as "betray". Why should my informant falter on just that word?'

'I cannot imagine.'

'Could it be because he himself was betrayed?' Fabian was still only probing for an opening, but this time the vigour of the riposte surprised him.

'It could or it could not, what the devil do I care?' The tone was now not only cold but angry. 'I heard you so long for my satisfaction, to know how far damned impudence would go. You're on the wrong errand, young man. I admit nothing and deny nothing, and you can take that back where you belong.'

Fabian stood his ground. 'Then there is something to deny?'

Dyer looked at him with an almost pitying contempt. 'If you expect me to buy your silence after all these years you're more fool than knave, and you seem to be neither. Who sent you? Where got you the verses?'

'No one sent me.' Fabian spoke slowly, his brain racing through the tangle. 'Yes, I see. This comes of trying our wits. I have stumbled on the wrong secret and should ask your pardon. Too witty is worse than witless.' He glanced away to the brilliant green grass and jewelled flowers, and back again in deprecation. 'You have admitted more than you know – what eyes can see is usually an open secret. But I am not concerned with amorous adventures. I ought to make that clear.'

'You do,' the poet said drily. 'Having put me in my place, could you perhaps make clear what you *are* concerned with?'

'I could,' agreed Fabian. He would show his cards, but one by one. Try a short cut first. 'What happens on 5th December or is to happen?'

Dyer stared. 'The beginning of Advent, near enough.'

It was, too: another point for the prosecution – the coming of our Lord, but of what else? For two pins there would be an additional charge of blasphemy. Oddly enough the thought had not occurred to him before, and he was shaken with sudden anger.

'Or the Nones of December? Who writes to you in Latin?'

'No one now.' For all his astonishment Dyer answered mildly. 'I am out of fashion, you see.'

'Or Spanish?'

He made no pretence of misunderstanding. 'This is the first time my loyalty has been questioned. I have not the tongue, as it happens.'

'Then why did Sir John use the word "betray"? Who other than yourself would know the error?'

Ask the ordinary man two questions at once and you confuse him immediately; give him a loophole in the form of counter-question and he will usually seize on it. 'Sir John who?' would be the expected rejoinder, unless he knew who was intended. A clever man could try to answer both; a man on his guard would choose whichever question was least inconvenient. Only the very simple would stick to the later one, or the stupid wait for them to be repeated singly: this man was neither. Fabian watched his face, more useful at this stage than any words he might say, and saw reflected in turn counter-question and possible answers and rejection of them all. He wondered what Dyer saw. What he said was unexpected.

'I am disposed to trust you, God knows why, but unless you trust me I cannot tell what you want.'

Not 'what you want to know'; the choice of words could be deliberate. What do I want? thought Fabian, and answered honestly.

'I want most of all to be reassured, but I think it is too late for that: and next to know the truth and end the matter. Yes, I will trust you–' and trust once more the impulse, act as he would in the days before ever it was called in question. A reasonable man must make experience his guide: certainly he had no other. At the worst it could scarce do harm; a time comes when there is nothing left to do but put the ferret down the hole.

'Then come to the real questions – who or what is betrayed? Who quoted the verses and where?'

Fabian told him.

Dyer was silent for a while. He had not exclaimed or shown any conventional sign of sympathy or horror, only his eyes were dull and he suddenly looked his age.

'It is worse than I thought,' he said at last. 'And impute not that to foreknowledge, my mind misgave since first you came into this garden like the raven, boding.' He found himself still holding his flowerpot, and set it down on the grass with pathetic care. 'What would you have me do?'

'May I question your servants?'

'Of course.'

'As a matter of form, to clear you of all suspicion.' There was none now in Fabian's mind, only the quick sure feeling of striding forward he had always had when a case took the right turning at last. So strong the sensation was that he gave impulse further rein.

'And one thing more – those verses: did he send them to you? A written copy?'

'If he did, there was no error in it. The change of word in your version will be accidental; few would know and none would care. No message would be sent that way.'

'No, no, that theorem is discarded. Did he send you a sheet of paper? Can you produce it?' Then as Dyer still hesitated, 'It will not harm him, it may even do him good. The paper that accuses him was folded like this sheet. He says it was in his wallet, with those verses, before the letter it bears is alleged to have been delivered to him. I must tell you no more; but papers in a wallet are commonly folded together –'

'– and if the folds are identical they prove his innocence?'

'Not prove, but give a strong presumption.'

'Come into the house.' He led the way rapidly. 'I cannot be sure I have it, these toys mean little to me now, but for his sake I hope –'

Indoors he flapped through his papers like a cat in a hencoop, till Fabian took a hand. By organising the search methodically he also assured himself there was nothing else to hide. No objection was raised, but as they drew cover after cover without success Dyer's spirits flagged, and he drooped tiredly into a chair.

'Think back,' said Fabian. 'Where were you when the

letter came? What time of the day did you read it? Remember the weather – was it raining, cold?'

'I have tried,' he said dejectedly. 'It was winter, I know; we had a cold autumn – the onions were in pickle –'

Fabian shrugged and left him, moving on into the next room. Suddenly a shout rang out behind him. 'Fool that I am! It was the day I read the lesson. There's a chance –'

They ran together. It stood at the stair-foot on a special table, a great book as big as the parish Bible – Fabian had seen it already and half looked for the chain. He lifted it by the covers and something fell to the floor.

Their hearts sank.

It was a tight little wad of paper, folded and re-folded. The older man stooped for it and silently opened it out, trying to smooth away the creases, but the task was hopeless. One line of the four verses stood out in blacker ink than the rest:

This was a dreame, it was not day...

They could not look at each other.

'Here it is,' said Dyer unnecessarily.

'And even I could not take it into court and convince a local magistrate, let alone the Star Chamber.' Fabian replaced the huge Bible with venomous gentleness. 'Well, it was worth trying.'

There was really nothing left to say. A meal was served, Dyer exerting himself to play the host; they talked on safe topics, the late harvest, the price of flour, the man who danced his way to Norwich. A dear old dame bustled in with a special posset 'against the damp', notwithstanding the hot sun outside. 'You see how it is,' the old bachelor grumbled good-humouredly, 'yield to no woman and you're under all their thumbs,' but he seemed rather to like it. Then he donned his gardening coat again and left Fabian to ask his questions.

There was little enough to ask; the essentials were soon

established. Life had closed in around Sir Edward Dyer. He seldom rode out now, and never farther than the next village: his visitors were the parson and a neighbouring landowner; books and the garden occupied his days. It had been so for several years now. Each member of the little household had the same story to tell.

Fabian sought him once more in the garden, and found him among the hives: telling the bees perhaps, lest trouble should light upon them too?

'If there is anything I should do – an affidavit perhaps?' He seemed relieved that Fabian thought this unnecessary. 'I could write to the Queen, but I have no influence now. Or I'll testify he wrote to me, and on what day, if it will help him. Only let me know.' He repeated this anxiously as they strolled back towards the courtyard, and again as Fabian took his leave. 'I will write, or I will testify if need be. Only the authorship of the verses,' he smiled a little, 'I neither confirm nor deny.'

Too late indeed, thought Fabian as he rode away: 'that time of year thou may'st in him behold' – too late for love or hate or toil or treason; the Land of Summer has him in its spell. For himself, he did not grudge the interlude; a day more or less would make no difference in the end. He was back on the case, only that mattered: the scene with Sir Edward had restored his confidence. Wasting no more time in metaphysical speculation, he swung Jewel into a brisk pace, accomplished the rest of the journey without incident, and was at home on the third day.

10

Mr Secretary

London, after his absence, seemed noisy, cramped and smellier than ever. He could not find Farmer at the Turk, and Seething Lane had not seen him these three days. He'd been sent for by the Chief, in a hurry, and had left no word: usual enough – but Fabian, his mind still running on old age and its concomitants, was oddly pricked with anxiety. It impelled him straightway across the water, to the neat little cottage at Bermondsey he had only once visited before.

Farmer was indoors; that is, he was stationed in an old rocking-chair in the open doorway with a small grandson on each knee, for the express purpose of seeing they did not run out under the horses' feet. No fear of that – they were riding Granddad, with shouts of joy and many a jump and stumble. 'I fancied you'd come,' he said placidly through the hubbub. 'Down you get, men – end of the journey. Go in to Mother and she'll give you a cake.' The little boys galloped happily away and a great peace descended.

They looked at each other. 'Well?' they said together.

'You're back, then. What was the weather like?'

'Rough at first, but it blew over. How's the city?'

'Quiet.' Farmer gazed reflectively into the roadway. 'So far. We had a bit of sunshine, but hardly so's to say enough to warm you. It's all right,' he continued in the same tone, 'he's with the waggon, been waiting for it to load. I thought at first he had his eye on you. Seen the Chief yet?'

'No.'

'I'd to make myself scarce and say nothing, so I just left you to find me. We've been put off the job.'

'It's finished, then?' Although he had been waiting for it, Fabian's heart sank.

'Not the way you're thinking. For you and me, yes. "No further action" he said: like that – "No further action," and his lips bit tight together.'

'But I thought you had proof.' This was not what he expected. 'I got your message, and thought it would be final.'

'That all fell through. Unless something new's cropped up, and I doubt it: new since Tuesday it'd have to be.'

'No proof? He's withdrawing the case?'

'Not him. He was wild about it.' Farmer looked offended. 'I told him straight, we've been combing London for two months and there's not even a smell of what you're after. And I'm not going to invent it, I said.'

'He affects me that way too. It's his manner,' said Fabian. 'I believe him to be honest. What then?'

'He clamped down. "Very well," he said, "no further action." And give up all the papers, which I did.'

'And no word for me?'

'Not a one.'

They considered this in silence for a while. There was more to it, of course; Farmer was building up to it in his own way and could not be hurried.

'You've been round the city?'

'Only to look for you. Why?'

'Ah, then you've not heard 'em yet. I told him,' Farmer continued, 'it's no use just leaving it, with all these rumours about. You want to go up Cheapside, I said, or round Aldgate on a Saturday night when they're properly warmed up, and listen.'

'It's spreading, is it?'

'Spreading! They've got ballads about it. Some on his side.' The pronoun had changed persons, but there was no mistaking whose. 'You know that saying of his? There's a rhyme to it now –

> Adey and Crooks, or Crooks and Adey,
> For Adey is crooked and Crooks is shady.

They dare not be seen out together – or alone, come to that. The crowd's still good-humoured, but something'll have to be done.'

For Farmer to say so the matter must be serious. Rumours were one thing and ran through the city like wildfire, but ballads were quite another: all the difference between a blind boil and an abscess which may burst into open eruption. Once in his lifetime Fabian had seen the many-headed monster; he had no wish to repeat that experience.

'You told him this?'

'Much as he'd let me. You know what the Chief is.'

He would learn it from others – assume he knew it all along: more reason to press on with the investigation and come at the truth. Does he yet know more than he will tell?

'What do you –' Fabian changed his question. 'What happened to your witness? I'd like to get this straight.'

There'd been two, it appeared. The first was circumstantial, time, place, shape of the letter, colour of the sender's eyes; he was a common pick-purse, taken in the act and only too willing to mitigate his sentence. The second, to all appearance an honest man, had come forward with some vague story of passing messages between two strange gentlemen: face to face with the prisoner he contradicted himself so often that the prosecution had to discard him. They had kept the pick-purse in reserve. When he too was confronted with Sir John the latter questioned him so adroitly that he was pinned down to the last week in April as the date of the occurrence, Sir John immediately proving without any trouble that he had been nowhere in the named vicinity. The man then tried to shift his ground, but in vain: he had been too definite to begin with. Cross-examination of the prisoner served only to discredit the witness still further; Sir John did not deny having seen the man before – asked when and where, he answer, 'In Paris Garden, the night the bear got loose; he was trying to climb a tree.' (The shorthand writer added 'Laughter'). Oddly enough it was the sedate young Fisher who confirmed the incident, which had come near to being nasty. Sir John himself prevented disaster, with Adey an able lieutenant, keeping the crowd back while he walked calmly up to the wretched animal and soothed it until the keeper arrived. He talked to it, Fisher said, as he would to his horse. Adey too had been quite cool and at once grasped what was intended, Sir John relying on him absolutely. Everyone had noticed the man in the tree and a dozen could be got to swear to him, including those that knew his trade. There was little doubt he had been there to ply it, and owed his knowledge of Sir John to the scene that evening. So the whole story of the letters was a fabrication, and they were once more back where they began.

Not wholly so: there was still the fact of Sir John preparing to leave England. That could not be ignored. He had not yet been taxed with it, as far as Farmer knew; it was presumably being kept in reserve. And there was still no trace of Gregory. And every other way of approach had now been closed.

And the Chief had called them off.

A voice rose up in Fabian's brain and whispered, It was his brother had the appointment Stadis should have got. In '88 or 9, was it? And the post in the Ordnance, his nominee? And farther back still, who ordered Stadis home – the Queen, of course, but at whose instigation? The long-forgotten instances flashed up before the mind's eye as legible as on a written page, or more so: a blind man could read between the lines.

But this was lunacy. The prisoner was either guilty, or an innocent victim; you could hardly have it both ways. Or could you? If plain injustice drove a man into the opposite camp, before God who was to blame? And what other construction could be put on the few facts established? If he were innocent, why try to leave the country? Fabian could think of a reason, perhaps not very convincing, but it would not account for the choice of a dubious lawyer to settle his affairs: it would not explain the missing agent, or the Latin letter with the conveniently ambiguous seal. It would do the case no harm to know whose camp – whose letter; it was nothing short of fantastic that they'd failed to discover it by now.

They were quiet so long that the children came creeping back to the doorway, but retreated on finding the stranger still there. Their grandfather ignored them. He had not taken his eyes from the younger man's face. He had done his best, and told his tale, and passed on his responsibility: but no case in all their long and friendly association had been quite like this. He was still anxious for Fabian, and Fabian knew it, and spoke at random.

'April was wrong, of course, I always thought so. Nothing moved until May. Though why I should be so sure of that –' He shrugged and dismissed it. A decision must be made. 'What do you truly think?'

'It's no London plot, that I *will* be sworn. We could hardly have missed it: someone would've broke before now. For the rest, God knows. Maybe it's not for me to judge. I can only say, and say again, there'll be clamour in the streets if something's not done soon.'

Something – anything; decision right or wrong: a decision predestined from the start? Fabian made his.

'Very well. You're right, we cannot leave it. I shall go to the Chief.' He grinned and relaxed. 'I have to anyhow; I have his precious packet on me.'

Farmer smiled back. 'I knew you'd not fail.' Here or in Plymouth, his tone of voice conveyed. 'Good luck.'

'Thanks, I shall need it. No, stay where you are, I'm going now. Can I count on you if need be?'

'Any time.'

'I'll leave word at the Turk. Rest while you can, then,' and he turned purposefully away.

It was still early evening. He was not fool enough to go straight to the Chief. He walked briskly for some distance in the opposite direction and back by devious ways, until if there had been a watcher he was truly shaken off. He found an eating-house on the bankside that smelled less greasy than most, made a leisurely meal, took care to leave with a crowd, and reached his destination inconspicuously at dusk.

Farmer's wishes were with him: he was not kept waiting above five minutes, and the Secretary was in gentler mood. He looked in fact far from well, tired, sunken-eyed and lined; pale he always was, like any man habitually overworked and never outdoors. He gave his usual impersonal attention to Fabian's brief tale, received the packet, examined it and locked it carefully away. 'You have done well,' he said, and scribbled a memorandum; the affair was done with. When he looked up again it was in surprise that Fabian still waited.

'Is there some other matter?'

Fabian regarded him steadily; there must be a way of piercing this Olympian detachment. He wondered if it were feigned.

'The matter, sir, that brought Farmer here on Tuesday.'

The Secretary went on writing, but the point of his pen snagged maddeningly against an unevenness in the paper and spattered ink in all directions. He took his time over sprinkling sand on the blot, tilting the paper about until it was absorbed, choosing a new pen. Fabian held still and willed him to speak next, and the silence lengthened till there could be no doubt it was deliberate.

'Tuesday,' he said at last, not bothering to make a query of it. 'You are too late, there is nothing to be done.'

'May I suppose, then, that you know the truth?'

'The truth,' he said levelly, 'is no concern of yours or mine. I will word myself clearer: nothing is to be done.' And he dipped his new pen in the ink.

'You must pardon me,' said Fabian with equal firmness. 'You are informed, I think, of the condition of the city. Truth, or a comprehensive explanation, will be needed quite soon.'

'It will be provided.'

'May I know it?' The Chief did not reply, and Fabian pursued his advantage. 'A provided explanation is of all things the least convincing. His popularity is greater than perhaps you are aware. On the other hand there is some feeling against his unfortunate followers. If you want (in Farmer's phrase) a clamour in the streets you're going the very way to obtain it.'

'When they hear, they will not question.' But he was worried; Fabian pressed home.

'There are facts that cannot be hidden, and surmise it might be difficult to curb. They will be hard to satisfy with anything less than the truth.'

'Which you have failed to produce.' He put the pen down and his fingers were twitching. 'You come to me now, having failed me, and take this tone –'

'Shall I be open with you?' said Fabian. 'To me, the most significant fact is the absence of conclusive proof. In denying me your confidence you force me to suspect your own actions. He is plainly not blameless, but who else is involved? Why was he not examined sooner? Who sent the letter, and who blurred the seal? Why has contact after contact been thrust under our noses, each as innocent as morning, while the main source stays wrapped in mystery? Who has always consistently opposed him, and how much has been deliberately concealed?'

The Chief had followed this speech with growing agitation. He took off his spectacles the better to listen, and now gazed closely at Fabian as if seeing him for the first time. He said 'You seem to be honest. Your remarks have some pith. But you are wrong if you suspect me.' He passed a hand wearily over his forehead. 'I have long struggled amongst duty and compassion and the fear of doing him injustice. There is between some sorts of men a fixed antipathy; so I deplore his way of life and he – despises mine. I *have* opposed him – rightly, I still think – his nature is too self-endeared to serve princes: but before God I am not his enemy. I was even glad at first when you found no proof. While I could, I resisted much pressure in the Council. Now –'

He was desperately sincere. The evening was chilly, but he sweated; he pulled out a square of linen and dabbed ineffectively at the palms of his hands. 'Now,' he said, and it sounded like a groan, 'it is too late. My instructions were definite. He must be put to the question, and a full confession enforced.'

Too late, and since Tuesday; Fabian felt rather sick. On Tuesday in Somerset that cloud had darkened the sunshine; if he came straight from Plymouth he could have been home by then. But ifs were idle.

'What does he say?'

'The interrogations have not been successful. I – shall be kept informed.

'And if you still learn nothing?'

'That too is provided for. I had to warn him once, years ago, for alchemical practices – studying the nature of things, as he called it. If all else fails, the charge will be witchcraft.'

'You told them that!' Fabian did not try to hide his disgust.

'It was my duty. You must surely see that. I have concealed nothing at all,' he repeated.

'It was something no one else could know; it was not in the file,' retorted Fabian. 'It was a filthy trick, worthy of – never mind. And you know it to be irrelevant. What sort of duty do you call it, to make sure he is your scapegoat? You say you are not his enemy – then who is? Who on the Council, how many, to outvote you?'

'There are – interests: not on the Council. The Council found it politic to agree. There are names I must not mention.' But his finger in the sand-tray traced 'S X', traced and obliterated. 'You call him scapegoat; perhaps you are right; but he cannot be blameless, you yourself said it. He will confess – he must confess, and the principals will be apprehended.'

'Unless they too are names you must not mention? There's no need to reply. My point,' said Fabian 'is that we ought to know – to have known, without resorting to this. The seal alone should have told us; there's something odd there if anywhere. Can you tell me the entire College of Heralds would not recognise it, however blurred? Have you been to our allies? Is there no Dutchman living whose life's work is all things Spanish? My men are helpless there, and you talk to me of failure.'

'The seal,' he answered quietly, 'is truly known to none within our reach. There were some possibles but the likeness is not great. And you know what he admitted. It is held sufficient, with the details he will shortly provide.' He picked up his pen again. 'Believe me, I did what I could. Read over the papers and see for yourself.'

It was probably so. Except for Farmer's summary, Fabian was four weeks out of touch. He took up the later papers in silence and settled down to fill the gap. But somehow he could not fix his attention: his eyes ran through the closely-written sheets mechanically, but the quick reason which should inform them was in abeyance. He had worked with the Chief for many years and thought he knew him by now. If so, there was more to come; he waited, turning the pages. And of course, as usual, Farmer had given him essentials; the words were different but the sense he knew already. A phrase or two stood out in his skimming. The episode of the pick-purse was exactly as Farmer had told it; new to him was the prisoner's outburst at the close of those proceedings: 'Take my life, gentlemen, if that is your will, but let us have no more of these pitiful counterfeits.' No later examination was recorded; possibly the interrogation since referred to had not yet been copied fair. There was the statement of the wretched lawyer, attested on oath. There was the Secretary's own memorandum scrawled at a Council meeting, the speakers indicated by initials: this, which Fabian knew would be entirely accurate, showed clearly he had indeed done as much and more in the cause of justice as one man could be expected to do. There was the material evidence re-summarised, with unsupported statements firmly ruled out. There was, finally, a sheet of paper with nothing on it but the inscription '29th August – Today.'

That *was* today.

Fabian looked across at his Chief, whose writing seemed to go no smoother with new pen than with old. He said aloud, 'Today,' and gathered up the papers. 'At least, sir, your former fears are groundless. The girl is not a suspect.'

'The girl!' He was once more discomforted. 'I had forgot: there is a letter.' He brought it from his pocket. 'Take it: it has not been copied. They discovered it today.'

So Sir John had written at last. Pen and paper had been provided from the start, they always were. In impassioned pleas for help a prisoner's guilt might be manifest; it was often especially revealing to know whom he would address. Here then were the first unprompted words since the arrest, more valuable perhaps than any amount of question and answer.

He had written to the girl.

'They say there are ambassadors arrived from Barbary, the place so called, but I know better. They do not come to me.

'If you hear of me from others, think no more than you please. I am accused of what I know not, and it is like to go hard with me. Let there be in this nothing to grieve you. Your uncle will call it a judgement: perhaps it is, yet other than he thinks.

'I will preach to you, Barbara. That man is good for whom the world goes well, so he does not abuse it. The little I achieved, of good or ill, was less always than the world's reporting. Now he that cannot learn from the good must make shift to be lessoned by the evil; the easy teaching being mastered, comes then the hard lesson that will be master. The child likes not its lesson, yet is not the teacher evil. The parable is clumsy. More plainly, what is to come my will must be toward, though not my liking. Think then that I have fallen not into the hands of men but in the hand of God.

'You must know I am not idle. I am much in the company of a great old tabby cat, a mouser like your Tom but not so handsome, videlicet he lacketh an ear, but we keep each other in exercise. He belongs here to one of the keepers, a good man but not a merry. When I am disposed to music he will furnish me with Dumps, or a doleful ballad, or songs sighing: as, 'If My Complaint Would Pity Move'; 'Weep, Weep Mine Eyes'; or, 'Alack, Why Does She So'? – if I would read, he brings me in Diet's Dry Dinner, or some old tragedy – till mine own proper brain has taken the infection and yields nothing but sad verses, or lines that taunt me with the past, to say, 'Time, loosely spent will not again be won'. My time is spent and I undone. Yet for all that I will not cry Miserrimus, nor waste the little that is left reproaching Fortune; from our own selves our fortune springs.

'I am well housed here, and better served than at the inn. There is a window looking to the river, and I watch the clouds come up and pass. Evenings are cold now, the gulls fly over: autumn is upon us. I think this quiet time is at an end.'

In that he was right.

The letter was unfinished. There was no date nor signature nor superscription; only lower, in a shakier hand, 'Dear Barbary.'

The two men in the little room were very still. As Fabian read, the Secretary watched him; when he reached the last words their eyes met.

'We have made a mistake. This man is innocent.' Fabian stood up suddenly, head and shoulders above the lamplight vanishing in shadow. 'You knew of this.'

'Today. Only today,' he whispered. 'And besides, this is not proof.'

'No,' said Fabian coldly. 'We have no proof,' and the Secretary shrivelled under his look. The situation was such that one could almost pity him, but more important things were to do. 'You will not need me for a few weeks: I am taking leave of absence. If there is one spark of feeling in you, countermand that order, or defer its further execution. The papers will be returned to you. I will bring you the whole story, or you may fill my office how you please.'

He caught them up roughly into a bundle in his cloak and walked out of the house unchallenged.

11

Nearer Home

They were all there, tidy and in order, not a mark to show what the Chief had thought at any point nor even that he had dealt with them at all: caution carried to the extreme, and it exasperated Fabian as never before. His own copious notes were spread out on the table. Farmer sat opposite, his round good-humoured face furrowed in concentration. The breakfast things had been cleared away.

The case was starting again, from a different viewpoint.

'If you call it different,' Farmer was grumbling. 'We thought him guilty and got no proof, we think him innocent and get none.'

'Just that,' said Fabian soberly. 'That *is* the difference. We must work from what we have.'

He began to sort the papers into separate heaps, leaving the job (it seemed) to his fingers and thinking aloud as he went.

'We believed him guilty on several counts, none of which we could fully explain. How much can be explained now we suppose him innocent? No proved contact with the enemy – because he had none: we can discard those who assert it. No consonance between his words and deeds – indeed, why should there be? We are none of us quite consistent, speak things we do not always feel, or fail to express our meaning: therefore discard all those who heard him say, or understood him to intend. The Gaier affair we had already discarded; suspicion of other associates has yielded nothing. What are we left with?' He dealt them out like playing-cards:

'The missing agent.

The anonymous letters.

Disposal of property.

Return to Orchard House the very
night of the search, and – of course –

The Latin letter.

In, I think that order.'

Farmer stirred. 'The property first – he gave most to the girl.'

'And that was two years ago. Yes', said Fabian, 'but grant him innocent and his explanation is quite credible: she is comfortable there, he did not wish to disturb her, it was as good a way as any of securing her future. Or if to you and me it seems unlikely, grant him innocent and the exact truth becomes none of our business; say only that's the reason he elected to give. Let us stick to the case against him, to this year's events and the five points that need explaining.'

Farmer recited them. 'The agent. The letters laying information. The lawyer business. The night of the search, and the Latin letter. Yes –'

'Can you think of any other?'

'I *was* just thinking,' said Farmer. 'I'm not saying it does, mind, but without going further, this new letter of his might explain a lot.'

'How do you mean?'

'According to how you see it. It convinced you he was innocent, but –'

'It could be twisted to show his guilt – "from my own self

my fortune springs". The Chief saw that, and gave it to me, the letter itself before a copy was taken.'

'It could mean something else,' Farmer insisted. 'It could be warning the girl.'

Fabian gave him a sharp glance. 'It strikes you like that?'

'I just thought it could be. Look, he says, I know nothing about this business, but whatever happens, I'm willing, as long as you keep out of it. And those songs he mentions – I suppose they *are* songs – they might be a way of asking for help: something about pity, and "why does she so?"'

'They're songs all right, the last one's "Jolly Robin", but he got a word wrong – "My lady is unkind, perdye, Alack why *is* she so?" Odd he should get a word wrong: natural mistake, perhaps. It *could* look as though he thought her guilty and that was his way of reproaching her. "Weep, weep mine eyes" is a madrigal. "If my complaint" I remember hearing somewhere – a lute song – Dowland, was it? No, someone taller: dark hair – Campion, that's the name.'

'A Jesuit name!'

Fabian laughed. 'A different man. "I am Cinna the poet, I am Cinna the poet, I'm not Cinna the conspirator." But the mob tore him in pieces just the same. That really happened,' he added, 'in Rome, the night that Caesar died: which shows how careful one has to be. The Council would read a hidden message into it, for sure.'

'But not you?'

Fabian did not answer at once. He was looking grim, and his grip on the letter in question had tightened.

He said slowly, 'There may be a message. If so, it is one he did not knowingly send.'

'You mean it was tampered with?'

'No. Not that. A message he could not help sending but did not know he had conveyed – a message he thought he had successfully kept out of it. You will not see it, perhaps. I wonder if she would?'

It was wrong to tease Farmer, who could hardly be expected to see the point but who was blessedly too wise to take offence. He was also used to Fabian's ways, and knew that his thinking aloud helped himself more than the hearer. Without pretending to understand, from long habit Farmer passed the ball back.

'Not in the songs, then?'

'Partly in the songs – in the kind of song: in what they have in common. Chiefly, perhaps, in the fact that he wrote at all. That he got a word wrong, in this as in an earlier quotation. That he has acted throughout – in the way he has acted. Words can be quite misleading, but what a man is we read from what he does.' Fabian shifted his big hands impatiently. 'I'm sorry. All this, if I'm right, had nothing to do with the problem. Put this letter, if you like, at the end of our five points as needing explanation: only then, to balance it, I put first the girl's letter to him. When was it?'

He rummaged through the papers. 'Of course! Remember I said nothing happened until after April, and could not think why I knew it? 19th May she wrote to him. I felt all the time the whole thing sprang from that. So it did, in a way. If I'm right.' He shook his head, returning Farmer's curious gaze. 'Grant me this for the present; her letter the unwitting prologue, his the epilogue to our drama – telling us something about the persons, but not part of the play itself.'

'As you like,' said Farmer obligingly. 'Meaning you know something but not enough.'

Meaning precisely that, thought Fabian, with a pox on it. All he knew – all he still knew for all their comings and goings – was the bare outline, the points he had enumerated: five acts without a cue. Consider them at their barest, divorced from suspicion and surmise. He put them, and they argued them back and forward, one by one.

First, the agent – 19th May, leaves Aldernaton for London: 28th May, arrives back with Sir John's message and leaves again carrying further letters. They now knew there were four, one for Wiltshire and three for Scotland, and he had started southward and not re-appeared at Aldernaton. The Scottish letters had been delivered, or one of them at least, the only confirmation a discreet enquirer could obtain: it was well into June, and a Monday. The calendar made that 9th June, allowing a reasonable journey: two days at least for Wiltshire, a full seven nights to reach the border – he might arrive in the Scottish capital by 7th June, but the next day was Sunday and he would know better than to knock on godly folks' doors on the Sabbath. Accept 9th June: then he had two more letters to deliver, and perhaps wait a day or so each for answers. Even if the other letters were a blind, he could not be back in London by 13th June, when the first anonymous note was received. He could have been expected back, allowing for slight delays, in another week or so – by Midsummer Eve, perhaps? – and might well have been supposed to go straight to Orchard House – but that was only conjecture. He might instead have fled to France: he might have been waylaid and robbed or even murdered: they might never learn the truth.

Second, the anonymous letters: there was no hope now of tracing the messengers, very little of the sender. There were the scraps of paper themselves, no more, vilely penned and blotted: Fabian passed them over.

'Look to sir J Stidds'

'Sir J. Stiddis goes too grenich'

'Try Orchd howse tonight'

He said, 'Does anything strike you?'

'Suppose,' said Farmer eagerly, 'it was the agent they were warning us of. "Look to Sir John" could mean guard him, not guard against him.'

It could: it would tangle the skein still further, they might have to face that; but that too was conjecture. When in doubt, look at the thing itself.

They were all on the same paper; it was demonstrably one sheet torn into three strips. The sender, therefore, was one. The hand that wrote them was unused to writing; and the brain that thought them -

'You can see something else,' said Farmer without rancour.

'Well, yes; how comes it that this unpractised writer, who cannot spell the same word twice the same way, should have "tonight" correctly?'

'Someone told him what to put.'

'Someone who was not sure of "to" but could remember 'night'? Or someone feigning to be a poor orthographer but whose invention gave out at the end? Who was interrupted, perhaps?' Why did that sound familiar? Fabian clutched at the flying idea, but it eluded him. The possibility at least was that the hand and brain represented different persons.

Third, Sir John's disposal of his property – intended disposal: there was no fresh argument on it, for the lawyer's testimony had been admirably full and concise. For a fee of twenty pounds he had undertaken, two weeks after a date to be notified, to deliver a letter to each of certain friends, to contact the agent Gregory at Aldernaton and to arrange with him the sale of the remaining Stadis land, all but one piece: out of the proceeds gifts were to be made to friends and servants, and the rent from one farm reserved to Sir John 'if he should return'. Not when but if: the statement expressed complete certainty as to the wording. The beneficiaries were all on Fabian's list, and nothing suspicious had been discovered about any except Gregory. The lawyer swore he knew nothing more.

Fourth, Sir John's return to Orchard House; this point had already been argued many times. Although the house had been shut up, the lease had not expired; the beds had been kept aired, Sir John of course kept the keys, there was nothing to prevent him coming back when he chose. That he chose an odd hour and that it should coincide with the search were doubtful points. They turned back to his statements, and even Farmer was disposed to admit his return might simply have happened that way. 'He'd had a bad jolt: the sort of thing that brings you up sharp and makes you look twice at yourself.' Two jolts in fact, in the persons of Penelope and James Gaier, and so incalculable are our vanities that the afternoon's might have hurt him worse than the night's. He might well have felt he could not face Deptford (if not Greenwich) for a day or two.

But that it should be the night of the search, there was the obstacle baulking all reason and belief.

Were the Gaiers really clear of suspicion? They were under skilled observation, and nothing had been found remotely worthy of notice.

Yet in some way the happenings of that day and night were all linked. Sir John had felt it. He had talked of a dream and of a similar feeling. Fabian wished he had made fuller notes of that conversation; as evidence the prosecution would gleefully wipe the floor with it, but it indicated something: it told him something, if he could only put his finger on it, about the sequence of events. What had they in common?

The prosecution would not care: they would be interested only in the fifth. The letter stood by itself. It was almost enough by itself, and might be strengthened yet by a 'confession', true or false – it would not matter then. It would not be deliberate injustice. The principle behind it had seemed sound enough once, official proof should be backed by personal admission. Did it take a case like this to show officialdom what the ordinary man had known for some time?

But unless he, Fabian, pulled his five wits together there was nothing officialdom could be shown.

Well then, fifth. He had only a copy, but his mind's eye still saw vividly the slightly yellowed sheet with the red seal smudged over one corner: the Latin on one side, written fair though with a bad, scratchy pen: the three Spanish words on the other, in a different ink and of different, flowing character, which Sir John had acknowledged as his own.

Why did he acknowledge them? Presuming now that his story was true, why should he not? The ink was paler and could certainly have been several years old. As a fluent correspondent he must have known there were many people who could swear to his handwriting, even of that date. There was no point in denying it.

Presuming he told the truth, the paper with those three words only was in his possession, in Orchard House, at a time now established as last winter by his letter to Dyer – received by Dyer 'the day he read the lesson', namely 24th November.

Some person, between then and 4th June when the house was shut up, had taken the paper, written or caused to be written on it part of a letter in Latin, and returned it to Orchard House. Someone had then laid information causing the house to be searched; perhaps even the same person?

There's something wrong there, Fabian was beginning to say, when the thought was driven out of his head by a new and startling one. Startling was the word: it stopped him in mid-career with his mouth open while the crazy conviction grew in him, stranger than any of the wild theories they had discarded. But it was not impossible. On the contrary, it was the only one so far that made sense.

He might have been standing like that an hour, so changed was his whole outlook. In fact, Farmer had just begun to look surprised when Fabian resumed his chair and went on speaking, the words changing in his mouth.

He said, 'The Latin is a forgery, of course.'

'If you believe his story, yes, it must be.'

'We knew if he spoke true the letter had been planted to incriminate him: we thought, or assumed, to shift the blame from the actual conspirators. Did we know, did we even guess, that there was no conspiracy at all?'

It was Farmer's turn to be dumbstruck.

'Plot, letters, the whole thing is a forgery: that's the only possible explanation. No one knows the seal; no one brought him the letter; we can find no sign of treason in himself or in his friends. Why? I said it myself ten minutes ago – because there *was* none. That must be the answer. For what said Pythagoras?'

Farmer rallied. 'Well, what said he amongst other things?'

'I forget what he said, but this is what he meant: if you're looking for an explanation of certain movements, the simplest is most likely to be true. He was talking of heavenly bodies, but it holds on earth, I fancy. Or could it have been Euclid? Never mind.' He was rattling along almost light-heartedly, but his eyes were still grave. 'Our job is now to prove it.'

They were both silent for a moment.

'But good Lord!' Farmer burst out. 'It's worse than before. It's hopeless.'

Fabian said quietly, 'It must not be that.' He made an effort to be cheerful and logical. 'We are looking now for something different: someone who wants Sir John out of the way. It ought to be easier – there cannot be so many.'

They made a fresh list of suspects, but tore up the first attempt, not for lack of material. In Sir John's London everybody knew everyone, and those who were not your friends were apt to be termed your enemies. In point of fact most of these were no more than petty ill-wishers, not above a piece of well-chosen slander but generally confining their dislike to the exchange of mutual sneers. It depended on the company you kept; your circle was at official loggerheads with the other. Most of the names appeared to be eliminated at once, as being out of London before June. The man they wanted had not only to get his forged document back into Orchard House but to attend to the anonymous letters, so well-timed in delivery that pre-arrangement was impossible. Had he had a confederate? They thought he must have, and their spirits fell even lower – unreasonably, Fabian pointed out: for like the quality of nothing, double-impossible was still no more than impossible; nor less, he added.

They re-wrote their list. Fabian fished through the relevant papers and read them again, vainly. Farmer said hopefully it might even be the parson: Sir John dead, he'd reckon on keeping his home. So indeed it might could they fit him with a confederate, but as he never travelled and he met no one else on the list the proposition was unlikely.

Except Gregory?

'No,' said Fabian loudly and firmly. 'If we start supposing confederates who would themselves need a confederate, God help us! I am tired of Gregory. Besides, I'm sure in my heart the thing is simpler than this.'

He began to pace up and down angrily.

'For the same reason, I refuse to believe in an unknown enemy. No long-lost brother suckled by she-bears and denied his rightful estate; no irate husband we have never heard of; no rival of his youth wreaking vengeance from the past. The cause – whatever the cause – is here and now.

'We can rule out in the same way, I think, several of these names: his enemies at court date mostly from the early years, they can have little to fear from him now. These at least –' he lightly scored through the names – 'the others will need continual watching, but as you see they have all been covered since midsummer. And as you said yourself, if it had been a London plot you'd have something before now.'

Farmer's lips thrust forward comically. 'But if we've been looking all this time for the wrong –'

'You've watched every known contact, no man could do

more. My only fear is that he was picked merely as a scapegoat, with no personal animosity, to distract the Council's attention from – others. But you *would* have found something.'

'And they would have thought up something more plausible. Are you sure of the Chief, though?'

'Certain. So far from hating him, he holds him in reluctant admiration. Although he is the success and Sir John the failure, he can never quite forgive himself for not winning his good opinion. No,' said Fabian, 'there's only one direction to be further explored: Worcestershire. I am going myself; excuse, to deliver this letter.'

'Today?'

'At once if I can. Will the city hold still?'

'If rumour does.'

He said savagely, 'I should have gone before. What about his people here – will they be in danger?'

Farmer shook his head. 'Not if they've any sense. The servants are hired out again and seem to be doing well. Adey's at the Waterman in Thames Street, gives out he's lodging there, but he's thick with the old man and helping on busy nights – after the daughter, perhaps. She's not the heir, though, there's a young brother dodging about. Crooks is with a carter at Wapping, lends a hand in the yard in exchange for his board. I can keep an eye on them.'

'Good. Act as if any one might be the confederate. Not that I see it – we've found no contact anywhere. Where's Nick?'

'His money ran out and he hied him home to father – last week. I sent Wilkins after him. That reminds me, how do we stand now when it comes to paying wages?'

Fabian pulled out a purse. 'Will this cover it?'

'This is your money,' began Farmer.

'I'll get it back,' he said shortly, and started to pack up the papers. 'I'm leaving these with you. Give me ten days, and unless I'm back return them to the Chief. If anything happens beforehand, you'll know what to do. I need hardly say, be careful: we have no standing at all. If he asks any questions –'

'I'll tell him what Py-jiggerum said.'

Thank God for Farmer, anyhow. But when he rode out of the city an hour later Fabian was not laughing.

It was grey weather, wind in the southwest, sweet-smelling enough but no warmth in it. September was still two days off but it felt like autumn; on many trees the leaves were turning already; vermilion lords-and-ladies in the dusty hedge-rows flashed out brilliant as evil. Each hoof-fall now was beating in relentless rhythm 'So little time, so little time'. He should have come himself in the first place. He should not have gone to Plymouth. He ought – but there was no telling what. He had tried reason and reason had failed him. Nothing was left now but blind personal conviction and that instinct which told him Aldernaton was the heart of the business. Very well then, he would obey instinct, sheer against all theory and not knowing whither it would lead. If he was right he would be no nearer uncovering the plot, but Sir John's own behaviour would be easier explained, and of that he must be quite sure. He told himself that with increasing emphasis. He might have to go into court yet with the little that he knew, if only as delaying action – the chance of success pitifully small – and it must in itself be convincing. In default of an answer, induce belief in the plausibility of the question: who stood to gain by Sir John's death, *ergo* who had sought to encompass it?

Meanwhile there was still method, a lifetime's habit not to be denied. He rehearsed over and over the principal facts in the case, and at Aylesbury in the privacy of an inn bed-chamber reduced them to shorthand. It was no use thinking any more; he would make this his daily exercise and leave the rest to instinct. He would read through the notes just once before sleeping – but he was tired, the candle guttered very near the socket, and he yielded gratefully to compulsion. He slept without a dream.

Next day being Sunday he was away late and was delayed still further at Oxford, where he arrived about noon as people were coming out of church. The town was crowded with notables summering from London and those who wanted to be thought so. To avoid remark, Fabian stabled Jewel on the outskirts and walked further into the town to get a meal, taking time enough to appear leisurely and keeping his ears wide open. He made no attempt to get in touch with his permanent agent; any news from that quarter could safely be left to the usual route. From the tattle that surrounded him he thought there was nothing of importance.

For himself, Fabian had no plans beyond the journey. He could not emulate Sir John's cross-country ride, but he did intend to reach Stratford that night – he had hoped Evesham, but that was now out of the question. With this lowering sky he would lose nearly an hour of travel; it would be dark soon after six. But the road was plain enough and he was confident Jewel could cover it. Hunched in his collar, the wind still obdurately on his left cheek, he settled down to four hours' hard going without leisure (he hoped) for vain thought.

Yet thought broke in. As they traversed the grey miles between deserted harvest fields, rough pasture or downright wilderness (and there was too much thistle hereabouts for even Fabian's town-bred eye): as Jewel clapped briskly through some drab-looking village street or stretched out again along the open road, imperceptibly the question was recurring. Who stood to gain? And thought could not refrain from pushing ahead in the direction they were going, where the answer seemed to lie: the parson – the rejected suitors – or the girl? The last suggestion ran counter to all his theories but he dared not overlook it: with Sir John out of the way she would be free to marry where she chose. True, in a year or so she would be fully of age and free in any case; to rid herself of his guardianship by the tortuous way of Tower Hill might gain nothing at all in point of time – but she might not know that. The same objection would apply to the suitors, if they still hoped to persuade her; from reports they seemed to have recognised defeat, but there'd been something unusual, surely, in the violence of that quarrel. They might well have put their heads together to concoct a revenge, but you'd think it would be simpler: plain murder, for instance. Had they the wit to work out this intricate indication of treason – or the restraint to leave it so, and not come leaping in on its heels with wild denunciation? For the man who planned it was subtle, and in his own way courageous: he could play a waiting game. He was also, arguing from the nature of the case, a shrewd judge of character, or at least knew Sir John well. As for the parson, his motive seemed insufficient, yet by all accounts he hated Sir John and his manner of life; he would rejoice in his downfall, whether or not he had a hand in it.

And that, thought Fabian bitterly, concludes the case for the defence! Would it even be listened to? Should he not be enlisting influence on Sir John's side to ask for a pardon, rather than riding on a wild-goose chase like this? What could he do here – see the suspects and form his own conclusions; trick someone into an admission? For he could no longer hope for proof. If there were proof it would be uncovered by now. If he proved collusion between a person with a motive and someone who'd had access to Orchard House, it was not in itself proof there had been no treason, and nothing else would serve. Without that, any story now put forward would be looked on as the misguided effort of friends to save him: so devilishly clever his enemy had been.

The collusion was the one near-certainty. Fabian had it by the tail in his remark to Farmer, that palpable mis-statement, interrupted before he could correct it. Farmer could work it out for himself, but would he see the connection? Was it even desirable he should? If the city stayed quiet, for God's sake leave it so. Farmer would do nothing rash, of course, and to prove opportunity was not to prove the deed; but the opportunity was there, and the paper must have been returned in that manner: on just which occasion he was not certain. The anonymous letters would need other confederates – or would they? There was a boy, any one of London's thousands – he would not count. The other notes could have been delivered, all could be contrived by one man: the same man? On Midsummer Eve he had been elsewhere. Or had he contrived somehow to make it appear so? That would be difficult short of witchcraft, and Fabian did not believe in witchcraft. He believed with all the force of grim experience that everything had a reasonable explanation, and that when reason boggled it was because someone of malice aforethought had so designed.

For all that, it was an uncomfortable time of day to think of witches – unless he could have borrowed a broomstick, or some other means of rapid transit. The afternoon was growing darker, and he still had several miles to go. He had never before cut a journey so fine; but he knew now what Jewel could do.

And suddenly he saw it, how it was and how it had been designed; and the two statements, so alike but with one trifling discrepancy; and the earlier statements, alike but all committing the same mistake as himself, that of making an assumption without evidence.

So he knew who the confederate was; could he prove it? He could prove it had been possible. He could have done that without coming north, if his brains were even fit for buttering. But who was the prime mover; whose, of all possibles, the compelling reason? He arrived at Stratford very much in the gloom.

* * *

First task next morning was to hire a horse – it would be to say the least impolitic to visit Sir John's old home on Sir John's own mount. But the best he could obtain was a poor substitute for Jewel. They plodded dully down to Evesham and circumambulated the valley beyond. He found himself reining in more frequently, scanning the weather, at cross-roads choosing the easier if longer road: all, he told himself, in kindness to the animal, but could it be his own theory he was trying to spare? If he was right, when he saw the girl he would know. He thought he was right, but discovered an odd reluctance to put it to the test, to destroy as it were the last stronghold of privacy. Destruction was so easy, a man's life and honour so blithely sworn away. If it failed to disprove treason, all coming here could do was add one more humiliation to those already in store. Yet it must be done, or the possibility neglected would haunt Fabian for ever.

He had taken the longest way indeed; once committed to the Shirecote road there were no short cuts. The entire Garner estate was surrounded by a high wall alongside which he rode eternally, hemmed in on the other side by trees and thick hedge. The day grew closer, the flies more and more troublesome, till he had to break off a leafy branch and beat them from about his head and the horse's. This was neither the proper road nor Sir John's alternative, both of which approached Aldernaton from the south; here he was completing nearly a circle and on the north side of the hill. There should be a road on his right then, snaking down from Baindon Heath to ascend again, Fisher's route in reverse. He had mapped it carefully in the primness of Seething Lane behind the muffled doors, but no map can show the look of things: proportion is not perspective – and how the dickens was he to have known the trees were of such a height he could not see a road if there was one? And in this, he reflected, behold your whole image: a fool on a fool's errand, putting his big feet down one after the other and not seeing the heart of the mystery until he had trodden on it.

But the woodland fell away at last (scrubby woodland – the impoverished Filpot property?) and was succeeded by patches of corn nearly ripe and fields where sheep and a few cattle grazed. And round the next bend he could see the heath, with a white thread running through the tawny bracken to resolve itself presently into the road. He swung left, and almost at once had to dismount and lead the hired horse by the bridle. It was a steep climb round a hidden curve; the animal did not balk, to do it justice, but took the hill wearily, as did Fabian himself. Blame the weather perhaps, but all of Worcestershire he'd seen so far he would readily exchange for Bankside; a dull, sad country, a country of clod and cloud. He climbed stubbornly; and suddenly they were at the top.

It was breathtaking. The wind leaped at him straight across Wales as if from the sea, he could taste the spray almost – spattered raindrops from the cloud-fringe being driven eastward at such speed. The view rebuked him utterly. There was no one feature of especial beauty; the plain below was English chequer-board, once down there it would be unremarkable; the blue-black irregular line that was the Welsh mountains might have been no more than another cloud formation: yet the breadth and splendour of it silenced and rejoiced. His first act was to stand straighter; his first thought, after the instant of surprise, a total comprehension. This was the Stadis inheritance. The proud, obstinate family had dug themselves into this windy hillside, looked out across this distance, and been still. And Sir John had given it away. In that, in the certainty of that stillness, Fabian's theory was doubly confirmed. His second act was to move quickly on, the searching air itself a grim reminder he was not here to enjoy it.

He was at the house within five minutes. The service was poor, as though visitors were infrequent, but his horse was taken and he himself brought at last into a room well-furnished, with a clutter of feminine belongings that cried aunt . He had asked for Mistress Dalbie, and was beginning to wonder whether they let the young lady receive company unattended when she walked in.

He was expecting what? The nymph of the ode, the little girl of the letters? She did come short of his two yards' height, but not by many inches. She had a straight back, a slim waist, hair black as a crow and strong-looking hands: old Henry's señorita, he thought fleetingly, but this girl would need no duenna, would tolerate none, the grey English eyes proclaimed. Not beautiful exactly, as the landscape was not beautiful and in much the same way – sullen to others, to those she trusted simple and forthright, she could not coax or flatter, blow hot and cold or be other than she seemed. Was he at his old trick of reading more into the lines than he saw written? Would he have seen so much had he come by the other road?

He made his bow and the speech he had decided on, watching her closely. If surprised she gave no sign.

'Your errand concerns this letter; you wish me to read it in your presence?'

He proffered it. 'If you please.'

She stiffened at sight, although she clearly recognised the writing; with hostility, suspicion that a stranger should bring it, or even – yes, of course, reluctance to open it within her aunt's domain. Yes, he was right (he felt again the quickening that never failed him), right both ways: for even on the thought she turned, saying, 'Into the garden' – at once, before decision cooled or anyone should come.

Outside, within view of the house but out of earshot, she seated herself on a low wall, Fabian standing a little apart where he could see her face. She read at first quickly, then slower and slower, expressionless save when the sheet was turned and her lips parted a moment. From the end she went back to the beginning and re-read the first part with care, then looked away and out across the hills, her fingers folding the letter with quick, sure movements, unseeing but deliberate. When only a narrow strip was visible she suddenly faced him.

'You have read this?'

'Yes.'

'Did he ask you to bring it?'

Truth was best; she would have to know the truth, but how –

'He knows nothing of my coming. It was taken from him while he slept.' Detail given unasked prevents sometimes the asking of other questions, less convenient to answer. Besides, how much did she know? No news had reached the village, yet she was strangely pale already: or did that shaft of watery sunlight striking through the cloud beguile him? He knew little of women, but supposed them to be human; man or woman was but small distinction in his trade. The unpremeditated movement, the sick clutching at heart that draws all colour from the lips, he had seen many times; bad news is like a blow, he had even seen it mortal. It was no proof of guilt or innocence, only of shock. She was moved in some way. He hoped she would not swoon, but nothing would surprise him.

She jumped up uncontrollably, stammering as she spoke, and he got his first surprise, for her emotion was anger.

'He would not have sent it. Never. You had no right –' she choked over the utterance – 'neither have I: a thing like that, between himself and God –'

A second surprise: she knows him very well, thought Fabian. Abandoning his half-formed version of events fit for a lady's ear, he found himself telling the story simply and as to an equal. What exactly he said he could never afterwards remember, but the treatment was right; she calmed at once, heard him intently without swooning or indeed interruption, and was willing to answer any question he could put. He asked for two things chiefly: other letters of Sir John's (which she fetched at once, and there was no doubt about the handwriting) and her account of the June visit. It was curiously enlightening to hear this from Barbara's point of view – the picture not the map, as it were: the hills rounded out and the trees took on leaf and greenness – especially the quarrel. She had Sir John's trick of vivid speech; Fabian might have been there (here, in this very garden, but closer under the windows) with the sun a dazzle and the quiet, shattered with harsh voices, flowing back as the impatient clatter of horse-hoofs disappeared. It was over then. She had heard no more of the affair, as Sir John promised.

'You heard them go *which* way?' said Fabian suddenly.

'Down the hill.'

'Their way lies up. Am I right? Both Baindon and Monks Croft, the direct road?'

'Yes. That must be why I remembered it. They were not going straight home.'

'Where, then?'

'To ride off their ill-temper, I supposed. Could it be –'

'We could guess, but how to prove it?' He was thinking aloud, almost as if this girl could understand him. 'They were home that evening, their households there to swear to it. Arranged? They all knew they were invited. An accomplice down the road somewhere, waiting; if the day goes well, no action, but if they lose, if the guardian is obdurate –'

'No.' She had not only followed but raced ahead of his argument. 'You see, the Filpots were with them.'

'What hinders? I said all.'

'Only this –' and suddenly she looked very young and determined – 'neither Martin nor James would do anything dishonourable. They could not.'

'You like them better than the others?'

'Infinitely more.'

'But not for a husband?'

'It is nothing like that,' she said impatiently. 'They are only boys. They have run wild since their father died, they are high-spirited and silly sometimes, no worse. I know them.'

'Very well: they all ride off together but part at the next road and – look,' he said abruptly: 'is there no one you would wed?'

'How could there be?'

He took that as perfunctory protest. 'You would ask his consent, Sir John's, of course.'

'No. I mean yes, he is still my guardian.'

'And there is no one else – if it *were* possible?'

'No. Oh no.'

She was not offended, she did not turn aside, but she had not looked him in the face. One way and another Fabian had his answer, and it gave him little comfort.

He spoke some words of apology; she did not seem to hear them but cast back directly.

'What can we do? Who are you?'

Said Fabian, 'I will tell you my name, but it means nothing. I can get at the truth, perhaps. I have the ear of one who can do more, but only with proof, proof positive and incontrovertible.'

'How will you get it?'

For answer he turned up empty hands.

'There must be a way!'

He said grimly, 'We could pray for a miracle.'

'Yes, yes,' cried Barbara, 'but *do* something too!' Her foot began to tap on the stone paving. 'I must go to the Countess. Can you take me into Wiltshire?'

Should he let her go? The suggestion was right, now was the time for influence, but a woman's intervention is tricky business. Besides, if the girl went haring off to Wiltshire four counties would want to know why. But as if she sensed his objection Barbara continued, 'He – commended me to her, and she wrote to me very kindly. I will give out that you come from her, to invite me on a visit – it will seem quite natural.'

There was nothing wrong with that. Her blend of simpleness and shrewdness he could only admire. 'It would be well, though, if I went before. Can someone in the house conduct you?'

'Trueman will come with me.' (She had decided that already.) 'Will you come now and speak to him? A pity Gregory's not here, but no matter, we can ask our way. Gregory is our agent,' she explained, 'we rely on him for everything: how much I never knew until a storm one night soon after he went, that blew down chimneys and left wreckage everywhere – thatch to mend, great trees across the road, a bridge swept away at Gapps End –'

'Yes indeed,' said Fabian, 'where is Gregory?'

'Scotland, I think,' she said indifferently. 'Mind your head in this doorway. Trueman will be somewhere about.'

It was neatly done, and he almost let himself be carried after her, wondering at the strength of woman's will. Yet noting her flushed face and fingers clasping and unclasping he could pity her too. He stood firm outside the threshold, summoned all his persuasiveness, and talked for several minutes. He convinced her, of course. She could not set off on a strange journey not even knowing if the Countess were at home to receive her; first write a letter, which Fabian would deliver, and let the Countess send a carriage for her in the proper way – Trueman could still ride with her if she wished, and bring word back of her safe arrival. Meanwhile, prepare her aunt and uncle in the way she had suggested. Yes; she agreed to everything he said, with outward calmness but despair in her eyes as if the shackles were being riveted upon her. Only then did Fabian relax and follow her back into the house.

She did not take long writing her letter, and as she returned with it he saw through a window his horse being brought round to the door. She was not offering him a meal, then; less, he thought, from hostility than preoccupation with the immediate task. He would not hold that against her – in his character of servant to the Countess he would have been forced into kitchen intimacy and doubted he could sustain it; anyhow, he preferred to be on his way. And Barbara was beginning to have qualms: 'She may not want me – there is little I can do –' She broke off. 'You will do all you can.'

It was a statement not a question, and yet her eyes implored him. Fabian, longing only to get away, found it difficult to answer her; the cheerful lie was not part of his equipment. He said, 'Try not to hope too much,' and (to mitigate it), 'south and west from here?'

She nodded. 'Turn right past the church. There is a little inn, they tell me, some way along, where you can ask again. You want the Swindon road.'

He bowed for thanks. A very old groom (not Trueman, he hoped) touched a very old hat and handed him the reins. The hired horse, rested, broke into a trot, and with a last salute he rode thankfully downhill.

His mind, released from company, began to work: a thought for what he had gained, the confirmation he came for and one other point of possible significance; a backward thought for Roger Dalbie's heir imprisoned in a woman's body and subservient to aunts; and, forward and most pressing, his own responsibility. He must go to the Countess as promised, but he had carefully not mentioned when. He must return this animal to the Stratford chandler – the horse that took him to Wiltshire would need Jewel's strength and speed. He must approach besides the Countess some half dozen more influential people now scattered to their diverse homes: soon to be back in London, but how soon, and dare he wait? He must speak to Farmer again; he must follow up in some way the only other thread in his hand; and he must decide very soon which to do first, for the church tower was already visible. The issue was too grave to be left to chance or caprice. What, he wondered, would Roger have done? Made a bee-line long ago for his own suspect and shaken the truth out of him somehow? Or been confronted with such semblance of innocence, such a cloud of opposing witnesses as to laugh him out of London? No, Roger could have carried it; his passionate sincerity shining in a corrupt world would have aroused the public conscience, that sea-monster, to demand further enquiry: a thing Fabian could not do were every hair a tongue to tell his story – he had no claim on their attention, he was nobody. For the first time in his career he regretted it.

But the church was here and here was the road, and using one's head instead of vain sentiment was the way to a decision – which after all was surprisingly easy. He was expected to turn right and he would do so (downhill still, he noticed), find this inn which was so conveniently situated, and make enquiries there of a rather different nature. He would then double back to Stratford and postpone further decision until needed. There must be other byways, since Wickins etc. had reached home that day without going through the village. It was likely that they had used that very inn for the final conference with their accomplice, whether joined by the Filpots or not. He was not so sanguine as to suppose the people at the inn would have overheard or remembered a three-months-old conversation (not sanguine at all, phlegmatic, he freely acknowledged), but they might remember a stranger in the company of local landowners. It was worth trying; no, hang it, it must be tried – lest any little thing be left undone.

So he came at last to the inn, a good two miles, with at least three tracks passable by horses leading off the road beforehand. It was a little low house scarcely more than a cottage, boasting no bush nor other sign, though a post alongside bore a rusty iron bracket which might have displayed one. But the door stood open, and a man in a fairly clean apron could be seen polishing a row of pint pots. When Fabian halted, this worthy hurried out to take the horse. The interior was so unexpectedly roomy and comfortable that despite all reason Fabian's spirits rose. He sat down and ordered a meal. The host, an oldish, cheerful-looking man, came in with it, and himself placed a steaming bowl and spoon on the scrubbed table.

'To start with, sir, if you're on a long journey, a dish of the wife's hot broth, good for the stomach, sir. Unless you've no fancy for it?' For Fabian, half risen from his seat, was staring like a booby.

It was the spoon; just a cheap latten spoon, an ordinary spoon, but where the handle broadened out it was embossed with a crude device: some sort of an animal, sketchily *rampant,* bearing across its forelegs a diagonal line that might be a *bend* or a staff...

'The spoon, sir? That's blacksmith's work, that is. My cousin down at Tuddle, he did 'em for me. Not big enough to show up properly on a spoon, though. You shoulda seen our sign, until that tempest banged it down, two months, nigh on three months ago – Hugh! When was it the wind fetched the old sign down? Middle of June? – and of course farmers comes first, she's still at the forge for mending. Begging your pardon, sir?'

'The sign, what is it? What do you call this place?'

'Why, sir, the Pig and Whistle.'

It was as simple as that.

Careful, now.

'It's very good. Like somebody's crest, or signet.'

'No one's I ever heard on. Funny you should say that, though. Somebody in here one day, June too that'd be, but earlier, the sign was still up then – borrowed one of them spoons to seal a letter. Right there where you re sitting, where the light's best, and made a joke about it.'

The miracle at last? Try not to force it –

'June, you say? A friend of mine was in these parts in June. I wonder. . .?

'What like is your friend, sir?'

Thank God for Farmer! Fabian described a person he had never seen.

'Aye, that'll be him.'

He risked another question. 'Would that be the day the gentlemen from Baindon were in here?'

'Come to think of it, so it were. You mean they know your friend, sir?'

'I think so,' said Fabian. 'I understood they were meeting hereabouts.'

The host shook his head. 'It must have been someone else, then. They come and gone without a word to the one I was talking of.'

No, it would not be as easy as that. 'Left a message, perhaps? Or did their business while you were not by?'

'No, sir, nothing like that, and I'll tell you for why. Mr Wickins, he come in rather far gone, as you might say, and I helped Mr Tom get him into the next room, private like. When they left I let 'em out through the kitchen. This other one was in here all the time, been here an hour at least a-writing of this letter, and smiling.'

An hour? Downhill from Aldernaton was twenty minutes or less. They could not have met earlier: Fisher's statement and the others made that clear.

'Look,' said Fabian, 'can you swear to that? A great deal may hang on it.'

He not only could but would, and the man Hugh confirmed it. No word or sign had passed. The letter was written and sealed before the Wickins' arrival. Hugh remembered that especially, for some wax had remained on the spoon handle and he was scraping it off when the gentlemen came in. They went straight through without setting eyes on this corner, which was so situated, Fabian would see for himself, as to be hidden when the door stood open. The writer of the letter, whom Hugh, unprompted, described very clearly, had sat on there until late evening – he was staying the night, and only stepped off the premises for a brief stroll about sunset. He left the next day, paying generously, with an air of being well pleased.

The testimony seemed conclusive: no treason – no confederates – no accomplice of any sort if you excluded unwitting messengers: one person alone was responsible for all. One brain, one hand –

But why? Why?

Think back to the beginning. It was all there, as Fabian had more than once declared – not only the material evidence (except this of the spoon) but the true cause, the prompting of the monstrous act.

He had come near to seeing it so often that for a moment the solution still eluded him, but suddenly, with the smoothness of absolute finality, everything slid into place.

12

'This Thing of Darkness'

Three weeks later, the earliest he could physically contrive it, a room was being prepared in the Tower. Fabian's chair was already placed but he could not bring himself to sit. He stood quietly in the window, watching men in aprons bring in the furniture required – a small table for the President, a posy of sweet herbs, an orange stuck with cloves (specific against plague), a cushion for each chair: taking their time about it, and as cheerfully unconcerned as players setting stage for a scene they would not take part in. They would not indeed. Apart from Fabian only those who had appeared in the enquiry were to be present – but all of them: the Chief saw the justice of that. The same lawyer, the same clerks were to attend. Lord Ambrose had been brought back secretly from Sussex as a guest of the Captain of the Tower, greeted by him loudly, for the public ear, as 'Mr Mannering'. Extraordinary measures had been taken to prevent the least wind of rumour blowing toward the city.

The clerks arrived; the aproned men withdrew. The legal representative came in, bestowing on Fabian the slightest of greetings, and took his seat aloofly – poor fellow: the case was without precedent and he liked it not. What Fabian disliked was the ceremony of it, the insistence on form even to the end. He had not been allowed to see Sir John beforehand; in the stringency of their precautions no one had. He hoped

Lord Ambrose would not be late. He hoped he need not say too much. Spoonfeed his lordship, he had been told, make it simple for him. Present the evidence concisely, but so as to leave no doubt. This must be his lordship now, with a white beard, being helped in by two attendants – to the wrong chair? Good God, it was Sir John.

He put the helping hands aside, not impatiently, and settled himself, fairly upright, sideways in the chair. In that position he seemed less shrunken, less a shadow of the self Fabian had last seen. The width of shoulder was there, some hint even of the power once behind it, but the strength itself was gone: he looked tired, too tired for pretence or argument. His eyes wandering round the room without curiosity at last met Fabian's, and somewhere in the depths of them still glimmered faintly a spark of the old mockery.

There was no time to speak, for Lord Ambrose was now entering: a big man, made bigger by the number of wraps and gowns he wore and the old-fashioned flat cap, like a pancake, sitting incongruously on top of a round wrinkled face. The voice that issued from it was thin and high, a tenor faded.

'Are we all present?'

'Yes, my lord.'

The heavy door was shut and locked, and covered by a heavy curtain.

'Then let us commence our business.' He seated himself with deliberation. 'It would of course be improper to anticipate the evidence, but I think Sir John should know at once what I am given to understand, namely that circumstances have come to light which exonerate him completely. If that is so indeed, we shall be glad to hear it – we shall all,' he added firmly, his glance travelling among them 'be very glad.'

There was a hurried murmur of assent.

'And now Mr – er – this gentleman, who is best acquainted

with the matter, will explain it. Please proceed.' He leaned back, and all eyes were on Fabian.

All but Sir John's? It was impossible to tell. He sat still at the odd angle that served to prop him; his hands, which made as if to move while the President was speaking, at once recollected themselves and again lay slackly on his knee. This new development could be to trick him: he would show nothing, neither hope nor incredulity. He had learned to show nothing. He did not turn to Fabian or appear even to recognise him; but the glimmer had been there, and to it Fabian addressed himself.

He began formally, a speech learned by heart to set things in motion while he felt for the correct approach. Once he had that, words would not matter, they would come of themselves.

'My lord, and gentlemen, you have followed the progress of this enquiry and I shall not weary you by describing it in detail. You have the letter before you whereby Sir John was accused. I propose to show now why it was written, and presently to produce its author. That will not take very long. But lest the truth seem stranger than the accusation, I must tell you also how it was discovered.

'And begin, I think, with an apology. Justice is hooded but she is not meant to be blind. The hand that holds the scales is only human, and in trying to be impartial we weight the scale against our personal feelings. In this case, alone of my experience, it was the wrong thing to do.

'But where there's smoke it is common to find fire. We cannot concern ourselves as to persons, we must find the fire and stamp it out. Only, in this case, we could find no fire at all.

'May I say straight away that there was no fire – neither treason nor intention of treason. There is no need for oaths or affirmations; we know Sir John to be guiltless. Even the guilty party has committed no act against the Queen's peace, only a private offence – a wicked one, but understandable perhaps.

'I will try to leave out private affairs except where they have a direct bearing on the matter. What put us most off the scent was the affair of James Gaier; occurring on the very night when Sir John's house was searched, it appeared to be part of the plot. Sir John himself believed the two incidents to be connected in some way, because of "a feeling he had", very like an earlier premonition in a dream. Coming from Sir John this impressed me, for he is a man not given to idle fancies. There was in fact a connection: the same person had contrived both. It was a long time before I saw how this could be.

'You must remember we were looking primarily for treason, no matter whose. Even after failing to trace it to Sir John we had still to search for the supposed actual traitors. The culprit may not have understood this fully, but it greatly favoured his design. Chance, Fate or what you choose to call it favoured him still further as one after the other each explanation put forward by Sir John turned out incapable of proof. He could not have foreseen this would be so. But the whole plan was built on chance, and he seized every chance most skilfully. He chanced to see a paper on which Sir John had once written three Spanish words; he had a smattering of tongues and chanced to know their meaning. He must have taken the paper and kept it by him, mischievously, without knowing to what use it might be put. But when later he found himself by chance at an inn whose spoons are embossed with the inn-sign in little, he was quick to see its possibilities as a signet; he sat down then and there to compose his sham letter. It was chance alone (or what we chose to call it) brought me in time to this same inn and the persons who could identify him.

'But, treason once disposed of, we should have guessed his identity sooner. I fell at first into the error of supposing the forged letter must have been planted before 4th June, when the house was shut up; if so, there were as many suspects as people who had the original opportunity to remove it. Two persons, in fact, had access to the house after 4th June, but there appeared no connection between them and anyone who had reason to wish Sir John ill.

'It is better to prove actions, and leave the reasons to prove themselves. Suppose one man alone could have contrived and executed this plan, what, by his actions, did we know of him? That he was quick – courageous – could write Latin, with schoolboy mistakes – had been in or near London sending anonymous warnings on 13th, 21st and 23rd June – had either the opportunity himself to plant the letter or means to cause someone else to do so. He knew Sir John intimately, not only his movements but in part his soul. He had also engineered in advance a quarrel between Sir John and James Gaier: for how else could it have been spoken of the same night in Eastcheap when it occurred privately, ten miles away, near sunset?

'There is one man, and only one, possessing all these qualities, and I now present him to you: Henry Adey.'

Fabian as he spoke flung open an inner door and two tall officers brought Adey forward: somewhat pale, his dark hair somewhat ruffled, but lips set arrogantly in a sneer.

The President leaned forward, joining his plump fingers.

'Do you know why you are brought here?'

'*He* told me' – with a jerk of the head towards Fabian.

('Your lordship,' growled one of the officers.)

'And what have you to say for yourself?'

'Nothing. My lord,' he added defiantly. 'I'm saying nothing. Let him prove it.'

'Very well,' said his lordship. 'We accuse no man except in his presence. You will stand aside – and you, sir, may continue.'

There was still no movement from Sir John. Adey with one

contemptuous glance round the room had not observed him, but kept his gaze fixed on Fabian; and Fabian, with much disquiet, kept his on Sir John.

'Your lordship will wish me to be precise. I take up the story from the beginning, omitting all conjecture: what I say now is proved already.

'Adey had been in Sir John's household, I cannot say employ, for about two years. He *was* employed on a variety of errands, some of which might be thought the duties of a servant; at the same time he was admitted to an intimacy which yet fell short of confidence. He was excluded from Sir John's private affairs; with his companion Richard Crooks he was the object of some merriment amongst the gentlemen who frequented Orchard House. Crooks is of a different sort, cares nothing for verbal sallies and will perform any task to which he is put: in Adey this treatment rankled. When he found the sheet of paper Sir John had tossed aside in his search for Dyer's verses, there was born in Adey's mind the chance of a revenge.

'He could not get at the Stadis signet, which was kept in a locked box; he would need to fake some kind of seal. In the Pig and Whistle, a few miles from Aldernaton, he discovered the thing for his purpose.

'I said he found himself there by chance, but that is only partly true. Sir John would never take his followers to Aldernaton – another thing that rankled. Adey and Crooks, with a young gentleman then in Sir John's company, had been left thirty miles away when Sir John went there on Friday, 6th June. But Adey disappeared early on the Saturday and returned on Sunday evening; he had been with a wench, they assumed. Instead, he had gone after Sir John to Aldernaton, to see the place for himself. There was no rain those two days and he could have followed the tracks quite easily. He would avoid hanging about too long in Aldernaton village, but it was only chance that he stayed at the Pig and

Whistle; and by pure chance (or Fate again) a heavy storm on Monday, 9th June damaged the inn-sign, so that when my men investigated the neighbourhood later there was nothing to show its connection with the seal.

'Meanwhile the party had returned to London, where for his own purposes Sir John lodged privately a while. He sent Adey and Crooks more than once to Orchard House to fetch clothes etc., and on each occasion they were instructed to air the beds. This entailed lighting a fire and preparing warming-pans, a lengthy operation of which Adey grumbled and which we may be sure Crooks was left to perform, giving Adey ample time to plant his paper unseen. There was also time, during the days when Sir John kept in retirement, for Adey to arrange dispatch of his mysterious warnings to the Secretary of State's London house.

'On 20th June Sir John was summoned to Greenwich and his followers took lodgings at Deptford. On 20th June the second anonymous note was received. On 22nd June James Gaier came to Greenwich and several people took pleasure in informing him that Sir John was paying attentions to his wife. On 23rd June occurred the only event I cannot prove, namely that Adey persuaded Gaier to their tavern: be that as it may, he came there, and was goaded into a frenzy by whom? Adey surely, neither Crooks nor Greenlee had the wit. He rushed out of the house in his rage, so the hoped-for quarrel did not at once take place; but an hour or so later he caught up with the party, not at all by chance – we have found the man who was paid and stationed, by one of Adey's height and colouring, to tell Gaier which way they went. Gaier forced a quarrel on Sir John, who dismissed his followers back to Deptford. This same day, already, a further note had been received warning us to search Orchard House, and the tale of the quarrel had been spread in Eastcheap.'

Adey cut in. 'While I was at Deptford.'

'I ask your lordship's patience,' Fabian responded, 'and

will presently explain this seeming contradiction. It puzzled me for some time. That I was finally enlightened is due to another chance Adey had not foreseen. His own mischief undid him – the Gaier quarrel was a piece of superfluous malice which seemed to dovetail with his plot. But Gaier was ill; Adey did not guess that Sir John, having tended him, would return by night to Orchard House. He had read Sir John's faults truly; his virtues were pages that he could not read.

'The house was being searched when Sir John arrived. I was there. I remarked that both he and his horse were very tired; the man with good reason, but why the horse? It had good staying power, I was later to prove, carried Sir John forty miles in a day and myself, riding heavier, a good thirty; yet on Midsummer Eve we were to suppose a mere twelve or fourteen miles had exhausted it? *Absurdum est.* The answer is that Adey had ridden this horse to London and back earlier in the day. His own was too slow, and Crooks', a piebald, might be too easily remembered; he took Jewel, and rode him hard; and if Sir John's mind had not been so exercised with the Gaier affair he would have perceived it.'

'It's a lie,' said Adey mechanically.

Fabian ignored him, and unfolded a paper. 'I went to the inn at Deptford riding Jewel, a chestnut with distinctive markings. The stable-man recognised the animal, in fact I had difficulty in persuading him I had not stolen it. He said (and will repeat before this court if your lordship wishes): "I've seen that horse before. Why, that's the horse belonging to the gentleman who disappeared – what's his name – the knight – the one in the Tower." Asked why he was so sure, "I groomed it often enough." Reminded that Sir John stayed there only three days, he agreed, "But it was in and out twice a day." Pointing out that on the third day he did not come back, "Ah, but the horse had been out twice already. They went in the morning as usual, Sir John and one of the others, the red-haired one it was that day, and the red-haired one brought it back as far as the street outside: there the dark-haired one meets him, takes the bridle from him, sends him (the red-haired one) off on an errand and himself rides away on the chestnut. I saw it, in a doorway. It was not the silly gentleman, he knew nothing of it, for he'd been that hour with the foils fighting his own shadow in the back yard, and if a shadow could hold a blade he'd been a dead man a dozen times, for a worse guard I never did see. No, it was Master Knowall without a word of a lie – him they called Adey – and he stood and watched the red-haired one out of sight before he mounted and rode off. He was gone two or three hours and came back with the poor beast in a sweat, and it's *Rub down this animal and look sharp about it.*" This evidence, my lord, was sworn to in my presence before a Justice of the Peace.' He passed up the paper.

'The next day Sir John and Gaier had disappeared, and it was Adey who instituted the search. But Adey did not think either party had been injured; he admitted that Sir John would not have harmed Gaier, and doubted Gaier could hurt Sir John. Why then did he make a search? His purpose could only be to deceive his companions, and anyone else who might enquire, into believing he knew nothing of the affair. He was in fact in the dark as much as any concerning Sir John's whereabouts, but the disappearance added suspicion to the circumstances of the plot, and he took advantage of it. When told he was in the Tower he showed fear and astonishment, repeating several times 'He has done nothing, they will have to let him go.' This passed for loyalty to his master. But I think the alarm was genuine, and that he had not expected his forgery to proceed so far. He would have been satisfied to humiliate and inconvenience Sir John, to bring upon him such ridicule as he himself had suffered; this would have been a fitting revenge. For there is, your lordship will observe, a likeness between them: ability that lacked employment.'

That much Fabian had to say; it was nearer home than he wanted to press, but anything to rouse Sir John from that unnatural stillness would be justified. It was; a faint gesture, ghost of the upflung hand when a point lands on the target, broke his pose. The President turned to him courteously.

'Do you wish to question him, Sir John?'

'No, my lord.' Quiet, but neither feeble nor held tense; he was simply waiting.

'Then let him stand before me.'

But Adey had seen Sir John, and his knees gave way. He had to be dragged forward.

'Now, fellow, what do you say?'

'Nothing.' But his teeth chattered and his face was ghastly.

Fabian said, 'I have more witnesses if need be. One is the boy Robert Carpenter, residing at the Waterman tavern in Thames Street where Adey has been lodging; he will testify that this man gave him a folded paper and bade him deliver it at the Secretary's gate. The two men at the Pig and Whistle have sworn their statement; they can be brought from Worcestershire to confront him, but I think this will not be necessary when you have heard the last evidence – that of Joan or Joanna Carpenter, the young woman who helped him to prepare the anonymous letters, on a sheet of paper similar to this from the stock kept for their customers –'

Adey broke; babbling, shuddering into speech.

'She knew nothing – I swear she knows nothing – she cannot write, but I guided her hand –'

He controlled himself suddenly, looking wildly about him, at the faces stern or contemptuous, and fell silent.

'That seems to be an admission,' said the President. 'This court has no power to try him, but he shall be closely kept until a form of charge can be prepared against him – he will do well to confess all before his punishment is doubled. Take him away.'

Sir John said, 'No.' His voice rang out clearly, with

authority, and everyone jumped as though a corpse had spoken.

'You have something to say?' asked the President (kindly, as to a child).

'I have. I say no. There shall be no charge.'

'Sir John, you must consider,' he said patiently, 'not only the grievous injury this man has done you, but the contempt into which due law and procedure have been brought–'

'I do consider it. If I let pass the injury, the law can have no claim against him – the action will not lie, is that your term? – and I suppose,' he added drily, 'you will not wish to spread this contempt abroad into the streets.'

'That is true,' the President agreed. 'I have a word to say yet. You have suffered injustice and we regret it sincerely; but you must know that apart from this man, all concerned have done nothing but their duty. You see yourself the danger of rumour. I am to ask if you will be good enough to join with this gentleman, in a way he will explain to you, to avert that danger.'

Sir John faced Fabian at last. 'First give me the explanation.' But the spark of merriment was back again, and a little colour burned in his cheeks from the exertion of argument; the miracle had been in time.

'Would you come to the Globe this afternoon, to let people see you well and at liberty? It may not stop tongues, but it will remove their sting.'

'On two conditions – no, three.' The spark danced a moment. 'One, that it be not a play I detest; two, that I may rid me of this grey beard beforehand; and third,' – he turned back to the President – 'in all seriousness, that you grant my former request.'

'I cannot think it right, Sir John. As our friend here might have said, Justice is hooded but she is not to be hoodwinked. Let Justice take her course.'

'Perhaps she has: if you heeded what our friend did say.'

He stood up with a sudden effort. 'It is my turn to make a speech, a very short one. I am not insensible, and I have had time enough for reflection. Adey's fault was my fault, bred and nourished by me. I have paid for it. If you conceive yourselves to owe me anything, do not add misery to misery, but let it end there.'

A little silence followed his words, until Lord Ambrose addressed Adey in gentler tone: 'Do you hear this great kindness? Have you yet no tongue?'

Sir John said, 'May he come to me?'

He moved like a sleepwalker, still with that stricken face, and the clock-tick was suddenly magnified in the stillness. While everyone present held his breath the two men looked at each other. Sir John at length held out his hand, speaking quietly, almost awkwardly.

'Well, Harry. We must learn to know each other better.'

That was all. If Adey spoke they did not hear him. The President rustled his papers and the uncomfortable moment was over.

'Besides, my lord,' Sir John's voice added cheerfully, 'we must be seen together – I shall need him at the Globe.'

'For God's sake, no!' Adey found his tongue at last. 'There'd be a riot. I dare not.'

'I suggest,' said the President 'that the presence of the man Crooks will suffice.'

'Not that,' cried Adey. 'If he's there without me they'll know – if he's not, they will suspect him too – you know what they've been singing –'

'You see?' Sir John said, but as if it proved a different point.

'Perhaps we should reconsider the – er – theatre,' Lord Ambrose demurred. 'There appears an element of risk.'

'Better a fire on the hearth than in the thatch,' said Fabian. 'We can control it there.'

Sir John took charge. 'There is no risk and there will be no riot. I'll have Crooks and Adey, if you know where Crooks is, which I doubt not. Stand up,' he said sharply to Adey. 'If I can do it, you can. You give us leave, my lord?'

The old man was actually smiling. 'I leave it in your hands. Now, gentlemen, there remain two things to be done. In the Queen's name I countersign the warrant she entrusted to me, giving order for Sir John's immediate release: and I direct that the whole of this enquiry be expunged from the records. This ends my commission.' He rose, gathering his shapeless wrappings. 'Congratulations,' he murmured, 'seem out of place, yet they are due all round, and perhaps most to this gentleman who must be nameless. You put your case ably, young man, and there is more than one who should be grateful. Sir John, your father was my dear friend; come and see me sometimes for his sake.'

They bowed. He trailed voluminously from the room, the officials filing after him; Adey was led back to the inner chamber, and Sir John and Fabian left alone.

'You still have not told me of the play.'

'Did I not?' said Fabian, steering him to the door. 'It is the one of Beatrice and Benedick – titled other – some proverb was it.'

'*Much Ado About Nothing*. Apt, I fancy.' Sir John laughed. What, man, look not so tragic, it is a comedy as I remember. Now bring me to your barber, and I'm for you!'

13

First Player

Fabian shaved him; they could trust nobody with the secret. It took half an hour, but he made a fair job of it, and Sir John, fingering his smooth chin, demanded a mirror.

'Well?' said Fabian, presenting it.

'Well enough. Younger, by the loss of a beard: older by – what else. The hair will do, think you?'

'It will pass in a poor light.'

'I doubt you've been too clever,' Sir John retorted, 'and no one will recognise me.'

'They'll recognise Crooks and Adey.'

'True enough.' It was not all white, not near so white as he'd feared, and the regained youthfulness of his face would contradict it. That was something to know. He looked round the small apartment, his home for so long, and it was strange already; the streets would be strange; his shaven face was a stranger.

I must not hurry him, thought Fabian, but it's close on twelve, and to get him there unperceived, myself to Seething Lane and see the messenger, and Crooks – if they find him – back to join his fellow, it will take some doing. But I must not rush him or all's lost. He has borne up so well.

'Are you ready, sir?'

Sir John roused himself. 'One moment.' The remains of his breakfast were on the table; he crumbled them into a plate and put it on the window ledge. 'My friend the cat,' he said, smiling. 'He'll know I am gone.' He had planned to do that on whatever was to be his last morning; no need to explain it now to his friend the man. The last shall be first. The evening and the morning were the first day. Halfway to the door he halted suddenly.

'Fabian.'

'Sir John?'

'I have not thanked you.'

'No need,' said Fabian.

'I know.' No need for thanks or oaths or explanation; only the direct miracle, instantaneous and persisting; only the straight look and the warm handclasp and truth the sun at noonday: only life.

'You're cold,' said Fabian practically. 'Take my cloak, it's thicker.'

Sir John grinned. 'Thank you at least for that.'

They traversed stairs and passages without meeting any one; they crossed the outer court, Sir John limping a little. The halberdiers saluted them incuriously. They were through the gates. The air was sweet and cold.

'Pull your hat well down,' advised Fabian. He smiled reassuringly, but glanced at his charge with some anxiety. The animated flush had faded, and in the keen daylight he looked thin and ill. 'Do you mind which way we go?'

Sir John shook his head. 'I am new-born into the world, you can lead me anywhere.'

'Take my arm, then.' He had meant them to walk further on and approach the river by way of Nightingale Lane, but not in this northeast wind. The devil take politic precaution: St Katherine's Stairs were nearest. Luckily there was a crowd coming down from the Minories and two more made little difference; they'd not be noticed in a boat-load. They got into the stern; he placed himself behind Sir John, to shield him with his own greater bulk from the wind. It really was bitter for September, and more than one passenger was muffled.

His lips to his companion's ear, he said, 'Will expects us. I had to tell him.'

Sir John nodded without speaking, as the little boat tossed through the wake of a larger vessel. The river was steel-grey and violent, the sky steel-white with a shine above the cloud. Light and motion confused him with their insistence. He shivered under the thick cloak, and eased his leg surreptitiously into a better position.

Fabian's square hand closed on his. 'How goes it?'

'Only the cramp.'

'Lean back on me. We're nearly there. Can you walk along Southwark Street?'

'Good God, I should hope so.' But he obeyed thankfully enough. Their muttered colloquy could not have carried; it must be Fabian's concern that was so obvious for a stout merchant to ask as they stepped ashore, 'Friend ill, sir?'

'The ague,' said Fabian promptly.

'Ah. Dreadful thing. Come on anywhere, once you've had it. It'll be this wind today. Far to go?'

'His brother lives near here, I'll see him safe. You'll get as far as William's, Humphrey?'

Sir John, achieving a wan smile, thought that he would, and they parted from the stout party with mutual good-days. The incident had its value – 'Humphrey, indeed,' Sir John snorted as they turned the corner. It took them to Bankside at a better pace than Fabian had dared hope.

It was the dinner-hour, the streets were almost empty. If anyone did see them going into the Globe, it would cause little comment; there were always visitors to see the building, some of whom would stay for a performance. No one they passed showed any sign of recognition. Let but this afternoon go smoothly and it would not matter if they had.

The doorkeeper said, 'Second door on your left, sir,' and

resumed his chunk of cold pie with no more interest in their existence. It could not have been better. Fabian tapped on the door and threw it open.

Will, in shirtsleeves, looked up from the littered table, sprang to his feet and grasped them each by a hand. 'Come in,' he said.

'I must leave you for an hour,' said Fabian. 'All's well so far. Take care of him.' And was gone.

Will put his head out into the passage and called, 'Boy!'

There was an answering cry of 'On my way, sir,' and a quick scurry of feet.

'And now,' said Will shutting the door, 'let's have a look at you. Lord, it's good to see you back.'

The well-known voice with its warm undertones dispelled for ever the last shreds of unreality. Sir John smiled back into the dancing eyes and returned the firm grip: he had come home.

'Food first, I think,' Will said. 'The boy's gone to fetch it. Come and sit down.' He swept props and costumes from the one comfortable chair. 'We have it all rehearsed, stage seats on the first balcony roped off and your company picked. You'll sit well forward for the crowd to observe –' he broke off, and the laughter-lines crinkled round his eyes. 'Shaved! ' he said. 'Oh lord!'

Sir John grinned apologetically. 'It was that or a white beard, impossible to hide.'

'Not easy, no. I talk too much, never heed me. It becomes you very well. Chins will be worn firmer this coming year.' (He threw away the last sentence, crossing to the door again.) 'Good boy, I'll take them.' These were two covered dishes from the cookhouse up the road, which he set before Sir John, clearing space neatly with his elbow. 'Get this inside you; there's time and to spare,' he said, 'and you can watch me dress for entertainment.'

Sir John obeyed. The food was simple and blessedly hot;

he had forgotten how good a hot meal could be. That disposed of, he leaned back in the chair, drowsily content, while Will put on his finery, adjusted a tawny wig over his thinning scalp, and sat down to the mirror. He painted sparingly, with quick sure strokes, but long before his handiwork was accomplished Sir John had drifted into sleep. Observing this, Will moved his equipment quietly aside, drew a tattered script and some clean paper towards him, and began to write.

Their positions were unchanged when Fabian knocked again. Will met him finger on lip, and together they gazed at the sleeper. He breathed lightly. Lacking the beard he looked curiously unprotected; the bones of his face stood out sharply under the skin.

'Can he do it, d'you think?' Fabian spoke in a low voice. 'Are we asking too much?'

'Too much,' Will agreed, 'but he'll do it. Sleep's the best medicine. Are your people ready?'

'Now, yes. They picked up Crooks in Wapping, so the party is complete.'

'Crooks without Adey seems a thing impossible.'

'It is,' said Fabian grimly. 'Adey's here.'

'He's what?'

'Here. At Sir John's request. He would not have him charged.'

Will said, 'S'truth!' and looked down at his friend with mingled exasperation and affection. 'That kills the rumour, sure –'

Sir John stirred. His face changed, in the second before waking, to a weary alertness that caught at their hearts. Then the cloud passed over, and he was beaming at them comfortably.

'The first time for months I've been warm. Have I slept too long?'

Will answered; for the moment Fabian could not. 'We have

just ten minutes. Lord, you could do with some colour. I'll see to that, if you can play your part?'

'I think so. Not on one of your vile little low stools, though.' He eased himself carefully upright. 'If I fidget, it's not that I do not like the play.'

'We'll get you a chair. Boy!' He shuffled rapidly through his papers. 'Take this to Mr Burbage, ask him from me to make this cut in his last speech: I'll rehearse it with him at the half-hour. It was something too close,' he added over his shoulder, 'there might have been trouble.'

'For God's sake,' Sir John said, nettled, 'make no cuts for me. I'm tougher than you think.'

'We know that, old boy,' Will retorted very kindly; 'but I'd as lief not be closed down by the Lord Chamberlain. First Essex and now you! We had a last act once. Ah well, it ends with the dance anyhow, let's hope no one will notice.' He reached for his colour-box. 'A touch, I think. Hold still.'

In a matter of minutes he was discreetly made up, given a heartening drink, and settled firmly in the first gallery in what looked like the throne from *Henry V*, disguised with cushions and a cloak thrown over it. A subdued Adey was wedged in on his left, and Crooks, cheerfully uncomprehending, on the right; the other seats and the bench behind were packed with stolid and reliable citizens. 'There,' said Will, 'seen but inaccessible – I hope,' and Fabian, 'I'll be in the audience somewhere. If anyone comes over, be careful what you say.'

He grinned up at them. 'I'm practised in that.'

'Good lad,' said Will. 'You'll come to supper, George?' Fabian nodded; they both wrung Sir John's hand again, and disappeared. The little boys dressing the stage looked at him with awed curiosity. The house was filling. The musicians took their places and began to tune: in dumb show as it seemed, for against the general hubbub not a note could be heard. He sat there placidly, taking in the warmth and cheer.

He did not speak to Adey; time enough for that yet, when they were once again used to each other's bodily presence. As for Dick, good old Dick, there was no change in him; elbows on the rail, he was watching the pit, shouting to any friend he saw there, roaring with laughter at the man who spilled his beer and the man down whose neck it was spilt: Dick Crooks to the life, the party's guarantee of success.

A trumpeter stepped forward and cleft the din once, twice, and retired; the audience began to settle. The inner curtains parted, discovering two boys dressed as ladies, in convincingly female attitudes; the short dark one bent over some sewing, the tall fair one sitting negligently with a book. Off stage, the trumpet sounded a third time. The ladies jumped up full of curiosity. To them entered dear old Gussie Phillips, the picture of apple-cheeked benevolence, with a paper in his hand: 'I learn in this letter that Don Pedro of Aragon comes this night to Messina . . .' And the comedy had begun.

He had seen it before more than once – a year ago, or a lifetime? The drift was pleasantly familiar, and a line here and there chimed in his memory; but he listened now as from a long distance, and watched the actors much as he had done the audience, a many-coloured crowd. What matter? It was enough for him to be there, present but unregarded, in the world of living men.

It was during the masked dance that he was first perceived. Neighbour nudged neighbour; the ripple was running through the house, that's Stadis there, left of the stage. The re-entry of Benedick and the delightful ramifications of the plot recaptured their attention, but at each lull speculation grew – without a beard: can it be? It must be – until there was no disregarding it. Will, entering for the garden scene, decided to make a virtue of necessity. He turned boldly to Sir John, and addressed 'See you where Benedick hath hid himself?' directly to him. The others quickly caught on, both parties taking him into their confidence; he responded as well as he could, leaning towards them, glad of the chance to shift his position and yet seem to take a lively interest. The audience loved it. At 'Hath any man seen him at the barber's?' such a shout of laughter went up that no one heard the reply. The Claudio missed his cue, Will was gagging outrageously, but nothing mattered. Burbage's pained dignity ('All this is no cure for the toothache') set everyone off again, and when he took Leonato aside the old man was wiping away genuine tears of mirth. From that moment there was no holding back. The action built up at a hurtling pace, each player, charged with that electric atmosphere, at the very top of his powers.

Despite the inevitable cramp, Sir John found himself enjoying the play. The 'watch' came on, with the new man who'd taken Kemp's place looking for all the world like the pompous alderman of Coleman Street. Instinctively, to share the joke, it was to Adey that he turned; and not in vain. The instant grin of appreciation, exchanged before thinking, was more than speech: though Adey flushed he did not withdraw. Sir John's hand came to rest on his shoulder in the most natural way.

The audience, who knew the alderman too, were withholding judgment on the newcomer. Cleverness alone would not avail him, nor a fine voice, nor a ready trick of imitation. Unless he could prove himself in some way worthy of his place in the company they would never accept him. But generosity was in the air. When he rolled out his preposterous injunctions with the straightest of straight faces, and followed up by a huge wink towards the guest of honour, they took him uproariously to their hearts.

Fabian, inconspicuous in the top gallery, hoped all would be well. He was beginning to regret his suggestion. With the house in this temper, supposing Benedick forgot his cut there was no knowing what would happen. (He had no fear of Will forgetting.) A public demonstration, however good-humoured, was the last thing they wanted. There were ladies present, too. The play was drawing to an end; Claudio and Hero were reunited, Beatrice and Benedick brought together at last, and the couples lined up for the dance were halted by the solemn messenger:

> 'My lord, your brother John is ta'en in flight
> And brought with armed men back to Messina –'

Don Pedro, silent for this once, turned with a helpless gesture to Benedick, who tossed off the sixteen words that remained of his speech, and to a gay coranto the company 'danced out the answer'. Nicely done, Will; well remembered, Richard: well played, pipers! A storm of applause broke out.

The 'ladies' sank into billowing curtseys, the men made a neat leg and one by one retired. The clapping continued. They came out again, grouped as in the play. The pit began stamping and whistling and would not let them go. Then inevitably, someone shouted, 'Stadis!' The call was taken up on all sides – 'Sir John Stadis! We want Sir John! Sir John!'

Here we go, thought Fabian. How do we get out of it now?

There was only one way out, and Burbage took it. With the friendly courtesy that made him so well loved, he moved towards Sir John's corner, holding out a hand of invitation. The applause redoubled.

Sir John looked right and left, put by his cloak and spoke to Adey, who grasped him by the arm; with a belated shove from Crooks he climbed stiffly over the railing and limped across the stage. The whole house rose and cheered.

They cheered for two solid minutes, till they must have been heard at Westminster, and suddenly Fabian knew his fears were groundless. Sir John stood there quite simply waiting and smiling – the little crooked smile that now showed nakedly on his lips; a solitary yet strangely authoritative figure, tired but at ease. Here as in his own home, as in the

Tower even, in court or cottage 'he shall be found like Brutus, like himself'. The playhouse now was Stadis Place. Whatever the situation, he would meet it and being what he was, would surely better it.

Under cover of the noise he was saying something to Will, who replied without hesitation, grinning broadly. When the cheering abated by the tiniest fraction, Sir John stepped forward unprompted, and it cut off at once as with a knife. In the warm silence his voice carried easily.

'My lords, ladies and gentlemen – good friends: I should first ask pardon to come halting before you –' (murmurs) 'a trifling injury; I got it falling up a doorstep –' (shrieks of delighted laughter; that must have been Will's contribution) 'and since I am something ashamed of it, by your leave we'll not discuss it further.' (Appreciative guffaws.) 'But in good earnest, to be back among friends repays all the pains of absence, and such friends, with such a welcome, as these friends of ours.' He gestured towards the company. 'This play is my favourite comedy. I have seen it many times, and I can truly say it never fails. It may even teach us a lesson, for not only is it *Much Ado About Nothing* – let bachelors remember –' (laughter) '– but in the words of another proverb, all's well that ends well. There's a title for you, Will, when times allow.' (A little quick hand-clapping.) 'And now, friends all, dismiss me – having spoke a poor kind of an epilogue – to join you in thanks, our very hearty thanks, to the players, and musicians, and all who have made possible this memorable afternoon.'

And so it was and would be, even for those who would never know why. The final outburst of applause, no longer urgent but confirmatory, moved full-fed to a satisfied close. The citizens gathered their belongings, the gallants invaded the platform by dozens, all who could claim the least acquaintance shook him by the hand. There were quips enough about his beard (which he parried automatically, each time with a different jest) but none on any dangerous topic. For this day at least curiosity was deflected.

The tall young Earl came striding over, the crowd opening before him. He seemed ill at ease. 'How are you, sir? Mother has sent the carriage for you. We'll meet later, I expect.' He nodded curtly to Will (a little coldness there?) and moved on, trailing a whole shoal of lesser people.

The Countess in London! This was an unexpected development. He had gone through the strange day in blind obedience, letting each moment look after itself, all thought of the future postponed; now there was again a future, one other thing to be faced. He said lightly, lest his moment of dismay had been visible, 'we must not keep her waiting.' His eyes sought Will, who looked assurance, adding, 'we'll cover your retreat.' So he was to accept the invitation. He remembered a word for Crooks and Adey, promising to look them up some time at the usual rendez-vous. Goodbye then to his new-won haven: the Globe first, now the universe – and no one who watched him go would guess with what reluctance.

The big travelling coach was drawn up at the main door, a liveried man at each horse's head, surrounded by half the audience and all the children of Southwark. Burbage goodnaturedly went first to create a diversion, and the adult crowd surged round him. The Earl's own servants handed Sir John up, to no greater commotion than a small shrill voice declaring, 'Garn – that ain't the Earl.'

It was dim in the stuffy interior: he could just make out the form of its occupant and the blue silk of her gown. He began, 'This is kind in you, madam,' but the noise of their progress covered his words. When the coach slowed at the Bridge he tried again. This time the lady held out a hand, which he saluted. She trembled at his touch, but said nothing. He would gladly himself have sat quiet, but the silence was unnatural: she might be ill or in trouble. When it had lasted long enough, he made as if to speak; at the same instant,with an oddly youthful movement she pulled the curtain aside, and faced him between laughter and tears. It was Barbara.

'Good God.' He was shaken into abruptness. 'What do you here?'

She said quickly, 'I was properly escorted. The play was good, I thought.'

'You thought!'

It might have been her uncle scolding. The corners of her mouth quivered; she said with unusual meekness, 'Was it wrong for me to go?'

'No, no.' He struggled for composure. Better a fatherly regard than sound like her uncle indeed. 'Nothing of Will's would harm you. I am glad you should see it. But to find you here –'

The laughter was uppermost. 'They wagered you would not know me.'

He said crossly, 'I knew you were not the Countess. And who, may I ask, were *they*?'

'The Earl and his friends. The Countess could not appear in public, she is still in mourning, you know. She is very kind. I have been with her a fortnight.'

'Indeed. So the Earl and his friends went off and left you –'

'To return with my guardian.' It was unanswerable. 'He has to see a man first, at White-hall. The barge was waiting.'

They were moving at last, ponderous and swaying. 'While you and I,' he muttered, 'crawl home in this – perambulating haystack. What a plague ailed her to send this monstrosity into London streets? We shall scarce clear the upper storeys.'

'She thought it would be more – private for you.'

He was silent, angry at his own weakness. He should not have met her like this, so miserably unprepared. It would be hard enough at any time. And that was no excuse for his damned cross-grained impatient answers; to vent his ill-humour on her was unpardonable. 'I must be sullen when (poor when) I most would pleasant be.' The coach was jolting horribly, and brought back the trouble in his hip. A wave of pain swept over him. When he opened his eyes it was to meet hers, distressed and understanding.

He said gently, 'It was only a cramp – it is gone again. I am sorry I was churlish.'

Her lips shaped 'No.'

'I must not be ungrateful, today of all days.' He grinned at her reassuringly. 'And I am very glad to see you, howsoever.'

It was easier now; he could see his way clear, and do in time what must be done. And that was much: life to take up again, a part to play the lines of which were set down for him already. 'Now no way can I stray.' The future was bound to the past, no need to talk of choice: he was chained, by his own actions, to the living and the dead. The freedom was to do it freely.

Meanwhile, accept the good hour as it offered: he had learned that at least. He sat quiet, watching her in a new-found tranquillity. The fashionable cap became her, setting off the rich dark hair, the fine bones, the delicate curve of the neck. He thought of her no longer as her father's daughter, but saw with a sense of wonder the child she was, the woman she had grown to, and from his enforced distance glimpsed the quintessential Barbara. Barbara. Had he spoken the name? She turned to him impulsively, her hands catching at his. He took them steadily. She would not feel the blood beat in his eardrums till it silenced even the wheels. He must be there securely while she needed him, the guardian still; by no word nor sign from him should she learn otherwise. He could bless his physical weakness whereby the violence that shook him was subdued.

So he smiled at her serenely, commended her dress, and began to speak about the play. He had always known how to cheer her, and it worked as of old. Soon she was talking freely again, with no touch of constraint: and then they were at

Ludgate – and passing Paul's – and swinging downhill to where the old red-sandstone castle glowered in the grey evening like a tepid inferno. There were servants waiting at the entrance. He was glad of two men's help to descend, galling though it was to need it. Barbara stepped down like a bird.

In the doorway she paused to drop a quick kiss on his cheek, and saying breathlessly, 'I must go and change,' ran lightly up the great stair and vanished from his sight.

He advanced to meet his hostess.

14

The Countess and –

'Mary, my dear, this is very kind.'

She had not altered at all. In her stiff black silk she looked as slim as a girl; there was scarce a grey hair in the light auburn, and she greeted him with the same wise and merry eye, in which there was now a mingling of concern.

'Come straight in here,' she said. 'I often begged my lord to pull down this gloomy place, but we are glad of it at times – there has been a fire in your room for two days and the warming-pans renewed. You are to stay as long as you like, and command us in every way.'

'Then you expected me?' he ventured.

She did not answer at once, but directed the placing of yet another log on the ample blaze. The room was small and comfortable, panelled in golden oak and rich with tapestry, a gracious contrast to the rough exterior. There was a big armchair piled with cushions nearest the fire, and facing it a smaller one, with a book laid down where she had been reading. More books were in the window.

'You can light the lamps, too, Jenkin. It will be dark soon enough; we'll shut out this London weather.'

When the servant had gone, she turned to him with the quick gesture he remembered, motioning him to the big chair. 'Oh John!' and the sparkle in her eyes was very like tears. 'How near we were to losing you I can comprehend only now. I would not admit the thought.'

'Would it be such a loss?' he countered.

'Truly it would.' She took the question seriously. 'There are none too many left, of your sort.'

He shook his head. 'Your logic is at fault this once. It is the old time you sigh for, the friends who are gone you would personify in me. A poor representative.'

She said, 'Your friends think otherwise.'

'I do not think it. – If pride precedes a fall, I have had mine.'

She could not answer. She looked down at her long fingers and was amazed to find them shaking.

He said, 'Life is not as we imaged. We were so wise, and prudent, and omniscient; we delved into the nature of things and lost sight of our own selves: while they that knew, and were true to the knowledge, spent what they had and gave themselves away. Make no mistake, the best men are all dead.'

'You shall not outreason me,' she replied, 'nor belittle yourself. Believe your friends and be happy in their knowledge.'

He said with a touch of irritation, 'My friends are too partial. I have done nothing to praise.'

'Not what you did, but what you would not do.' She looked away from him into the leaping flames, and seemed to find courage there. 'The man Fabian came to me: rightly, for there was no time to lose. He told us – all that he thought fit. I know you did not name one name, nor write to any friend, lest other men be drawn into your misfortune. Few, I think, would have held to that.'

'Happily there was nothing to conceal.' His shoulder hurt and his foot hurt and he was weary of this verbal fencing. 'If there were I would have told it.'

That was too frank for her. She poked the fire and

pretended not to have heard. He thought longingly of bed, or better, of some homely little parlour where Will and Fabian would be sitting over supper. George Fabian! Well, why not? He had met him only three times, yet it seemed incredible there should be anything about him still to know.

But Mary was speaking. 'You sit stiller than you used,' she said.

'Yes.' Again the feeling of impatience, but for her goodness, for the sake of the dead, and because he was twice today convicted of discourtesy he must not show it. He smiled instead, and her expression changed. He was suddenly aware, without possibility of error, that he could be her second husband. As a boy he had loved her, but her birth demanded a better match; he had gone away, and come back to find her married. She had lived happily with her elderly husband, brought up two sons, managed their vast estates, become a personage in her own right and patron to the liberal arts. Now the storm had swept him to her side again, and this time she had only herself to please. In the wreck of all his life here was comfort offered, a comfort he might legitimately take. He had simply to say the word: but he could not say it. He could only meet her eyes, and let her read the answer in his own.

In one brief searching glance she construed it honestly.

'It is too late then.' The quiet statement was sufficient.

He answered in the same tone, 'Yes.'

'I knew it. You have gone beyond me, John.'

'Say rather, we have taken different ways.' He smiled again disarmingly. 'I sing but indifferently, I do not write, nor rhyme, nor play upon an instrument. There is no place for me in your world.'

She said with warmth, 'Your place could be anywhere you choose.'

'Stadis Place. They told you that too?' He laughed shortly. 'No, but I mean it. I gave – I tried to give what was required of me. It was so little always. When more is needed, then I fail: there's nothing here to give. Only–' his voice softened – 'to you for ever, friendship and thanks, thanks overflowing; both for myself, and what you have done for Barbara.'

'We do what we can.' She looked at him oddly. 'Yes, of course. We must talk about Barbara.'

'She told me you have been very good to her.' That was the right note, a father would speak so; he could hold that easily.

'I will do better yet,' said the Countess. 'How long have you loved her?'

'How long? Why, twenty years, I suppose.' Keep the touch light.

'You know quite well what I mean, John. When did you fall in love? There is no need to dissemble, and you do it very poorly.'

'So it would seem,' he retorted. 'Well, as you have guessed I must admit it.'

'Was it two years ago, when you gave her Aldernaton?'

'Before that.' It was his turn to gaze at the fire. 'I could not tell you when: she grew into my heart.' The little crooked smile was back. 'What a fool I have been. You need not say it – even my one good deed I botched from the beginning. I should have stayed where I belonged, seen to the land myself not farmed it out to others; held it for her, and sent her to you sooner. Would you have taken her?'

'Suppose I had, what would that have gained?'

'She would be safely married long since and Aldernaton her wedding-gift.'

'And the profit – to yourself?'

He said wryly 'It might have helped. I should have been away before this.'

'Away?' She was startled.

'I ought not to have mentioned it. Tell no one, till the Queen shall give me leave.'

'But where would you go?'

'Virginia – the Indies – anywhere.'

'Was that the meaning of your preparation –'

'That was the desperate plot.' He laughed into her shocked face.

'But did you not explain?'

'I told the truth, which was sufficiently unconvincing. Further urging, such lame and sorry reasons, would have seemed proof of guilt.' He got slowly to his feet. 'Well – now you know the whole story, such as it is.'

'I think no one will know the whole of it. Oh John!' she said again. 'And what will you do now?'

'I do not know. Stay at least for the wedding, then go, I think, if anyone will have me. They say more settlers are always needed.'

'Whose wedding?' she demanded.

'Why, Barbara's.'

'And whom do you suppose she will wed?'

'That will be her concern, and yours.'

'Hers for certain – I think you flatter *me*. But my dear, you cannot marry her off so quickly. There are plenty would like to marry her. I need not tell you it is not the same thing.' She turned to him earnestly. 'Look, John. I do not mean to badger you – but have you never thought of yourself?'

'Myself?' He stared at her. 'You must be mad.'

'Why? When you love her.'

'Good God,' he said with energy, 'that's different. That's something I cannot help. To think more would be fantastic. I? – a reputation in shreds, every purpose of my worthless life miscarried, a battered hulk fit for the breaker's yard – and old enough to be her father.'

'My lord was older.'

'I beg your pardon; but there's no comparison.'

'And my mother married for love and was happy too. It seems to me you have both advantages. She loves you, John.'

'As a guardian, yes.'

'More than that.' She rose purposefully and crossed to her books. 'I am going to betray a confidence, for her sake as well as yours. Read this.'

It was a single sheet, in Barbara's straight up-and-down hand:

Thinke of me sometimes without knowing why,
A quaint half-thought dismiss'd with half a smile,
And I will bear this absence for a while
That only time and you can remedy.
In the early morning on the day's young tide,
In the rhythm of some simple occupation,
Or as I saw you once at Aldernaton
Quiet, withdrawne, all contact laid aside –
Thinke of me then (when the instant does not cumber
With tedious business) as a dream should rise,
Drifting from thought to thought without surprise
Until you find me there, times without number:
For all these times look forward to the season
When you will thinke of me, and know the reason.

He read it through twice, and stood oblivious, fingering the paper as though it were rarest silk.

'Well, John,' said the Countess at last. He left his private thought with a start.

'"A play to wear out weary times".' He made to return it, but she ignored the movement.

'Which signifies?'

'"Fantastic passions, vows and rhymes".'

'Oh,' she said, 'Lyly. That old stuff. You are too apt; is that what you think it? Her sonnet is true.'

'And you,' he replied, smiling, 'are an authority on sonnets.'

'I am not speaking of the verse. She means it, every word.'

'Yes, I think she does. She has known so little company. That's where you can help her.'

'I tell you, she will not look at another man, in respect of marriage. She judges all by you.'

'Then I must go even sooner,' he answered calmly. 'I am glad you told me. Can you add to your great kindness and bring me to the Queen?'

'It is arranged – she will see us in ten days. But John, you cannot disappear in this way.'

'Why not?'

'If you go, you may never see Barbara again.'

'Perhaps,' he said, 'in some little corner of eternity.'

He still spoke lightly, but his face was grey. The Countess, between pity and anger, played her last card.

'Sit down,' she commanded. 'You will not leave her now, knowing that she loves you?'

'For her own good I must. She will understand.'

She mused aloud, 'You two are very sure of each other.'

'What do you mean?'

'Only that she said the same of you. "If he knew he would forgive: he always understands."'

'Forgive?' he repeated stupidly. 'Knew what? What is there to forgive?'

'I am trying to tell you, although I do not well understand her myself. A strange girl, some would say hard: God knows where she gets it, for Roger was all impulse, and her mother a poor spiritless thing I always thought.'

'Well, well,' he said impatiently.

'She was wary of me at first – I mean Barbara – but ready to face the Queen herself if need be. (I dissuaded her from *that.*) By the time we arrived here, she was softening towards me – we came from Wiltshire in two days, what think you? I always take three.'

'Is all this pertinent?'

'You'll see.' She noted with triumph the colour back in his cheeks, the rough edge to his voice. 'It took twice as long to reach the Queen. I was frantic, and Barbara calm as a rock.'

She smiled briefly. 'I think she knew then she need not fear me as a rival: plainly, I could not live up to you. But when it was over, when we knew for certain you were saved, then she wept in my arms. It was only the once. And then of course she told me; upbraiding herself all the while for selfishness. Do you see it, for candidly I cannot?'

'She told you what?'

'Everything. That she loves you. That you had given her all and would take nothing, not even the only thing she had to give. Yes, John, she said that.'

She glanced quickly at him, and stopped there. He was gripping the arms of the chair with painful intensity, a wash of pallor in his face again. He spoke carefully.

'I have travelled a long way today, from death to life: I am slow of apprehension. If there is anything in this – of hope for me – I pray you to unfold it.'

'I have told you,' she said with pardonable shortness. 'What more do you want? She is breaking her heart for you.'

'Broken hearts do not kill.'

'No, John: but tell me what they do?'

'Dry up the sense; lose friends; suspend judgement; lead us into temptation and deliver us to evil.' He looked up then, with the ghost of a smile. 'Yes, yes, I own it.'

'Then on my salvation,' cried the Countess, 'I can follow neither one of you: her the less, there's some excuse for you. But Barbara! Not a tremor on your account – the tears were all for her: it is not natural. She said it herself; she had no fear for you, whatever the outcome.'

'She said that?'

He leapt from his chair with a vigour that astonished her.

'She did. Make sense of it if you can.'

'The best sense in the world.'

He did not attempt to explain, but it was clearly a restorative. Hope and purpose flooded back, he stood firm and erect, re-made before her eyes. She saw that she had never really known him, only an *idea* cherished through the years: now it paled before his visible strength and integrity, actual but far different from her image. Being wise as well as honest, she could admit it and leave it at that.

'Well, John: have I finally convinced you?'

He turned to her from the world's distance, in the old easy way, and for the last time her heart stood still.

'Was it so hard? Forgive me. I will struggle no further, but accept my fortune humbly.'

Try as she would, there was a tartness in her reply. 'Humbly? You, John?'

He said, 'Alas, my reputation!'

Skill comes in the doing; she laughed with him, and rose.

'You're a match for her, John, and I truly believe she is for you. May you both be very happy.' She paused in the doorway. 'I will send her to you, for fifteen minutes. Try not to waste them in argument.'

'A hit,' he acknowledged, saluting with the sonnet for sword-hilt.

The Countess tucked her book under the right arm and extended the other: she had not two grown sons for nothing.

'Left hand, is it not – like this – after a bout?'

They shook hands cordially in the fencers' manner. He said, 'Thank you again, for everything;' she smiled kindly, imitated his salute, and withdrew.

When she had gone he stood quite still, his hands held loosely as they were with the paper still between thumb and finger, not daring either to clench or relax them; emptying his mind of conscious thought and desire. If it is to be let it be, let not my will precede it, nor arrogate to self what self has not deserved. If there be anything ... any thing ... if my whole life ...

The door opened slowly.

Barbara.

She was so like his solitary visions that he stood motionless;

only the dark corners of the room were filled with light, the light shone in his eyes and was reflected from them. Yet all he saw was a girl in a yellow gown the colour of thick cream, her dark hair done simply without ornament.

And what did Barbara see? Her first impulse always was to run to him, to run and to hold tight; now something held her back, not pride nor bashfulness. Meeting him for the first time on equal terms, she saw him in that one instant as a stranger: a man of middle height, no longer young; a figure of strong contradictions, greying hair with hairless chin, latent power and present gentleness, passionate yet restrained, still but the pulsing centre of life. He smiled, and was her old friend too, but with every former barrier removed; he raised his head, and their eyes met with the force of lightning, leaving her dazzled, shaken and exultant.

She had taken one step into the room; he had completed his sole movement: it was so nearly instantaneous.

Until that moment she had had no real hope, only the illogicalities love feeds on, which thanks to her uncle she was scholar enough to recognise. (One of these now recurred, *we are exactly of a height.*) Alone, she could pretend confidence – a confidence in self? – which the presence of even one other person could disturb; it had no firm foundation. The drive back from Southwark was most disturbing of all, as if there had ridden with them a third grim figure whose face she could not see, whose name she must not ask. In such company self could not intrude. She had acted the dutiful ward, he had behaved as a kindly guardian, but for one incident that gave her in retrospect a wild, irrational joy; and then the stern Mentor was again between them. She feared it was her fault: she scoffed at herself for presuming a connection: she knew at least she could do nothing but wait, if it were till doomsday. And now suddenly the sky cracked open, and in the brilliance, if she dared to see it, was a portrait whole: the masked sternness too was his, one face among many. And the many were all one, like the different coloured fires in a dewdrop or a tear. And like every truth in the moment of knowing, she had known it all the time.

She took her second step forward. The door closed soundlessly behind her.

After all, he was waiting for her to speak.

'I writ you a sonnet – it was very ill penned.'

'With one or two false rhymes,' he teased her. She could take that too: the new relationship must include the old, as future contains past.

She murmured, 'Not the ending.'

He quoted from memory,

> 'For all these times look forward to the season
> When you will thinke of me, and know the reason.'

There was a tiny pause. 'I knew the reason long ago.'

He folded the paper abstractedly and bestowed it somewhere in his coat. To Barbara, even in her new excitement, each movement he made was a separate delight.

'At first I would not think. I tried to keep away, for every year it grew harder. Then when it seemed my life was near an end, there was no harm in thinking. In the last weeks chiefly, I have thought of you: during the unlikeliest of – occupations.'

'I did not mean – it was written long before –'

'True's true, you need not withdraw it. Even at the worst, you were there. Beneath the fear and the acceptance, past the point of thought you were there: you are so part of me. It was no easier, I'll not pretend to you. It made no difference, but it made sense.'

She said, 'We are part of each other.'

'Yes; but what part? We have to see it clearly. Until ten minutes back I would have gone without speaking, but in that I was mistaken. It is right that you should know and choose.'

He spoke seriously, without emotion, deliberately playing it level.

'You know what they say of me. Take it that your uncle was right, near enough, that I am fitter for the stews than for your company, that my time has been squandered without grace or merit. As you are part of me, the one good part, I am of you the worthless and the rubbish.'

'Is Aldernaton worthless? Is all that you have done and given?'

He said, paraphrasing the Countess, 'We do what we have to do.'

'Tell me one thing truly.' She was feeling her way, but growing surer. 'How much does it yet trouble you – the past that you have squandered?'

He answered her directly, as only he in all her life had done. 'Now, not at all. Somehow I feel forgiven.'

'You have spent only the dross, and saved the proper coin.'

'If I have, it is yours.

'My own, to keep?'

'To keep or to spend, take or give or throw away: clipped and worn and lacking in true value, but yours.'

'Then – please – not to throw it away. I want it all, the base coin and the gold, all you gave and all you have withheld until now.'

'Are you quite certain?'

'Of nothing else but you. You are my certainty. Only–' this was harder to say – 'there are things perhaps – I have no right – you may not wish to share...' And she in turn was proffering a paper. 'You wrote it. Fabian brought it.'

'I see.' But he looked at her, not the paper. 'I had a bad night when that vanished, trying to remember each word, as careful as I'd been.'

'He should not have brought it.'

He shook his head. 'I should not have written it. The common urge, self-justification.' Then, because she was still troubled, 'we owe a lot to Fabian. I can have no secrets from him, and none from you. It has served its turn. By your leave –' and he dropped it, still folded, into the fire. 'This is rather like the play; our own hands against our hearts.'

'Burn mine too.'

'Your first sonnet?' he protested.

'And last. I'll never write another.'

'Pity. I meant to call you Sappho.'

'Try it!' she flashed.

He smiled, and fished in a pocket. 'Here, then. Burn it if you wish, though it's good for a beginner. The heart that thought it will survive.'

They stood watching the flames lick over and consume it. When the last corner was grey ash she looked up, to find him serious again.

'In a month's time I shall be twice your age.'

She answered, 'Need we wait so long?'

'Dear heart,' he said, laughter leaping behind his voice, 'only for your safeguard: to look longer at the world before you choose, to get experience.'

'If the world means London, I have seen it, and for experience, you have enough for two.'

'Yes, by God!' he retorted with feeling, and Barbara laughed back triumphantly. She was right; the thing between them was in motion, they were both breathing faster in the race that they must win or lose together. He was even a little flushed with the effort, as fair skins light up under the surface, but the depths were untroubled. As sometimes in a clear stream the sunlight seems to come *up* through the water, and even the pebbles on the bottom shine, so his whole self lay open before her, every minute detail visible and precious to her own. For one blissful moment they stood at gaze, delighting in each other.

The conversation was not broken by their silence, advanced rather. When he spoke next it continued from new ground.

'You must not feel bound to me, for that or any cause. As duty, gratitude, affection, pity–'

'Pity least of all.'

'No,' he said, 'there is no need of that where we inhabit. Look though, look carefully. It is your future, not mine, we must consider. I can find some way of living usefully elsewhere. But if you truly choose – such as I am – I am not diseased or decrepit, there is nothing wrong that exercise and right diet will not cure – then, then –'

Words began to be meaningless.

They were moving, literally drawn to each other without apparent volition, like Gilbert's electrics.

She said, a little breathless, 'This must be like learning to swim.'

His two strong hands reached out to her. 'The water is deep and the current swift. Come in.'

A generous half-hour later, someone outside had trouble with the door-latch.

It was only the Countess.

'Well, children? Yes, I see it is.'

Their faces glowed, not only with the firelight. The girl, she thought, was almost beautiful, and as for John, she would not see that look again this side of heaven. They were both in the big chair, and holding hands as if they'd grow together. There was no need to pretend; she was genuinely touched by their happiness.

It was Barbara who answered. 'He takes me for the estate, but that's all one, we were both his from the beginning.'

Well, really! thought the Countess, did I say she was strange? And he kisses her hand and adores her. Aloud she said, 'There remains but one question: what will you do with the uncle?'

Barbara only smiled, drowsily carefree: nothing could

shake her now. Sir John grinned ruefully. 'Faith, we must build a parsonage.'

'Or better still: the Earl has two livings in gift. If we could persuade him to accept preferment – I will not promise, but I think we can do something. When is the wedding?'

They looked at each other and laughed. Such lesser matters had been quite forgotten.

'Well, you can talk of that tomorrow. I am taking Barbara away now – no protests! You need a good night's sleep. You ought not to be under the same roof, but we can forget that until the betrothal is announced. Meanwhile, here's someone else you will be glad to see.'

A tall figure appeared behind her in the doorway.

'Gregory! Thank God,' cried Sir John. 'Come and rescue me from these pestilent women!'

15

The Queen

There was one river yet to ford: the next week's audience.

Gregory appointed himself nurse, groom and trainer, and exercised his charge relentlessly. He walked, rode, fenced with him, even had him on the river taking turns at the oars. If the Countess protested at their early rising, she would have been more horrified still to learn how they spent the hours. 'But it's no use, your ladyship,' said Gregory cheerfully, 'we are old campaigners, you must let us alone to kill or cure ourselves as we may.' For Gregory too needed exercise; his disappearance had been due to a bad fall and a twisted ankle on his way back through Yorkshire. He met with such hospitality that one month lengthened into two, and his good hosts, finding he was sought, closed round to conceal him – they had no love for Southerners and feared the worst on his behalf. And he had stayed willingly, pleading his ankle as excuse – 'For you cry, "Oh, doctor, my foot hurts when I walk on it" and who's to gainsay you?' He had promised to return next year, and they gathered he would be bringing home a bride; 'And there goes another one of us,' Sir John would groan with a twinkle. So they persevered together, in the brisk wind that whipped colour into pale cheeks and stimulated appetite. With natural movement, companionship, and Barbara awaiting him, Sir John began to feel himself again: not the old self entirely, a part of which was gone (he hoped) for ever, but with enough of its former attributes to take pleasure in the forthcoming encounter.

When Wednesday came he dressed with especial care. His clothes and personal effects from Orchard House he had found here in his room, and Jewel already installed in the castle stables, mildly supercilious of the mere carriage horses. He would have Fabian to thank for that. Fabian had vanished into London: with reason, of course, and it would be imprudent to seek him out. But there was no hurry. They would meet again.

Meanwhile, for the court: his story had been talked of; the anterooms would be thronged to see him, an audience more critical and a great deal more hostile than he had to face at the Globe. He must expect both question and implication, honest or malicious: the enemies he had made so carelessly would never let such an occasion slip. He thought he would not care. Now the time had come, to his surprise he cared considerably; the heart reopened, like a wound, is tenderer than before. The wonder of deliverance was still on him, could overtake him still in the middle of a word or gesture; time would dull it – it was mellowing already – but now, on this sharp October morning, sense and perception were intensified. He felt, and was content to have it so. Life spared, and to so fair a promise, had been spared upon condition; he would do all that was required of him, and do it as befitted, in the high style of comedy.

So he chose black, but the living black of velvet, warm and rich; and white, in innumerable crisp ruchings goffered to perfection, at the wrists and neck; boots and gloves of black Spanish leather, gold-fringed; a cloak lined with scarlet; and his father's plain sword in a plain hanger – an unexpectedly sober note that only Gregory (or perhaps Fabian?) might have understood. The whole household, willing slaves, were up before dawn to prepare him; with no word spoken, everyone seemed to know the circumstances and to wish him well. In the old days he would have cared little for that either, or found it matter for mirth; now he was touched to humility – although, as the Countess doubtless would have said, he hid it passing well. The measure of his change was that he knew it. He had the right word for everyone, thanks and banter mixed: a grip of the hand for Gregory, cheer for Barbara (who with some hours yet to wait for her presentation was beginning to tremble), for the Countess his deepest bow and to the Earl's tousled head emerging from his window a salute from the saddle; then off he rode, on a Jewel polished till he shone.

Through the streets freely, meeting recognition kindly or in kind according to the age, sex and conversation of those who hailed him; through the Palace gates and outer halls, the target of sympathetic or curious glances he moved, and (wondrous indeed) the inner doors swung open to receive him. The long room, without being crowded, was full of people whom he knew. All turned towards him as the Queen herself called to him across the length of it:

'Come in, come in, Sir John! If you linger in the doorway we shall think you cannot walk.'

At the cruel jest someone's breath caught audibly. Sir John came forward at once: he knew his sovereign in this mood. She was being typically Gloriana; the red wig piled high and of a harsher hue than ever shrieked against a purple gown and the dead white of her face. But he had not seen her for a year and was shocked at her appearance; the very skin seemed to have changed texture and be stretched tight, only her eyes were bright and alive still in the ageing skull. The moment he had dreaded was swallowed up in pity for her. It no longer seemed desperately important that his bearing should be upright, his stupid foot not drag; let him stumble would it do her good. As a result, of course, he did not even limp in his slow progress up the room.

'So this is that Sir John who has been ill-used in our name.'

'Your Grace will not hear me complain of it. To be saved board and lodging all the summer –'

That pleased her. She grunted, 'You do not say that to all who ask.'

'No, madam. I remember instead an old housedog we had at home when I was a boy. She could never tell friend from foe, and bit me many times; but I would hear no word against her, I was too fond of the old bitch.'

There was a moment's horrified silence, broken at last by the Queen's harsh cackle of laughter. She was plainly delighted. Those nearest her permitted themselves to smile.

He had come now to her footstool and went to kneel; that was harder. She raised him immediately, giving both hands to assist him. 'No, no,' she said. 'Get up, Sir John.'

He smiled. 'Have I earned it now?'

This time the hush was ominous. For months the whole court had been carefully avoiding such allusions. The creation of knighthood, once given to Leicester, since usurped by Essex, was her most jealously guarded power; at the mere mention of recent knights she would fly into a rage. The anxious faces turned to one another, and quickly back to miss no instant of the spectacle. One hand still lay on Sir John's arm, and the knuckles whitened, but her anger was not for him. She cried, 'Pack off, the lot of you! Here's a man at last.' Then, commanding herself, she added in a clear carrying. voice, 'Sir John, you were not doubted. We think scorn of those who learn us to distrust our friends. And yet you wish to leave us.'

'To serve you always, madam, but in my own place.'

She said, it might be wistfully, 'Stadis Place?'

'Your Grace does know everything: we always swore it.'

The room relaxed. He kissed her hand; she drew him into the window, called for cushions, and remained with him in earnest talk for nearly half an hour. What they said there was overheard by no one, but some averred that at the end of it she wiped away a tear.

With these marks of royal favour Sir John discovered more friends than he ever had, and time soon passed until the afternoon, when the Countess and Barbara were to be privately received. The arrangements were really private. A page brought him a pre-arranged message, and he excused himself quietly from the little group he stood with, leaving the building and returning by a side door. It was her Majesty's own wish he should be present at the audience; he wondered why (their morning talk had not touched further on his private affairs), but was grateful for the privilege. Other people do not always see those we love with quite the same eye; he thought (and if the thought was vanity, forgive him) that Barbara would shine brighter in his presence. The day was surely gone when the Queen, however chagrined, would forbid the marriage; prevent it she could not, but her displeasure could bring that notoriety they were trying to avoid. And on the other hand, he did not want even his beloved, with the unconscious cruelty of youth, to misjudge their sovereign lady. He remembered his own early days at court and the irreverent comments of his friends. Time had brought tolerance, then understanding and respect and real affection. Her tongue was rough but her judgement generally sound; only those resented it who could not face it.

There was one anxious moment. 'So this is Roger's girl.' The piercing scrutiny could devastate; if she should follow it with 'Well, mistress?' the lady had been found wanting. Barbara's direct gaze did not falter, but her lover held his breath until the Queen continued.

'He was a boy, no more than a boy for all his black beard: impetuous to the end. It seems only yesterday–' But she was looking out across the years, the long years that had swallowed all her fine young men. And Barbara, with her father's daring but an understanding all her own, did something Sir John would always remember with deep gratitude: took one step forward and kissed the royal cheek.

It was so quickly done the Countess could not prevent it, and so simply offered that there could be no offence. Her Majesty said 'God bless me, child, who taught you that trick?' but did not expect an answer. 'We should have had you near us, but the world is evil and would misconstrue it. You have done better for yourself, what say you?'

It was a test question, but put without malice. Once more Barbara's own heart taught her the answer.

'All that I have is given, madam, and all good, so good the evil cannot touch it.'

'No, cannot? Has it not already? Ask Sir John.'

He said, smiling equally at both of them, 'All that I am given has been very well worth while.'

The three looked at each other in a bond of mutual understanding. 'Well, well,' said her Majesty, 'we talk in riddles and the Countess disapproves of us. Advise me, Mary; shall we let them leave us now?'

The Countess, who to say truth had thought the conversation in poor taste, was yet relieved it was so cordial; she had worked very hard to that end. 'I think so, madam; with the commands you have to lay on them.'

'The same on each: to wed none but the other, and that as soon as they can find a priest to tie them; and another for Sir John which will be sent you under seal. Off you go, for the State awaits me, and (what was the phrase now?) "light a fire for tomorrow".'

So it was presently known, and spread widely, that Sir John Stadis was appointed Justice of the Peace for his corner of Worcestershire; that the marriage would take place on the 23rd, the Countess having come to London specially to arrange it, and her son the young Earl would give away the bride; and that the couple were then leaving London directly to stay a few days with several old friends of both families, and thus gradually home. London dearly loves a wedding, and although dark doings were yet hinted, on the whole the city must conclude all other rumours false. Sir John removed back to Orchard House on a special short lease, and needed it; he had much hospitality to return within the three weeks yet remaining. Then too there were farewells to pay in the city, with Crooks, Adey and a varied company; he discharged these punctiliously, more so perhaps than his more formal commitments. On such occasions he met with plainer speaking, and an equal warmth of goodwill which everywhere astonished him.

One visit was to the Quartern. His reception was almost tearful.

Said Alice Thorn, 'When we heard you was in the Tower – lord, I thought me 'eart would've stood still.'

'What, for me?' he chaffed her. 'You would have seen me disembowelled without moving an eyelash.'

'Ow, S' John, I'd 'a' cried me eyes out. Sure you'd 'a' died beautiful, S' John.'

Absently he agreed, ' I would so, Alice.'

He was thinking, but without bitterness, women, how like they are; with all their differences, from the Virgin Queen with her gaunt bony grip to this gross survivor of three husbands, the whole gamut: and core of his core, fixed firmly in the centre, Barbara, who had not been afraid for him. It seemed there was this property of his nature, through no merit of his, that they all craved. What he had to give was so little, let him render it with goodwill – as willingly at least as the price he might have paid. He was still holding Alice's hand. In this new mood, neither pride nor humility but compact of both, he raised it to his lips.

'S' John!' She was shocked and a little frightened.

'For a moment,' he assured her 'I thought you were the Queen.'

The men laughed, thinking it a good joke, but surprisingly (or not, perhaps: was that the next lesson he must learn?) she understood him. 'She – we are all very proud of you. We'll never forget you, S' John, will we, Winkle?'

'And that,' he summed up cheerfully, 'is a great deal more than I expected.'

16

Goodbye

In a private room at the Mitre Sir John, with Will and Fabian, spent his last bachelor night. They had left a larger party of well-wishers behind at the Mermaid; for whoever friended him to church (and for honour's sake they must be many) he would have these two nearest, who knew the best and the worst of him and loved him notwithstanding.

A little soft rain fell as they walked up Bread Street, hushing the city. Inside, firelight danced on the ceiling.

Fabian looked about him with satisfaction. 'This is London. Can the shires offer more?'

'Mine can!' came from the other two in unison. They laughed, and Will added, 'I'll not be long behind you. In a few years now – Heming can take my place here –'

They were silent for a while, each dreaming of his heaven. Fabian applied himself quietly to tobacco, saying when his pipe drew well, 'I could not ask permission, you were a hundred miles away.'

They apologised solemnly. Sir John asked Will, 'Do you not join him? I never use it myself.'

He shook his head. 'Too busy. A man of any occupation –'

'Laugh on,' said Fabian placidly. 'Though I partly agree: when there's work to do I cannot take it. The herb requires leisure and a mind at ease.'

'Requires, or induces as some say?'

'It's the same thing, you know. Custom brings easiness. The great thing is to sit down and practise it.'

'Hence the Indians' rite?'

'I think so. For what is teaching but repetition – as in the schools – until the teachers have forgotton the reason, and attribute some magic to the operation itself.'

'"Use not vain repetition, as the heathen do".'

'Exactly. Yet the property of easiness remains. But how often must we examine our reasons, how many heresies and schisms must there be in every generation to hold us to the heart of truth?'

'So you will set up Saint Tobacco, and Sir John and I dissent from you; and the devil will come along in the likeness of a pretty puritan maid and tempt you to forswear him.'

'You hold by the cap and bells; no mistaking *your* occupation.'

'Talking of which,' Sir John said, 'I have promised to ask no awkward questions, but there's one thing I would much like to know: how the Exchequer accounts for your salary.'

Fabian smiled. 'I never thought to ask. Not directly, you may be sure.'

'Ratsbane for the Palace of Westminster,' Will suggested.

'Nothing so important: a rushlight for the scullery perhaps.'

'Yet you have lit up greater halls,' said Sir John.

'Greater, and darker. Yours was a pleasant arbour in comparison.'

'And you knew it all at the first glance, or very nearly.'

'Not quite,' confessed Fabian. 'I can never forgive myself for not discovering it sooner. But the pleasant part, I admit – your Deed of Gift, for instance – the real reason was obvious to me: a man gives away his dearest possession only to his dearest love. It accounted for everything – your changed habits, your absence from Aldernaton, your attempts to leave the country – everything but that infernal letter. And all this was still compatible with treason; to give up what you hold dear would need an overriding cause. I thought I had it – that your love was not returned. Then I saw the lady and spoke with her, and the last prop for my feeble case was swept away.'

'You knew then that she loved me?' Sir John was incredulous.

'She told me so: unknowingly, of course. I could only resolve to keep the knowledge to myself, especially at the Enquiry. I hope I succeeded; and I can only hope I did not force your hand with Adey.'

'You are not by chance apologising,' said Sir John 'for saving my life? Adey's all right, you know. He'll marry his Joan and make a good thing of the Waterman, latest fashion.'

'Wait a moment,' exclaimed Will and Fabian together.

'You've been giving him money –'

'What about the father and brother –'

Sir John very nearly blushed.

'The father agreed to retire. It was only a wedding present. Besides, I could not turn him on the parish. No, you did not force my hand: I'd worked that part out for myself. I might have followed the whole thing, the clues were in my hand, but there's none so blind as he who will not see. I knew you knew my secret from all you were careful not to say. As for Barbara's, why, I did not know it myself.'

Then of course they both laughed and proclaimed him the living instance of love's blindness, and how the whole of his troubles flowed directly from that source; and certain healths were drunk and the party grew somewhat hilarious, to the point of rivalling that at the Mermaid; and Will sang them several stanzas of a ditty he wanted to fit into the next play, to a very well-known tune with an outrageous rhythmical innovation in the last line, of which only one verse was anything like printable:

Old Plato was a worthy peer,
His kingdom cost him half a crown,
He chucked the poets out on their ear
And the pur-i-tans brought – them
tu-umbling down.

And before they had done assuring him it would never be passed for performance, the landlord was knocking on the door and begging them for his reputation to be quieter. But he was a friend too, and joined them in another cup for old times' sake, made up the fire for them and left them bedroom candles, and they settled down to comfortable talk again like the middle-aged men they ought to be.

They talked Sir John's story out, declaring in the old days he would have had a dukedom for it – 'and lost your head into the bargain,' added Will. Both, both, he admitted. 'We'll fit you with a title. Worcester, Surrey are bespoke: the Duke of Bankside? Earl of Kent?' It seemed to stir a train of thought, for he spoke more seriously. 'Should you leave the court yet? God knows what is coming, and honest men will be needed.'

Sir John shook his head. 'I could do nothing. If need be, I hope I would; but any influence I have is with the Queen herself, no further.'

'When will it be, do you think?' They all knew what *it* was.

'Not long. Three or four years, perhaps. She is withering visibly.'

'And then?'

'Scotland, for certain. Gregory was not the only post who rode north this summer. Ah well – it may be for the best.'

'No danger from Europe?'

'I think not. The time's gone by. Our dangers are within.'

'What about Essex?'

'Impudent, overgrown puppy! He should have learned his lesson. In any case people would never accept him; his ambition is boundless and he is quite unfit to govern. The way he speaks to the Queen if nothing else is unforgivable.'

'How should she be spoken to?' Fabian asked. 'She is to see me, I believe – later, when all this has blown over.'

'Speak out, then, as frankly as you would to one of us: she prefers it and deserves no less.'

'And you should know,' murmured Will. 'They're laying wagers now on what you said to her in private.'

Sir John smiled. 'She did most of the talking. There'll be changes, I think, if she is spared, but it's slow going and they oppose her. No one can forget she is a woman; it infuriates her, and then she loses her temper and proves it.'

'You managed well enough.'

'With me she almost forgot. She could even quote to me "Do me right and do me reason" without fear of being misunderstood.'

Will grinned. 'You might have quoted it to her.'

'Perhaps I did. At least we both took the allusion.'

'Next boy!' Will pointed at Fabian, who mildly finished the couplet:

'"Cruelty is cursed treason"?'

'Top of the form. Did you ever fail in anything?'

'Often at school. Once since, if that's what you mean. The Hurstleigh diamonds, to be precise – but there may have been reasons. I always thought your friend Sir Walter could have told us something about them. And, very nearly, this time.'

They sat quiet a while, till twelve struck from innumerable churches, a pleasant discord.

Sir John quoted softly:

> 'This is my birth day: time has come round
> And where I did begin there I shall end –'

'But not for many happy years.'

'Amen to that, and a last drink to confirm it.'

'No more for me.' He picked up his candle. 'Are they calling us before six?'

'It's pitch dark at six still. You'll be called, never fear.'

They escorted him to his door and shut him firmly inside it, then grinned at each other, suddenly tired.

They were called in good time. Sir John threw open the shutters. 'How do I look?' he said in the grey light.

'Pale but resolute –' that was Fabian.

'Not a day older than forty –' from Will.

He laughed, and clapped a hand on either shoulder.

'God bless you both. What is it, Will?'

'Nothing. Words stirring:

> Friends of my heart, you twain –
> We three now part, whether to meet again –'

'We'll meet,' he said; and then the music was at the door.

The next hour or two were a whirl.

Everyone kissed the bride: the bride kissed everyone.

Will bowed over her hand. 'Do they keep the shearing feast still in your parts?'

'Yes, indeed.'

'Then if you should see two elderly strangers, heavily disguised, at your next sheep-shearing – use them kindly, madam, for old sakes.'

It was Greek to her, but she laughed and promised.

'Goodbye! Goodbye!'

So they rode away together, and the rout followed them nearly to St Albans. The journey had been carefully spaced for easy travel, now the evenings were drawing in: at each halt a kind welcome awaited them. The weather was green and russet, perfect autumn; and in a week or so, before the first frosts nipped it, the bells of Aldernaton would ring them home.